I0782131

… italics …

O Wonderful, Wonderful Wizard of Oz

W. Frank Schulte

Adapted from the original, *The Wonderful Wizard of Oz,*

by L. Frank Baum.

With illustrations by Elizabeth Pieroni.

Burlington, Vermont

Onion River Press
191 Bank Street
Burlington, Vermont 05401

ISBN: 978-1-957184-04-3 Print Edition
ISBN: 978-1-957184-05-0 eBook

Library of Congress Control Number: 2022909498

This book is set in Sabon LT Pro/Monotype

Contents

Author's Dedication

To Ivy, who inspired this story,
and to all my grandchildren:
Lorien, Ivy, Caelyn, Rowan, Everly, Jacob, Layla, and Grace

To Thine Own Self Be True

Author's Acknowledgements

With gratitude for my advance readers, June M. Schulte and Robin L. Schulte, for their unfailing support, encouragement, suggestions, and proof-reading of this rendition. And with gratitude for Elizabeth Pieroni for her patience, collaboration, creativity, and delightful artwork! And, as well, with gratitude for Jonah S. Schulte for his technical wizardry, without which this work of imagination would not have become a reality.

My heart is a heart replete with thankfulness for their loving support.

Illustrator's Dedication

As a deep supporter of Arts in Education, I wish to dedicate the illustrations of this book to all the art kids of the world and those who dare to dream big, push boundaries and stand up to injustices. Art is hope and acceptance. For the lovers and dreamers, art is like the moment Dorothy realizes she is not in Kansas anymore. Stepping into the art world and out of the black and white of every day opens the possibility to see all the colors in between.

Prologue

"Ivy, how are things in school?" asked Grandad of his granddaughter Ivy, then age 11.

"Fine," she answered.

"Are you doing anything with Shakespeare?" asked Grandad.

"No," answered Ivy, "but I know who Shakespeare is.   He wrote *Romeo and Juliet*."

"Yes!" said Grandad.

"And *The Wizard of Oz*," continued Ivy.

"*The Wizard of Oz*?" asked Grandad.

"Well, maybe not *The Wizard of Oz*," replied Ivy.

"Well, maybe…" thought Grandad.

Chapter I

The Tempest[1]

On the Kansas prairie, wild and gray, full nineteen hundred years since blessèd feet walked[2] the Holy Land, stood there an honest house.[3] In sooth, 'twas but a single room resting on its poor foundation. Its occupants, as the house itself, wast elderly and weathered, and, so too, wast they kind, for they received into their care and trust a belovèd niece,[4] one Dorothy, orphaned some twelvemonth since,[5] and Toto too, her little dog by whose dear love[6] was her sweet soul made whole. And blessed was she in her imagination, wherein was she heartened in her isolation on that lonely prairie. In her mind's eye,[7] kings and queens[8] and knights in shining armor and, this above all,[9] therewithal didst true-hearted friends abound.

Her Auntie Em and Uncle Henry thought her coming providential, for Dorothy, in nature as in name,[10] didst prove to be a heavenly gift. I' sooth, her merry laugh, elicited by her playful times with Toto, didst brighten their elsewise drab existence and made the solitude and monotony of prairie life more bearable. For, in late summer season, a season now upon them, the sun didst render even simple chores most onerous, and baked the country all about dull, dry, and drab, so far as one could see.[11]

Yet not all was drab. Now and again, after drenching rain, when the golden sun burst forth, didst the welkin dance indeed with colour[12] as Iris, goddess of the rainbow, for her own delight didst paint a heavenly bow.[13] A bow, whose sweet perfection,[14] by yet another hue,[15] could not be more exalted.

Yet still didst the heavens have other moods, when either there is civil strife in heaven, or else the world, too saucy with the gods, incenses them to send destruction.[16] On one such day came forth the sharp north wind.[17] And from the south came threatening clouds, withal, and scolding winds[18] with a deafening voice to herald doom upon that humble house! Who'ever knew the heavens menace so?[19]

"A cyclone!" shouted Uncle Henry, above the mighty roar! "Inside! Anon! Take shelter 'neath the cabin! Give now thanks that you have lived so long!"[20]

"All lost! To prayers! To prayers! All lost!"[21] cried Auntie Em, as she hurried to find Dorothy. Yet, even then, not every hope was lost, for 'neath the house, in preparation for such time as this, a shelter from the tempest's[1] rage there was. In the darkened earth was there yet safe-haven to be had, not so wide as a church-door, nor so deep as a well[22] i'sooth, yet with ample room for Dorothy, her kin, and even one small dog.

"I am for the horses, pigs, and sheep!" cried Uncle Henry to Auntie Em, through the open cabin door. "Free must they be from sheepcote,[23] pen, and stall that they may fly before the storm! Perchance some may yet 'scape[24] so baneful a calamity![25] Get Dorothy to the cellarage,[26] and pray it be not her grave!"[27]

Auntie Em, much afeard,[28] pulled back a woven mat, uncovering the trapdoor to the cellarage at the center of the cabin. With Toto underarm, Dorothy hastened after Auntie Em with firm intent to join her in the darkness of that depth. But as she started her descent, Toto leapt from her embrace and raced outside to rail against the storm, his noble heart so big, to hold so much![29] No threat could be so great, but still would he affix himself 'twixt such danger[30] and his beloved Dorothy. O, he that hath a heart of that fine frame, to pay this debt of love but to his mistress![31] What doth he know? Too well what love little dogs to little girls may owe![32]

"Toto!" shouted Dorothy, as she started after him. "Dorothy!" shouted Auntie Em, reaching up to grasp her hem, but missing, and so didst Dorothy fly away into the storm. Out o' the door and into such bursts of horrid thunder, such groans of roaring wind and rain, as none can e'er remember to have heard,[33] calling the while,[34] "Toto! Toto!" By his bark, barely to be heard above the roaring wind, didst Dorothy then find him in the whirling, blinding dust-devils.

"Dorothy!" shouted Uncle Henry from the barn, as he held the bridle of a panic'd mare, urging doubt to calm her fear.[35] "Get thee to the cellarage! Get thee to the cellarage! Anon! Anon!" Then, holding Toto with one arm, and shielding her eyes with the other, Dorothy pressed against the wind and once more gained the safety of the cabin, and still the wind grew stronger! As she hastened to the trapdoor, with Auntie Em yet calling from below, such a violent gust then struck the house that it didst tilt on its foundation, and so was Dorothy thrown to her corner bed with Toto in her arms.

Rising altogether then, the house began to turn o' the toe like a parish-top,[36] as all went dark about.

Chapter II

The Undiscover'd Country₁

Throughout that day, then night, the cyclone held the house aloft in the heaven's firmament.₂ In time, and in contempt of every expectation, the house came to rest once more, yet with a jarring jolt, between the elements of air and earth.₃ Still intact was that dwelling, and still didst Dorothy persist for hours in her unconscious state. At last, at Toto's gentle nudging, as much to say, "Awake, dear heart, awake! Thou hast slept well. Awake!"₄ didst she then, i' faith, awake. A new day it was, and brilliant sunlight, in quality and tone more golden than any she had e'er known, didst flood the little room. Rising from her bed she found her balance and her bearing were elusive, for the cant of that familiar room played false with her best senses. With outstretched arms, and with Toto at her heels, Dorothy teetered to the door and opened it unto an undiscover'd country,₁ beyond imagination.

I' faith, 'twas a paradise of emerald hues without a name as none save Eden had e'er known before, and with sweet beds of flowers.₅ Then, too, were there orchards, laden with exotic fruits, beyond the rounded houses nestled in the lavish scene. And here and there flew rare birds of brilliant plumage, that didst jet under their advancing plumes.₆

And nearby, withal, a small brook sang, upon whose banks wild thyme and nodding violets grew, and canopied over all were luscious bowers of woodbine, sweet musk-roses, and eglantine.₇ The sweet sound of that brook came o'er her ear in strains that had a dying fall.₈ The cool, fragrant morning air, and the melody of that brook, were most refreshing to a prairie girl, accustomed as she was to torrid days of dry and dusty heat.

As Dorothy felt this scene's perfection with an invisible and subtle stealth to creep in at her eyes,₉ she saw approach a trio of diminutive men, all dressed in blue and, too, a taller, older lady, all dressed in white, advancing along a road of yellow bricks. They approached with trepidation, yet with a clear desire to make her better acquaintance.[10]

Very short in stature were these men in blue, most certain. I' faith, no taller than herself, and yet were they decidedly advanced in years, and notably official too. Even so, they were most deferential in demeanor and most humble in their tentative approach.

Bowing deeply, the eldest said, "O you wonder! Be you maid or no?"[11]

"No wonder, sir," answered Dorothy, "but certainly a maid."[12]

At this the three conferred and then continued, "Wherefore have you killed the wicked witch who ruled this land for years and years gone by? Have you come to rule us in her stead?"

"I'm sure you do mistake,"[13] insisted Dorothy, "for no harm could I ever bring to any living thing, and most certain t'would be madness to strike at so fantastical[14] a being as a wicked witch!"

"Though this be madness," said the lady all in white, "yet there is method in 't.[15] For, yonder, 'neath that sill lies the Wicked Witch of the East, and dead as a doornail[16] is she."

Turning, Dorothy saw slippered feet protruding from beneath her house. She ran to the place exclaiming, "O, peace, peace![17] Art thou hurt a'tall? O, I prithee! Do come away, come away, anon!"[18]

"'Tis no use," spoke the lady in white once more, "for there is no spell, nor e'er there was, to quicken they that are now dead."

Dorothy felt that, upon the least occasion more, her eyes would tell tales of her.[19] But the lady in white then asked her gently, kindly, "Whence came you, dear?[20] How camest thou hither, tell me, and wherefore?"[21]

With resignation in her voice, Dorothy answered softly, "From Kansas. And I can say little more[22] than a terrible storm bore Toto and me, in this very house, from Earth to heaven, then from heaven to Earth,[23] falling as we did to the misfortune of this witch."

"Sweet are the uses of adversity,"[24] observed the lady in white, as she kissed Dorothy's forehead. "Now are the Munchkins free of the reign of this wicked witch, she who rendered mischiefs manifold, sorceries,[24] and unmitigable rage[26] too terrible to tell. Forever will they hold thee in their hearts, my dear, for this, their great deliverance."

"I beg your pardon,"[27] said Dorothy, "but who are the Munchkins? Shall ye present me to them?[28] Art thou a Munchkin thyself?" asked Dorothy of the lady all in white. But afore that kind soul could answer, the Munchkin people suddenly appeared from every point, emerging from their houses, and from every hidden place amongst the greenery, emboldened in their approach by the lady in white's tender embrace of Dorothy. And the children, too, who had never known a dog, didst eagerly acquaint themselves with Toto. And Toto too, in return, didst eagerly accept their fond attentions. For who'ver lov'd that lov'd not at first sight?[29]

"The Munchkins save my labor by their own approach,"[30] said the lady all in white, smiling at the scene. Then, to Dorothy, she said, "Though my home is in the north, yet am I a denizen of Munchkinland, and so too am I a benefactress to the Munchkin people. They love me, as I love them. The Munchkins soon passed word[31] of thy arrival, and of the timely end of this Wicked Witch of the East, and thus I came, anon. Ye must know of me then, my dear, I am called[32] the Good Witch of the North."

"Gracious me!" exclaimed Dorothy! "Is it even so?[33] But thou art benevolent and beloved! Witches are nefarious and despised, are they not? In sooth, can ye truly be a witch?"

"I' faith, I am," smiled the Good Witch of the North. "'Tis true this witch whom ye destroyed was wicked, as is her sister in the West, but I am a good witch, as is Glinda, the Good Witch of the South. Yet, though I be a good witch, I am not so powerful as was this Wicked Witch of the East, else would I have freed the Munchkin people long ago, myself. But free are they at last, by thy cherished hand."[34]

"And now tell us, my dear," she asked, "what is thy name and thy parentage?"[35]

"O! Pardon, I beseech you!"[36] exclaimed Dorothy, as she curtsied to that lady. "O, forgive my rudeness[37] and please know that I am Dorothy of Kansas, and this is little Toto."

Then, in th' very moment[38] that Dorothy spake these words, did the Munchkins gasp as one and gesticulate. I' faith they pointed to the very place where the slippered feet were last seen. For the sun that early morn did shine[39] and traced a course ordained when Creation was but new and, with travel so demure,[40] diminished both the shadows and the morning dew. And as the first rays of that sunlight touched the feet of that wicked witch, instantly they shriveled and then disappeared entirely underneath the house. Left there then, as a certain proof of her demise, were the silver slippers she once wore. These the Good Witch of the North did vouchsafe[41] Dorothy, proclaiming they now rightfully belonged to her.

"Don anon these silver slippers, for they possess a cryptic power and enchantment," said the Good Witch then to Dorothy. "Wear them always, as protection, so long as ye remain in Oz. These slippers, and the kiss I set upon thy brow, are thy best security."

"I'm so sorry," said Dorothy then, "what maleficence must I fear?"

"'Tis true the Wicked Witch of the East be dead, but do recall her sister, the Wicked Witch of the West, lives on. She will be enraged when she learns her sister lives no more. Yet, take heart, my dear, for so ever long as ye wear these slippers and shun the western lands, wherein her castle lies, ye shall see none to fear,"[42] explained the Good Witch of the North.

"Very well," said Dorothy, "since you deem it wise." As she replaced her shoes with the enchanted slippers, she found their fit perfection, as if they had been made with her in mind.

Then, tugging at her sleeve to gain attention, the eldest of the trio whispered in the ear of the Good Witch of the North. Smiling and nodding her consent, she turned to Dorothy and said, "The Munchkin people ask thee to name thy heart's desire.[43] They will be pleased to grant it if it falls within their power, or mine, so to do."

"O!" exclaimed Dorothy! "In sooth, I know no answer!"[44] Then, upon reflection, she said, "All I truly do desire is to see once more Kansas and my Auntie Em and Uncle Henry. I know them as I know myself, and so I know how worried they will be. I prithee, kindly tell me in which way Kansas lies."

At this the Munchkins and the Good Witch of the North looked at one another, and then to Dorothy, and slowly shook their heads,[45] for there was none who knew.

"I am afraid, my dear," said the Good Witch of the North, "there is none amongst us who know in which way Kansas lies. E'en should we know, a great desert encircles this country, so great as none may ever cross. I think it best, my dear, that ye shall now, and evermore, abide with us, and most gladly are ye welcome hither, as is the spring unto the earth."[46]

Dorothy's eyes brimmed with tears at her estate, at how her own occasion was so far from mellow,[47] for too well she knew that she and Toto might ne'er again see Auntie Em, Uncle Henry, or the fields of Kansas. She dropped then to the road of yellow bricks and sobbed as Toto climbed into her lap and softly whined in consolation. At this, each Munchkin, to a person, produced a handkerchief[48] and wept, withal, in heartfelt sympathy with her.

"There is still one who may yet know how ye may return," said the Good Witch of the North. At this, Dorothy looked up and met her gaze through her tears. "The Great and Powerful Oz." At the mention of this name, the Munchkin people hushed and then bowed deeply where they stood, in obeisance.[49]

"Who is this 'Great and Powerful Oz'?" asked Dorothy, as she took heart and dried her tears.

"He is the most powerful being in this land. In sooth, the first amongst us. He is a great, great wizard," answered the Good Witch of the North.

"But is he a good man?" asked Dorothy. "Will he help me, a'tall?"

"I cannot say if he is a man," said the Good Witch of the North, "for I have never seen him. And some say there is nothing either good or bad, but thinking makes it so.[50] But I believe him to be a good wizard. And the only way to know if he will help thee is to seek his audience and humbly beseech his effectual aid."

"How do I find him?" asked Dorothy.

"That is both simple and difficult," answered the Good Witch of the North. "To find him, simply follow this yellow brick road and it will lead thee to the Emerald City, where that wizard rules. The difficulty is that the road is long, and the journey may be perilous."

"Must I go alone? Nor will you not that you go with me?"[51]

"No, my dear, I cannot," she replied. "But ye wear the silver slippers and ye bear the kiss of the Good Witch of the North upon thy brow. None will dare to harm thee. When ye meet the Great Wizard of Oz, though in his stars he be above thee, be not afraid of greatness,[52] but simply tell thy tale and beseech him to assist thee."

"Sure, if Oz be as Great and Powerful as it is spoke, he never will admit me,"[53] objected Dorothy. "My journey then will be for nought, and 'twill be called a wild-goose chase."[54]

"My dear, ye must be clamorous and leap all civil bounds rather than make unprofited journey!"[55] insisted the Good Witch of the North. "Ye cannot leave this land as ye didst come, and so in course must ye humbly beseech the Great Wizard to lend thee his good entertainment.[56] It is thy one hope if ye be resolute[57] to once more see thy kin and Kansas. The gentleness of all the gods go with thee.[58] Fare thee well at once."[59]

"Very well," conceded Dorothy. "Come thy ways,[60] Toto, we are bound for the Emerald City."[61]

And so, after filling her basket with all things good, the Munchkins, with a rousing farewell,[61] sent Dorothy and Toto packing[62] down the auspicious yellow brick road.

Chapter III

How Dorothy Didst Render Scarecrow Free

When Dorothy and Toto were but a league without the town,₁ no longer were quaint dwellings to be seen. Here bucolic pastures didst abound and withal, amber crops of wheat and sweet, ripe summer corn. And here the yellow bricks found shade, the first that they had seen since bidding Munchkinland farewell.

The cool, moist air and filtered light of the green and shady glen invited them to rest awhile. Sitting then upon a stile,₂ Dorothy thus took her ease as she gazed out o'er the green cornfield,₃ leaning her cheek upon her hand,₄ and spied nearby a Scarecrow on a pole, raised above the corn. Its painted face could not have been more unlike her own, for her damask cheeks,₅ whose blend of red and white Nature's own sweet and cunning hand laid on, 'twas beauty truly blent.₆ Yet the Scarecrow's eyes were bright and blue and, as she met their gaze, she would be sworn₇ she saw one wink.

"'Tis but my imagination gone awry!" said Dorothy at this. "Such tricks hath strong imagination, that, if it would but apprehend some joy, it comprehends some bringer of that joy; or, in the night, imagining some fear, how easy is a bush supposed a bear!"₈

"How Now! Good morrow, friends!"₉ spoke the Scarecrow then to Dorothy in a husky, yet kind and gracious, voice.

"Didst thou speak, a'tall?" she asked, with such inestimable wonder.₁₀

"I' faith, I did. And who, child, might ye be?" inquired he.

"I am Dorothy," answered she, cautiously, as she strained to keep incredulity and wariness from her countenance, so charged was she in manners, the rather to express herself.₁₁ "And this is Toto," gesturing to her little dog who, at the mention of his name, promptly barked a warning to that Scarecrow.

"How now! And how are ye both, on so fine day as this?" continued he, cheerfully.

"I am very well, thank ye," answered she. "And thee? Art thou very well, withal?"

"N'ere well, a'tall," said the Scarecrow sadly. "Here I hang, in this field of green and yellow melancholy,[12] upon this weathered pole. A feckless fool am I, accosting heedless crows that feed upon[13] yon ripened corn. Yet," said he, in his philosophy,[14] "have I heard it said, 'he that is well hanged in this world needs to fear no colours'.[15] In sooth, I have no fears a'tall, save a lighted match."

"Of course!" said Dorothy, "Who could have more reason? In sooth, 'tis but a wise and sensible concern."

The direful spectacle of the impaled Scarecrow touched in Dorothy the very virtue of compassion,[16] and so was she resolved to free him from his lonely fate. With gentle ease didst she lift him from his pole, for slight of weight was he being but of straw, and she set his grateful soul down amongst the stalks of corn.

"A thousand, thousand sighs to save![17] If you will not murder me for my love, let me be your servant,"[18] said the Scarecrow, from an abundance of gratitude for his deliverance.

"I' sooth, I've never known a servant," answered Dorothy, "and I could never murder anyone, save one wicked witch, and never with intent."

"How now! How didst one so young, and so untender,[19] defeat so omnipotent a foe?" asked the Scarecrow in his astonishment.

"My tale indeed provokes that question,"[20] answered Dorothy. "And I prithee, do think me young but not untender. In sooth, my house dropped from the heavens[21] and didst but fall upon herself. 'Come away, come away,'[22] spoke I to her. 'Courage witch, the hurt cannot be much!'[23] But dead as a doornail[24] was she," related Dorothy in recollected terms.[25]

Dorothy gazed thoughtfully at the Scarecrow

"Thy tale, child, would cure deafness,"[26] said the Scarecrow, "Perchance that's how I hear thee now, though I have but painted ears," reflected he. "Even so, was this not a deed well done? To lead such wickedness to the grave and leave the world no copy?"[27]

"So some do think," said Dorothy, "though 'twas no intent of mine. Yet lives her sister still, the Wicked Witch of the West."

"Ay, there's the rub,"[28] said the Scarecrow.

"Marry, for cursed am I in her one eye and, even now, she doth threaten to appear and render mischiefs manifold,"[29] said Dorothy.

Standing on his toes the Scarecrow glanced from side to side then, stooping down, he whispered, "Wherefore doth that wicked witch not, in this very hour, in this very place, destroy thy very self?"[30]

"By these very slippers, and by the very kiss upon my brow, she durst not!"[31] answered Dorothy.

Then did he perceive the enchantment of those slippers, to the increase of his wonder, yet still more then did he apprehend the enchantment of the child who stood before him.

"Whence came thee, child?"[32] asked the Scarecrow then. "And let me yet know of thee whither you are bound."[33]

"Kansas is my home," answered Dorothy, "and my determinate voyage[34] is to the Emerald City, by way of these yellow bricks."

"Speak to me of Kansas," said the Scarecrow. "Is it a better world than this?"[35]

"I' faith, it hath a beauty of its own," answered Dorothy, "yet none to 'pare with this. Even so, it hath one hold on my affection that no other land can ever claim, and there begins my sadness.[36] You see, my Auntie Em and Uncle Henry do but love me so. And, even now, they must be pale and sick with grief,[37] and quite besides themselves,[38] withal, at my radical departure, to speak nothing of their home and cattle lost to a mighty storm's embrace. Therefore, dost ye see, must I find some method home or forever will they mourn my loss, in their sad remembrance."[39]

"If I but had a brain, perchance my thoughts would yield such means as would affect thy safe return," sighed the Scarecrow.

"Dost thou truly have no brain?" asked Dorothy. "How can this be true? Is it even so?"[40]

"A wiser man than I must answer this, for no answer do I know,"[41] said the Scarecrow. "In sooth, no more brains have I than does a stone."[42]

"Well now," reflected Dorothy, "perchance thy Fates open their hands[43] and smile upon thee yet. As good luck would have it,[44] my purpose is, indeed, to seek as wise a one as lives. None other than the Great and Powerful Oz, ruler of the Emerald City, to ask him to affect my safe return to Kansas. Perchance, withal, would he bestow in thee a brain if thou, with such humility, beseech his entertainment."[45]

"Where be this Emerald City?" asked the Scarecrow.

"'Tis far off, along this yellow road, and rather like a dream than an assurance,"[46] answered Dorothy.

"However long this journey be," said the Scarecrow then to Dorothy, "my soul will keep yours company on the way to Oz!"[47]

"I thank thee too for thy society,"[48] smiled Dorothy in return as they started down the yellow brick road, as Toto led the way.

Chapter IV

The Road Through the Forest₁

As Dorothy and Toto, and so now, too, the Scarecrow, didst wend their way o'er the yellow bricks, the fields of corn and wheat on either side gave way to untilled slopes of deciduous trees and conifers, and to old and twisted orchards, now long ago abandoned. The several farms passed earlier that day were sadly lacking in good husbandry, and now none a'tall were to be seen. To pass the time as they walked along, Dorothy asked the Scarecrow what he could tell her of himself.

"Very little," replied he, "for only yesterday was I but made. Two Munchkin brothers made me of these clothes I wear, which they didst find in a chest of drawers in some old and dusty attic. None can say to whom these clothes and hat belonged, though these old boots once belonged to a now deceased relation on their mother's side. My stuffing is simply straw left behind at harvest time, in some neighbor's field."

"The farmers reasoned I would be the more convincing man if I but had a face and ears," continued he. "I' faith, in th' very moment₂ they didst paint ears on either side of my head, so too could I then hear their conversation! And no sooner didst they paint mine eyes of blue, so too could I then see them! They gave me next a nose and mouth, but no thought had I of speaking 'til today, when first I greeted thee."

"I am so grateful that ye did," said Dorothy, "or, even now, I should be alone."

"It seems to me," said the Scarecrow, continuing his own line of thought, "that there was nothing notable in the straw the farmers in the sun didst use to stuff me.₃ And so this life I am now living must, perforce, be due to some enchantment in these clothes. Perhaps it is akin to the enchantment of thy silver slippers, whatever that enchantment may yet prove to be."

Perchance the night would pass more safely here than in those yonder woods.

"I think thou'rt i' the right,"[4] said Dorothy, "for once I heard my Uncle Henry say, 'The apparel oft proclaims the man.'[5] I might add, withal, thy argument is very sound and, so too, is it well-reasoned. Art thou certain thou hast no brain?"

"Quite certain," answered he, "for I didst hear one farmer tell the other that I didst want for nothing more, save but for a brain. And then I heard the other say, 'No matter, for the crows will not engage him in such witty conversation as we ourselves enjoy.'"

As the sunset fast approached, the brick road brought them to a forest's edge, and Dorothy was hesitant to enter. "Perchance the night would pass more safely here than in those yonder woods, where the light is quickly fading and where what's to come is still unsure,"[6] said Dorothy. "Yet hither will be dark anon, and shelter must we find before it falls. I could wish we had a lantern, for soon it shall be quite impossible to see."

"I prefer we had no lamp," replied the Scarecrow then, "for, in sooth, flame shall never be a friend o' mine. And as for seeing in the dark, I see quite as well in darkness as in light. Do not ask me wherefore this should be, for no answer do I know,[7] yet 'tis but my true nature."[8]

"How fortunate am I to hast a friend with such a sensibility!" exclaimed Dorothy! "If I may take thy arm,[9] I would happily venture forth.[10] I prithee, let me know anon if ye dost spy any sort of dwelling where we might pass the night."

And anon it 'twas the Scarecrow didst but spy a rustic cabin, just a little distant from the road. "Shall we approach and ask if we might stay this night within?" inquired the Scarecrow then of Dorothy.

"Indeed!" said she, "I pray, bear with me; I cannot go no further."[11]

They found the door ajar, and the cabin seemed abandoned. Entering, the Scarecrow noted, by reason of such absence, there was nothing to be found,[12] save an oilcan on a shelf and a bed of dried leaves in one corner. Dorothy laid down at once and, no sooner was Toto nestled in, then she was fast asleep.

For his part, the Scarecrow, who was never tired a'tall, stood sentry in the doorway and patiently awaited the dawning of another day.

Chapter V

Another Part of the Forest₁
The Emancipation of the Tin Woodman

On the morrow,₂ when the sun rose to a height to illuminate the rustic cabin, Dorothy awoke without the smallest notion of locality. And Toto, who was ever by her side, was nowhere to be seen. Her dreams were strange and disconcerting, in her remembrance,₃ as were yesterday's happenings, now waking in her mind; the violent storm, Munchkinland, miniature men in blue, witches dead and witches 'live, some wicked and some good, a scarecrow that didst speak, and, to end i'tall, a dark, foreboding forest. All had meddled with her dreams,₄ and all didst seem a most rare vision,₅ one that continued even now. But 'twas not a vision, nor was it a dream, for there in the doorway, of whatever place this was, stood the Scarecrow, keeping watch.

"How now, good morrow, friend,"₆ said the Scarecrow softly, "didst thou sleep well? Art thou quite refreshed?"

"Ay, I believe so," answered Dorothy, for the Scarecrow's voice instantly brought order to her mind. His spoken words dispelled all residual confusion and cast,₇ at once, the images of her unsettled dreams. His gentle tone reminded her she was not without a friend, and was not forsaken in this place, e'en though she keenly missed the warm embrace of those she loved.

Rising from the bed of leaves she asked, "I pray, sir, tell me,₈ where is Toto?"

"He has been yonder i' the sun practicing behavior to his own shadow this half hour,₉ his nose upon the ground. The cur is excellent at faults.₁₀ Shall we look for him?" asked the Scarecrow.

"Ay, I prithee," answered Dorothy as she brushed dried leaves from her dress and hair, "perchance, in his hunt, he hath found some woodland stream where I might drink and wash my face and hands."

The Scarecrow soon spied Toto but a short way from the cabin. He observed, withal, that Toto had made some notable discovery which, with lifted leg,[11] he was now saluting. As Dorothy and the Scarecrow neared the scene of Toto's prize, they saw it was a statue, all but covered now by woodland ivy that hid its princely trunk,[12] in its constant climb for light.

'Twas, in form, a woodsman, made entirely of tin, save for a rusted axe it held aloft. As they admired this unexpected sculpture and wondered wherefore it should be in such purlieu,[13] they distinctly heard a squeak. Startled, Toto sharply turned and barked a message of reproach at this man of tin. In response, the statue squeaked again.

"Perhaps my intuition is too brisk," said the Scarecrow, "yet I apprehend more hither than 't would at first appear." Taking then the jaw into his hand, he examined one side o' its face and then the other. And, as he did, he felt the slightest movement of the jaw. Springing back in his surprise, he fell upon the ground. Dorothy then dropped her basket and rushed to help him up.

"O, whatever is the matter?" cried Dorothy in her alarm. "Art thou hurt[14] a'tall?"

"Nay, nay, I am unharmed," answered he, with his gaze fixed intently on the statue. "But, by your leave,[15] must I hastily retrieve an apparatus from yon cabin. Pray wait hither but a moment. I will return, anon."

Returning, he held the oilcan he didst note when first they entered that dark cabin. In his watch the previous night,[16] he had pondered wherefore it was there, for nought else was there to be seen. Not food, nor clothes, nor vestiges of anything that one is wont to find in such a dwelling, save the bed of leaves.

With haste didst the Scarecrow then ply oil to the rusted jaw of that Tin Woodman. And in th' very moment[17] of that urgent application didst they but hear him speak.[18]

"Who, who art thou?" stammered the Tin Woodman, "and wherefore art thou[19] in this forest, away from all ye love?"

'Twas, in form, a woodsman, made entirely of tin.

"I prithee, I am Dorothy of Kansas," answered Dorothy, with a curtsy to that unexpected soul. "And this is little Toto, whose acquaintance, I do fear, thou hast already made. And this Scarecrow is my friend, who joins me in my journey to the Emerald City of Oz."

"O, I prithee,"[20] entreated he, "ply now oil to my articulated arm that I may, at long last, put down this weighty axe." At once didst they comply with this, his urgent plea, and still more. Thus, anon, was he released from his immotile pose.

"How didst ye ever come to be in this most pitiful and miserable estate?"[21] inquired Dorothy.

"Twelvemonth since,[22] and somewhat more, was I chopping wood not above a quarter league from hence,[23] when, of a sudden,[8] didst I feel a drop of rain. Instantly I ceased my labor and didst, posthaste, address my gait unto[24] my cabin, lest such torrential downpour should, perchance, follow aft that single drop. And sure, in course, the skies didst open and the rain didst drench me proper. Before I could but gain the shelter of yon cabin, didst I rust solidly in place, ne'er to move again. And hither have I watched the seasons pass, and so too travelers on the yellow road, 'til this moment when ye didst find me. The ivy[12] that adorned me, and kept me company, didst hide my form from every passerby, and so would I be hidden yet, but for thy little friend."

"On behalf of little Toto then, I welcome thee once more into the company of friends," smiled Dorothy.

This brought tears to his eyes, which Dorothy quickly dried. He then asked of her, "And what of thee? Wherefore dost ye venture to the Emerald City of Oz?"

"No mere extravagancy, our determinate journey[25] is from Munchkinland to the Emerald City where we seek the Great and Powerful Wizard of Oz."

Upon hearing 'Munchkinland' the Tin Woodman startled and then quickly asked, "Have ye truly come from Munchkinland? What tidings dost thou bring? For once I hailed from that fair country and so do hunger for any scruple[26] of glad tidings."

"The good news we bring from Munchkinland is anything but small," said the Scarecrow in reply. "For this is she who killed the Wicked Witch of the East and who, even now, bears upon her brow the kiss of the Good Witch of the North."

"Is it even so?[27] How can this be true? Is that wicked witch now dead?" asked he, in disbelief. And yet, before any could reply, he felt certain it was true. Dropping then his axe, and humbly upon his bended knee,[28] he took Dorothy's hand in his and kissed it, saying, "Too well didst I but know[29] that Wicked Witch, for by her art[30] am I made of tin and by her hand[31] was I banished[32] to these woods."

Then did the Tin Woodman tell his tale. In time gone by, he fell in love with a Munchkin maid, herself bound in service to the Wicked Witch of the East. Though she didst requite his love,[33] yet still was she forbidden followers[34] by that Wicked Witch. When the Witch discovered their true love she cast a spell to make of him a man of tin and, withal, she exiled[35] him from Munchkinland to this lonely forest, therewithal to be her woodsman for all time.

"And when she turned me into tin, no heart set she within my breast," continued he, "else would such a heart, come what may,[36] compel me back to her, my love."

"Dost thou truly have no heart?" asked Dorothy.

"None a'tall," answered the Tin Woodman. "In my mind I know that I still love this maid, for how ever could I not? But without a heart to feel affection, my affection cannot hold the bent.[37] I only pray she loves me yet," said he, "though I be made of tin."

"How could she ever not?" asked Dorothy, "for thou art as a knight[38] in shining armor."

At this, the Tin Woodman would have blushed had he been of flesh and blood.[39] Lovingly he gazed at her, with gratitude for freedom from immobility, and from the Wicked Witch, but more grateful still for the comfort of these words, that love does not alter when it alteration finds,[40] and thus love might yet endure.

"Be thou blessed for thy good comfort,"[41] whispered he. Then, with desire to turn their conversation, he asked of her, "Wherefore do you seek an audience with The Great and Powerful Oz?"

"My desire is to return to Kansas, and my intent is to beseech The Great and Powerful Oz to affect my safe return," answered Dorothy. And so, once more, she spoke of Kansas and of her Auntie Em and Uncle Henry, for whose dear love, said she, would she abjure the company and sight of all, save them.[42]

"I understand," said the Tin Woodman, "For I was adored once too.[43] Mine own affairs acquaint me with the awesome power of love, and thy love of kin and country speaks for authority the like of it."[44]

"My Auntie Em is wont to say, 'The course of true love never did run smooth',"[45] reflected Dorothy, "and in thy tale I see the very truth and meaning of her words."

"Well," continued she, "there is but one thing to be done. We must find for thee a heart and thereby make thee whole."

"Is 't possible?"[46] asked he.

"Things deemed unlikely, e'en impossible, experience oft hath proven to be true,"[47] assured Dorothy, "or so it seems, hither in this Land of Oz."

"Indeed," said the Scarecrow. "Mine own hope is that The Great Oz shall liken me to one whose skull Jove cram with brains,[48] for in my head of straw have I no brain a'tall."

"Do come with us anon to the Emerald City of Oz and beseech of that Great Wizard a heart to make thee whole once more!" invited Dorothy.

"By thy leave[15] I shall," responded he, "Only place thou my oilcan in thy basket,[49] as phylactery against inclement weather that may, of a sudden,[8] rain down."

And so didst she anon, and so didst they all, now three, and Toto too, turn once again to the yellow brick road.

Chapter VI

Yet Another Part of the Forest[1]
The Pusillanimous[2] Lion

"I would not wish any companions in the world but ye,"[3] said Dorothy to the Tin Woodman and the Scarecrow as they wound their way through the forest, along the yellow brick road.

"There is flattery in friendship,"[4] replied the Scarecrow, "but, i' faith, thy sentiment is shared."

In sooth, was Dorothy grateful for their society and friendship and, withal, protection. For growing in her heart was there now some unknown fear,[5] instilled, perhaps, but the uninviting forest. The edges of the yellow road in this part of the forest were serrated by encroaching roots of trees. So, too, didst fallen leaves and branches, missing bricks, and vicissitudes, now and again, cause the Scarecrow to trip and stumble, and so didst slow their pace.

"How long," asked Dorothy of the Tin Woodman, "before we leave this forest?"

"I know no answer,"[6] said the Tin Woodman. "But once, in my remembrance,[7] when I was but a boy of flesh and blood,[8] my father made this very journey to the Emerald City. He said these woods were menacing but, then too, he said the countryside beyond is more beautiful than even Munchkinland."

"O, do speak comfort of the beauty of that place," implored Dorothy, "or so too any account of good things to come! It may check my rising apprehension of these woods! The sky hither will not show itself[9] for reason o' this o'er arching canopy of trees. How well I know there is a world elsewhere,[10] a world I would return to, with sky in such abundance! In silent night, save but for cricket song, innumerous little stars do make the face of heaven so fine that all of Kansas must be in love with night![11] O, my soul is in that sky!"[12]

"We must be patient," said the Scarecrow then, "for the world is broad and wide.[13] Take heart and do recall thy silver slippers and the kiss upon thy brow. Remember, too, the Tin Woodman wields his axe and, withal, such stuff as I am made of[14] can come to no more harm than can a dream."

"But what of little Toto?" asked Dorothy. "In what quarter lies his safety?"

"We ourselves must see to his protection, and provide effectual aid, should any danger threaten," said the Tin Woodman.

"Thou'rt i' the right,[15] of course" replied Dorothy. "Perhaps my fears are quite unfounded." And yet she could not quite dispel her apprehension of some inimical surveillance close at hand. Thought she then, "An we had eyes behind us we might find more detraction at our heels than fortunes before us."[16]

Dorothy noted, withal, woodland sounds were not so pleasing as the songs of meadowlarks, nor as the wind makes as it whispers through amber fields of wheat. Hoot owls, distant barks and calls, movements in the underbrush, and snapping twigs all heightened her disquiet.

Then, too, didst Toto sniff the air and follow scents along the ground, and he didst prick his ears at sounds that none, save he, could hear. He did so now and, withal, he began to growl.

"What unsettles Toto's wits?"[17] asked the Tin Woodman then. "He is much out of quiet."[18]

Before any could conjecture, there came a terrible roar before them, as none could e'er remember to have heard[19] in life or in imagination. Standing proud upon a boulder stood the largest lion e'er there was! With tremendous spring didst he but leap from his high pedestal unto the road before them. Then, by a powerful stroke of his right paw, was the Scarecrow easily tossed aside. And, with another of his left paw, was the Tin Woodman swept away before any thought had he of raising his sharp axe.

Then didst the Lion challenge Dorothy and Toto! At once didst Toto hasten to accost[20] this mortal foe, barking all the while![21] The Lion bared his teeth and growled! Toto responded then in kind!

Don't ye dare bite little Toto, ye ought to be ashamed of thyself!

Then, in th' very moment,[22] with the Lion poised to pounce to put an end to Toto, didst Dorothy, heedless of the danger, rush to and slap him hard upon the nose, crying out, "Don't ye dare bite little Toto, ye ought to be ashamed of thyself, such a beast as thou, to bite a little dog!"

Aside then said the Scarecrow to the Tin Woodman, "Though she be but little, she is fierce!"[23]

"Wherefore didst thou slap my tender nose?" cried the Lion, as the tears welled in his eyes. "I didst not bite him!"

"Nay, but 'twas thy clear intent!" retorted Dorothy, angrily, as she helped the Scarecrow to his feet and patted him into shape once more.

"Nay, 'twas no intent of mine," said the Lion.

"Didst thou, or didst thou not, display thy very fangs of malice?"[24] demanded Dorothy, who believed the Lion to be giving her the lie.[25]

"Would ye have me comprehend thy intent was but to challenge him the field and then to break promise and make a fool of him?[26] Thou art but a pusillanimous[2] lion!"

"Just so, just so," replied the Lion, ashamedly. "'Tis pity and, pity 'tis 'tis true."[27]

"Wherefore wouldst thou behave with such dishonor?"[28] asked the Tin Woodman, rising to his feet, his axe in hand.

"My purpose was to frighten him away and, so too, ye all," answered the Lion.

"Again," demanded Dorothy, "Wherefore wouldst thou act in such rude manner?"

"That, by thy hand,[29] no harm might come to me," answered he.

"And yet, with profound irony," noted the Scarecrow to the Lion, "thy wanton[30] challenge begot that very end!"

"In thy denial I find no sense, I do not understand it,"[31] continued Dorothy. "Art thou not King of Cats?"[32]

"How can you say to me, I am king?"[33] asked the Lion. "As glory titles go, 'tis but an outward honor for an inward toil."[34]

Then did the Lion tell his tale.

"When I was but a lion cub, with my mother's milk scarce out of me,[35] in my innocence I knew not the doctrine of ill-doing, nor dream'd that any did.[36] But then came a day when Kalidah laid claim to Lion realm. On that day were the Kalidah repelled, but the elders of my pride did not return, and so I was left a foundling."

"Alas, poor Lion, searching of thy wound, I have by hard adventure found mine own,"[37] sighed Dorothy, "for I too am an orphan."

"In my youth I made my den amongst boulders where none larger than myself could go. Perforce did I put myself into the trick of singularity,[38] for none do fear the roaring of a lion's whelp.[39] But, in time, my voice so deepened that it terrified all who heard. Thus, was I preserved but, so too, was I alone."

"I pray, sir, tell me,[40] what are Kalidah?" asked the Scarecrow of the Lion. "Are they akin to bears, or maybe yet to tigers?"

"I' faith they resemble each, in part," the Lion answered, "and thus are they greatly to be feared."

"I' faith they resemble each, in part," the Lion answered.

"Just now as we came hither, I felt keen eyes upon my humbled neck,"41 recalled Dorothy, "though I do not feel them still. Perchance it was some Kalidah who, by reason of thy mighty roar, hath retreated now in haste."

"Perhaps," replied the Lion, "though I am frightened by the thought, for 'twould mean the Kalildah are far without their realm. So too, I know it is my birthright to be free, learn'd, and valiant,42 but I have never learned such ways, and now I fear I am too late to learn these noble lessons."

"Courage is as love," offered the Tin Woodman, "it must have hope for nourishment.43 And, in hope have you been long deprived, to the depth of your remembrance. Mine own neglect is for a heart, and I pray the Great and Powerful Wizard of Oz will restore one to my bosom."44

"So too am I deficient for, i' faith, I hast no brain," said the Scarecrow then. "Yet, if the Great Oz may impart a heart and, withal, constrain a brain, why would he not incline thy spine with such courage as none, save Hercules,45 e'er knew before?"

"I have lived my life in fear, and I have acted with dishonor, as when I challenged this small fellow," said the Lion then of Toto. "Indeed, in my orisons be all my sins remember'd.46 I would be ashamed to meet this Great Oz and beg his help when I am such a coward."

"All do mistake in life and so do all regret," said the Tin Woodman, "save perhaps this Scarecrow, who was but lately made. I' faith, some certain dregs of conscience are within me yet,47 and conscience doth make cowards of us all.48 With stronger blood, I should have answer'd heaven boldly, 'not guilty!'49 Yet, the quality of mercy is not strain'd. It droppeth as the gentle rain from heaven upon the place beneath.50 Therefore, i'faith and hope, we journey to the Emerald City to seek an audience with The Great and Powerful Oz. Perchance he will be merciful and will not count the ways51 whereby we fail in his esteem."

"Indeed," said Dorothy. "Therefore, we face our fears, and we invite thee, do as much! Take thou a measure of our hope and, withal, take comfort in the company of friends! Come with us to the Emerald City!"

"Well then," said the Lion, "if ye truly do not mind the society of a coward, I will be pleased to join ye in this quest, for my life is simply unbearable without a bit of courage."[52]

"Of course," said Dorothy, and so said all. Toto too, who was at first wary of this new companion, anon became his bosom friend, now that his aggressive posture was no more.

"Follow closely, my newfound friends," said the Lion then. "I will lead ye to a place where we can safely pass this night, for the sunset fadeth in the west, which by and by black night doth take away."[53]

"I thank thee," said Dorothy, "lead us on."[54]

Chapter VII

Yet Another Night in the Forest[1]

In the twilight of that day,[2] with light quickly fading in the forest, the Lion led the travelers o'er meandering ways, through underbrush and thickets, to a clearing near a stream, a furlong from the yellow road. As Toto waded in the stream and drank deeply of the clear, refreshing water, the Lion said, "On summer nights, warm and dry, I sleep soundly hither, and hither shall we all be safe this night. Withal, in yonder stream, where Toto hath stepped in so far that, should he wade no more, returning were as tedious as going o'er,[3] there do fish abide. I' faith, some will I fetch, anon, that we may feast together, e'er we take our rest."[4]

"If you would fetch our wood and make our fire,"[5] asked Dorothy of the Tin Woodman, "whilst daylight doth still linger, I will gather stones together.[6] The Munchkins, in their kindness, placed matches in my basket, and I would fain[7] have fish roasted o'er a fire with my bread, and so would Toto too. Withal, a fire will yield us light, for a great cause of the night is lack of the sun."[8]

Soon, all gathered round the glowing of such fire,[9] save the Scarecrow who stood apart and took such pains[10] to stay to windward of the sparks and lively flames. The Lion spoke in recollected terms[11] of how once, when he was young, he nearly drowned whilst fishing in a river. For he misjudged its depth, and as he pounced to catch a fish, the current swiftly carried him away. In time didst he but gain the shore, though cold and spent was he, and so was he resolved to henceforth only fish in streams.

"Yet I have no fear of fire," continued he, "unless it rages wildly through the forest, as once it did in my remembrance, when lightning struck an ancient tree. But the Kalidah dost fear it greatly so, I prithee, sustain this fire till morn, and we shall find our safety manifested."[12]

As evening passed, and tales were told, appeared then in the Lion's countenance a notable passion of wonder.[13] For Dorothy spoke of how the storm carried her to Munchkinland and of how her house killed the Wicked Witch and, withal, she spoke of the unknown magic of her slippers. So too the Scarecrow spoke of his construction and of his unexpected life. And the Tin Woodman shared how he became a man of tin, and, withal, how he had loved and lost.[14]

All then listened as the Lion spoke of all he knew of the Eastern Forest and its many creatures.

"Are there no other lions in this forest?" asked Dorothy of him. "Hast thou no kin a'tall close by?"

"None that I have seen since I was but a cub," replied the Lion, "for my parents hid me well before they went to war. Then, when I emerged, none were to be seen. In respect that my life is solitary, I like it very well; but in respect that it is private, it is a very vile life.[15] Yet vast this forest be, and I have often thought that I might yet find prides in its more distant parts. But hither have I stayed, rather to bear those ills I have than to fly to others I know not of.[16] Hither have I lived in safety, at the far edge of this forest."

"I must ask," said Dorothy, "how much of yonder yellow road remains before we leave this forest?" At this all skittish motion ceased,[17] as all didst strain to hear the Lion's answer to this question, a question that was much upon their minds.

"In sooth, not above a quarter league, from whence[18] we first didst meet, doth this forest end. And there, the hills of rolling green begin," said he, "for the Emerald City itself is not a day's travel from this very place.[19] At this very hour on the morrow shall we take our rest within the city limits."

"O! I thank my stars I am happy!"[20] exclaimed Dorothy! She then asked the Lion, "As thou art a king thyself, how dost thou think The Great Oz will receive us?"

"If he be akin to royalty, so too will he have the spirit and humour of state.[21] After a demure travel of regard,[22] thus will he deign to make our better acquaintance."[23]

"What means this augurer?"[24] whispered the Tin Woodman aside then to the Scarecrow.

"I know no answer,"[25] whispered the Scarecrow in reply.

When it was time for that day to be rounded with a sleep,[26] Dorothy took her rest upon a bed of leaves as the Scarecrow had prepared for her. Anon was she asleep, and the Scarecrow covered her with more. Then, as others slept, he stood watch o'er the camp whilst the Tin Woodman kept the bonfire burning brightly all throughout that night.

Toto, who didst e'er sleep with Dorothy, this night chose instead to lie within the Lion's warm embrace. This posture both surprised the Lion and, withal, affected him profoundly. For he had never known, since last he knew his parents, any kind of kinship, nor any faithful friend.[27] Toto's presence next to him, under his protection, evoked within the Lion a remembrance of a bond from deep within his memory. And in his dreams that night there was a lioness[28] who, in life, had been his mother.

As Dorothy and the Lion, and perchance Toto too, didst dream, the Scarecrow on his watch observed notable movements in the underbrush that didst increase with each passing hour. Clearly were these movements in his sight, as though 'twas midday, for he didst see the same in night as in day.

On his watch the night before, in the cabin doorway, so too he saw movements in the night, but these movements now were different, for they were not extravagant but determinate,[29] and they came ever closer. To be sure, the fire checked their tentative approach and, i' faith, they were pausing now in place, not a quarter furlong hence. He then whispered to the Tin Woodman, "Cease thy tending of the fire and hasten hither, I prithee!"

"I do not now fool myself, to let imagination jade me, for every reason excites to this,[30] that the Kalidah approach and are lying now in wait," warned the Scarecrow. "Daylight discovers not more, this is open."[31]

"Anon must we wake the Lion and seek his good counsel and advice," replied the Tin Woodman, "too well he knows the Kalidah and he will know whither our preservation lies."

Upon waking, the Lion didst attend most carefully as the Scarecrow told all that he had seen and heard.

"Kalidah have tracked me hither and find me out of my guard.[32] Be thou blessed for thy keen sight,"[33] said the Lion, "and, withal, for the keeping of this healthy blaze, else should we, even now, be heaven-bound. They await the dying of these flames, or else for our return to the yellow road by that same way that led us hither, and so they lie in wait. They do oft employ surprise, as on that day so long ago when I became a foundling. 'Tis the method of their madness."[34]

"If the Kalidah approach this camp, I'll soon dispatch them with my axe!" proclaimed the Tin Woodman. "Indeed!" said the Scarecrow. "And that may you be bold to say![35] Though ever do I fear such fire, yet will I brandish such a blazing torch[36] that none shall dare approach!"

"Nay," replied the Lion, "whilst I admire thy courage, their numbers are too great. Perforce, would we be lost, even unto Dorothy and Toto. Nay, we must not engage the Kalidah in battle, this night or to-morrow.[37] I' sooth, must we 'scape a brawl,[38] lest we all should perish."

"And, withal, the Kalidah would die with the greater honor," said the Tin Woodman, upon reflection, "for 'tis said, 'How much better to fall before the lion than the wolf!'[39]"

"I rather think behavior," said the Lion, "and not so rank or birth, is honor's firm foundation. I am much concerned with honor. Indeed, if it be a sin to covet honor, I am the most offending soul alive."[40]

"Mine own opinion," said the Scarecrow in rebuke, "is that there is a proper time for philosophy,[41] and now is not such time!"

"Thou'rt i' the right,[42] of course," replied the Lion. "In this hour, the better part of valor is discretion, in the which better part may we save our lives.[43] We must depart anon, by such other way, with such invisibility and subtle stealth[44] as we may e'er discov'r, before yon grey becomes the morning's eye."[45] Aside then to the Tin Woodman he added, "I pray you are well-oiled!"

Commanded then the Lion, "Wake Dorothy anon and gently 'prise her of our peril and, withal, feed this fire, for these dying flames invite[46] the Kalidahs' approach!"

"I pray you, what is 't o'clock?"[47] asked Dorothy then, as she rubbed her eyes and struggled to sit upright in her bed of leaves.

"There's no clock in the forest,"[48] said the Scarecrow, "but 'tis almost morning, and we must all be gone."[49]

"Whereto and wherefore?" asked Dorothy.

The Scarecrow then, in whispers, told Dorothy all that he had seen in his watch that night, and of their great need to leave the camp anon. Toto, sensing her rising apprehension, stayed nearby as Dorothy asked the Lion this, "Say there is such way as 'twill lead us 'way from hither, say what then?[50] Won't the Kalidah pursue us thither?"

"Beyond this stream doth lie another way, that I think likely is unknown to them," replied the Lion. "It leads through purlieus once fenced in by walls of stone, and it will bring us to the forest's edge, near the yellow road. The Kalidah likely know it not, by reason they are far without their realm."

"Anon I will carry each of you across this stream and, withal, the stream shall fault our scent. The Kalidah will not approach whilst this fire burns and dawn hath yet to break. When at last they do, they will find that we, as spirits, have melted into air, into thin air.[51] Even should they mend their fault, i' faith, by then will we have left this forest, to where they would be loath to follow, for fear of the unknown."

"I prithee, hold Toto close in thy embrace lest, in his courage, he doth race to make his challenge to the Kalidah and thereby break the sinews of our plot!"[52]

Anon didst the Tin Woodman lift both Dorothy and Toto onto the Lion's back. With silent feet, the Lion carried them o'er the stream, to a darken'd place beyond. In like manner, the Scarecrow, holding Dorothy's basket firm didst follow, and so too the Tin Woodman, holding firm his axe, didst then join them thither. Then, with Dorothy and Toto on his back once more, the Lion, with a determined step, led them on to safety.

Chapter VIII

The Deadly Poppy₁ Field

"O! Do but look!" exclaimed Dorothy! "What envious streaks do lace the severing clouds in yonder east!"₂ For they had reached the forest's edge, with Dorothy yet on the Lion's back, and the first light of the new day didst relieve her passion much.₃ And hither didst the welkin dance indeed,₄ for stars could yet be seen in the still dark western sky.

"I pray, sir, tell me,"₅ asked Dorothy of the Lion, "where lies the yellow brick road? Have we lost our way?"

"In sooth, 'tis not far a'tall," answered he. "If we but follow this forest's edge then, anon, will we find it under foot and paw. Yet I pray thee,₆ let us still pursue a course of our own making, and not approach the yellow road whilst forest eyes may yet observe. Withal, we are leeward of the forest, which is much credit to us,₇ for so may I sense the Kalidah and so may I know that we have not been followed. As through the forest we have gone,₈ let us keep to yonder field, and not fetch the yellow road 'til we are far beyond the Kalidahs' cruel reach."

"This is wisely done,"₉ concurred the Scarecrow. And so didst they proceed for hours, 'til nought of the forest could they see behind them.

Then said the Lion to Dorothy, "The fringèd curtain of thine eye advance and say what thou seest yond."₁₀

"Nought but a hill, sir," answered she.

"When we shall come to th' top of that same hill₁₁ yet will we see, again, the yellow road and more," replied the Lion. "For upon such height shall you glimpse the Emerald City of Oz! I, myself, have come thus near,₁₂ yet no nearer, to that majestic city."

"Oh, let us hence! I stand on sudden haste!"₁₃ exclaimed Dorothy! "I do so long to gaze upon the sight!"

"To climb steep hills requires slow pace at first,"₁₄ cautioned the Lion.

"Wisely and slow,"[15] said the Scarecrow. "They stumble that run fast,"[15] added the Tin Woodman.

"O! Do bid me to run fast, and I will strive with things impossible!"[16] said Dorothy, as she slid from the Lion's back with Toto under arm. And, so saying, didst she and Toto run o'er that grassy field, and to that yonder hill.

I' sooth, the hilltop vista was magnificent. Before them stood the Emerald City, not three hours' travel from that very place.[17] Below them wound the yellow road through rolling hills and shady glens and poppy fields and, so too, it crossed a winding river that sparkled in the distance. And o'er all, was there a rainbow and a sky of such deep blue that Dorothy didst ache for Kansas.

Behind them now, far distant, could the forest then be seen. Summer clouds and summer haze hung o'er it, and it seemed but a dream. Said Dorothy then, but to herself, "Through the forest I have gone."[8]

Anon didst they descend to join the yellow brick road, to where it flowed into such beautiful estate, through such a field of dark red poppies[1] that all but covered the road ahead.

"One such touch of nature makes the whole world kin,[18] doth it not?" smiled Dorothy. Then, to the Tin Woodman, "Thy father didst speak truly of the beauty of this land!"

Eagerly they entered the poppy field and anon were they immersed in its fragrant beauty. To start, their walk was most brisk and giddy-paced,[19] for the Emerald City was now in distant view.

But, anon, their gait didst slow, and Toto, who was wont to lead, fell behind and paused in place. Dorothy returned to him and, lifting him to herself, found him limp and drowsy. "Toto! Are you ill, or what are you that you should sleep at this time of the day?"[20] asked she.

Yet no response made he, for he was fast asleep. Collapsing to the yellow bricks, with Toto in her arms, she said, "He is but exhausted from so long a journey or, perhaps, from such an early waking. Perhaps we might all rest awhile. I' faith, I could wish myself asleep, for I cannot keep my drooping eyelids open.[21] To sleep, perchance to dream…"[22] said she, and then she too was sound asleep.

The hilltop vista was magnificent!

Anon didst the Scarecrow and Tin Woodman turn back to Dorothy and Toto. Said the Scarecrow then, "How now! How strange that they should, of a sudden,₅ sleep so in this place, upon these yellow bricks. I will carry Toto and, so too, her basket, but you must lift Dorothy onto the Lion's back once more, if e'er we are to reach the Emerald City."

Yet, when they turned to beckon the Lion hither, they found he too was fast asleep! "What shall we do?" exclaimed the Scarecrow! "Dorothy and Toto might we carry, but the Lion doth weigh thirty stone and is so far beyond our meager measure!"

"Each capricious zephyr breathes upon these banks of poppies,₂₃ stealing and giving odour! Enough, no more!"₂₄ exclaimed the Tin Woodman. "'Tis not so sweet now as it was before!₂₅ These sweet beds of flowers₂₆ are like to be their graves,₂₇ and shall adorn them so, if they should linger hither, never to awaken!"

Then, at a single tear on the Tin Woodman's face, the Scarecrow cried, "No time is this for tears, you'll rust again! Our business must now be the extrication of these three!"

"If I but had a heart," replied the Tin Woodman, "then, at this sight, most surely it would break. But i'sooth, I have yet to shed a single tear."

But then another and another appeared upon his face as the heavens opened and a drenching flood burst forth. Once more did Iris, goddess of the rainbow, smile upon this wayward child as the rain washed away[28] the fragrance of the poppies. In its stead followed cool, clean air and the sweet petrichor of the wholesome earth that ever follows rain. First Toto, then Dorothy, then didst the Lion stir and wake refreshed from so brief a slumber but left now shivering in the rain. The summer shower passed quickly and a heavenly bow[29] arched o'er all with brilliance and with promise.

"Alas," said the Scarecrow of the Tin Woodman, "he hath rusted firm again! Whilst I oil him, get ye all three[30] out of this poppy field anon afore the deadly fragrance doth return! Not even mandragora, nor all the drowsy syrups of the world,[1] are more potent than are these pretty poppies!"

With Dorothy and Toto mounted on his back once more, the Lion flew along the yellow road, and whe'r he ran or flew they knew not whether; for through his mane and tail the high wind sang[31] 'til they had gained the safety of the lush, green grass beyond the poppy field.

Through his tail and mane the high wind sang!

Within that very hour didst the Tin Woodman and the Scarecrow at last arrive there too, to find Dorothy and the Lion resting and drying in the warm afternoon sun. Toto, noting their approach, ran in haste to greet them, barking all the while. Now gladly reunited, they were, once again, bound for the Emerald City.

Chapter IX

The River

"The rain hath ruined the last of my good bread," said Dorothy, examining her basket, "and so too are my matches wet. 'Tis well we are so near the Emerald City."

"Alas," said the Scarecrow, "the property of rain is to wet.[1] There was not time, nor means, to shield thy basket from such sudden rain."

"Still," replied Dorothy, "the rain was such a blessing! All doth appear now fresh,[2] for it washed away not just the deadly poppy scent but, so too, it laid the summer's dust[3] from this yellow road. Withal, the Emerald City of Oz is nigh and, anon shall its palatial gate come into view! Let us hasten hence!"

Once more didst they address their gait[4] unto the Emerald City. And, anon, they came to that same river as first they spied from high upon the hilltop. Arching o'er the river was an ancient bridge of stone, long since collapsed midway. Whether or not by intent, the breach[5] barr'd all who would approach from the eastern realms or from the northern woods.

Putting a finger to the side of his head, the Scarecrow said, "Nay, but first, let me see, let me see, let me see."[6]

"How now, sir?" asked the Tin Woodman of the Scarecrow. "Are you reasoning with yourself?"[7]

"Indeed," replied the Scarecrow, "I am contemplating how might we cross this river. 'Tis not so very wide, but 'tis enough, and so too is it deep.[8] Withal, it flows most unnaturally swift in this late summer season. Perhaps the recent deluge[9] from the heavens provides the reason. 'Twill ne'er be crossed so easily as was the stream this morning afore the break of day."[10]

"I know!" cried the Tin Woodman! "From yonder glen could I fell such a tree as would span this rushing river!" The Scarecrow pondered this, but sadly said, "Nay, I fear 'twill not do. Thou may fell such a tree, of course, but there ends all success of such endeavor. For we lack the means to place it on this bridge, to span from one side to the other."

"Take heart, dear friend," said Dorothy. "Thou art so good to offer thy entertainment[11] in this, our time of need. Perchance some other means to cross will yet come into mind."

"Well, what of this? Suppose I hew smaller trees and build for us a raft?" suggested he.

"Again," said the Scarecrow, "this is a noble thought.[12] But swiftly flows this river, and so too westerly, and therewithal lies the castle of the Wicked Witch of the West, she whom we must avoid. If we should lose control, the raft would carry us away from the Emerald City and toward that forbidden land."

The Scarecrow thought once more and then said aloud, "Perchance, perchance." To the Lion then he said, "Recall yesterday when we first met, when ye approached us with such leaps and bounds, the like of which we, nor any, had e'er seen before."

Replied the Lion then, "O, I do but beg your pardon![13] Forgive me now so rude an introduction!"

"Nay, do but hear my reason for these recollected terms,"[14] said the Scarecrow with a quiet reassurance. "'Tis my belief that one so powerful could leap the gulf that doth exist between the remnant portions of this bridge."

"O! Nay!" exclaimed the Lion! "While strength I do possess, yet still hast I no courage equal to such action! Leap across this flowing river? If I should fail, and thus fall in, it would carry me to the setting sun, to that land ruled by the Wicked Witch!"

"Courage Lion!" said the Scarecrow. "Our doubts are traitors and make us lose the good we oft might win by fearing to attempt![15] I believe ye will succeed in this great leap. But even should ye fall into the river, do recall that ye can swim. The Witch's realm is yet a distant land, and ye should not fear on that account."

"I, too, believe in thee," said Dorothy, "with all my heart. I would exult[16] in thy success!"

"Perhaps," suggested the Tin Woodman, "ye might approach the bridge at a galloping pace[17] and so fly from one side to the other."

At this the Lion said, "Very well. By thy faith will I take courage, and thus will I attempt. But I shall make this leap as cats are wont to do."

The Lion then approached the precipice[18] and crouched there with the water rushing past, as if poised to pounce on some unsuspecting prey. He then sprang with a mighty leap[18] and so flew across the river! With ease did he land upon the other side! At his success, his companions cheered, and so too did Toto bark in the excitement! With yet another leap did he once more return to be amongst his friends, there to celebrate his conquered fear.

"Scarecrow," said the Tin Woodman then, "I marvel[19] at this feat and yet I cannot see how this brave display of aerobatics serves us in our objective. For we are still on this side of the river, and the obstacle remains."

"Quite so," replied the Scarecrow. He then asked, "Lion, could ye make this noble leap with a scarecrow on thy back? Or even this Tin Woodman? Or still again with Dorothy and Toto?"

"I' faith I could," replied the Lion. "Every confidence hast I now in my power to bring ye safely, one and all, and Toto too, to the other side. As ye hast seen, I am more than equal to this task, and gladly do I undertake it." And so, anon, were the travelers across the river and on their way once more.

Chapter X

The Guardian of the Gates

"Even now, on a moderate pace, we have since arrived but hither,"[1] declared Dorothy, upon their arrival at the outer gate of the Emerald City, where the road of yellow bricks abruptly ended. Embedded in the gate were multitudes of sparkling emeralds and, withal, was there a bell at hand, which Dorothy didst strike upon.[2]

Yet there came no answer to this summons.

"Why doth this bell not invite us[3] hither?" asked Dorothy of the others. "'Tis a sweet bell, not jangled, nor out of tune, nor harsh."[4]

"Perchance 'twas not heard within," suggested the Tin Woodman. "Let me knock upon this iron gate[5] with my weighty axe."

At this didst they distinctly hear a muttering within, and, withal, a jangling of keys. "Here's a knocking indeed! If a man were porter of hell-gate, he should turn old with turning o' the key![6] Knock, knock! Who's there, in th' other devil's name?"[7] as they distinctly heard a voice within to grumble.

Slowly then an inner door didst open, and appeared there a small man, not unlike a Munchkin, dressed all in green, and who, perhaps, had recently awoken from a nap or who, perhaps, had drunk himself out of his five senses.[8] And whe'r he napped or drank, they knew not whether.[9] He declared himself to be The Guardian of the Gates and, in a loud and official voice, he demanded, "Who be ye and wherefore seek ye entrance to the Emerald City of Oz?"

"I am Dorothy of Kansas," answered she. "And these are my true companions, the Scarecrow, the Tin Woodman, and the Lion, and this is little Toto. We seek an audience with The Great and Powerful Oz."

"Before my God, I might not this believe without the sensible and true avouch of mine own eyes![10] The Wizard of Oz will ne'er be seen by so motley[11] a crew as ye! Be gone! Anon!" said the Guardian emphatically.

At this the Lion turned his head and thought, but to himself, "How quickly leads this yellow brick road away from this churlish[12] fellow."

"'Tis true we have seen better days,[13] and yet why such incivility?" demanded the Tin Woodman.

"I do not like her name!"[14] blurted out the Guardian, who would give no reason near the truth for his rude behavior.

"There was no thought of pleasing you when she was christened!"[15] shouted the Scarecrow in retort!

"O, peace, peace!"[16] implored Dorothy. Then, recalling the advice of the Good Witch of the North to be clamorous and leap all civil bounds,[17] she said, "Sirrah,[18] I will stand at your door like a Sheriff's Post and be the supporter to a bench, but I *will* speak with[19] The Great and Powerful Oz! Here my fixed foot shall grow 'til I have audience!"[20]

"Much good may it do ye," derided the Guardian, haughtily, "for I see none to fear."[21]

"And that may you be bold to say in your foolery,"[22] exclaimed the Scarecrow, "for this is she who killed the Wicked Witch of the East! In sooth, she wears her slippers yet!"

Patience itself would startle at this[23] and so then did the Guardian! "O, now, now,"[24] stammered he, "'twas ever my intent that ye shall enter, one and all," as he quickly advanced to unlock and open wide the gate. Bowing then with profound humility, he said, "I shall present ye,[25] anon, that ye may humbly petition The Great and Powerful Oz."

"My purpose is, indeed, a horse of that color,"[26] declared Dorothy, boldly. "I thank thee, lead me on."[27]

The Guardian of the Gates

Chapter XI

The Emerald City and The Great and Powerful Oz

"The Captain of the Guard, who will of thy arrival be full joyous,₁ shall hast the honor of presenting ye to the Palace," said The Guardian of the Gates. "I prithee, wait hither whilst I inform him. Anon shall I return."

The ante-chamber₂ amazed where thus long they stood,₃ for 'twas ornate, in green marble and windowed in stained-glass of verdant scenes. And, withal, 'twas all of a dark mahogany. Closed before them were large oaken doors that opened to the city. Dorothy, holding Toto, took comfort in a stately chair of green velvet, and the chair in which she sat was like a burnish'd throne.₄ All then waited patiently for the Guardian's return.

The Captain of the Guard, upon perceiving truth in the Guardian's report,₅ promptly issued orders to him. "Pass word₆ anon to The Great and Powerful Oz! Ceremoniously let us prepare some welcome for this maid,₇ she who killed the Wicked Witch! The proud Court of Guard₈ assemble! Beat loud the tambourines, let the trumpets blow, that this great maid may her welcome know!"₉

Entered then the Captain, tall of stature and with a long and flowing beard of green, to welcome Dorothy, and all. "On behalf of The Great and Powerful Oz, and of the Emerald City proper, to thee and thy company I bid a hearty welcome!₁₀ Withal, my lady, a general welcome from his Grace salutes thee, and ye all."₁₁

"I prithee," replied Dorothy, "and I'll thank thee bounteously,₁₂ bring us anon to The Great and Powerful Oz, for we stand on sudden haste₁₃ to speak with him."

"Ay," replied the Captain, "ay, but first, wilt thou not cast thy humble slough and appear fresh?₁₄ For with long travel are ye not stiff and weary?₁₅ Dost ye not wish, when ye are first presented₁₆ to his Grace,₁₇ to honor him with thy best version of thy eternal self?"₁₈

"O, ay!" exclaimed Dorothy! "I 'faith, we must needs[19] show him every regard! Then, ay, upon reflection, we wouldst fain accept thy deeds of hospitality."[20]

"Excellent! Anon shall I bring ye to the Palace! Thy arrival is most timely," added he, "for this night I hold an old accustom'd feast, whereto I have invited many a guest, such as I love; and you among the store, four more, most welcome, makes my number more."[21]

And in th' very moment,[22] as these warm greetings were bestowed, so too were the Captain's orders then set in motion. Assembled just beyond the oaken doors stood the Court of Guard[8] in close formation, prepared to draw their swords.[23] Withal, the Palace Band awaited thither a signal to strike up a lively tune, by which strain[24] the Captain would escort the honored guests through the emerald streets, to the Palace gate beyond.

And word then passed[6] not only to The Great and Powerful Oz but, withal, throughout the city it was fresh in murmur[25] who 'twas had come amongst them, no less than she who killed the Wicked Witch of the East! For what great ones do the less will prattle of.[26] Then too, was she well attended[27] by a talking scarecrow, a man of tin, a large lion, and a small, furry creature entirely unknown to them. The entire city was turning out to look upon the sight!

"And one thing more,"[28] said the Captain. "Before entering the city proper, the Guardian of the Gates must fit ye with green spectacles lest the brilliance of our city should blind well-seeing[29] eyes."

This done, the Tin Woodman lifted Dorothy onto the Lion's back once more. All then didst tend to th' Captain's sharp green whistle[30] as the doors to the city opened and the Court of Guard[8] presented arms to the sound of trumpets blaring![31] Then did the Captain of the Guard lead them about the streets,[32] wherein they received five thousand welcomes,[33] as the Court of Guard[8] and Palace Band marched on, in perfect step, behind!

Which was the more astonish'd,[34] which could say?[35] The company didst marvel[36] at the majesty of the city, built upon green marble and adorned in sparkling emeralds. But so too were the people struck with awe to see Dorothy ride upon a lion through the civil streets.[37] All strained to see the silver slippers, and many didst note the kiss upon her brow.[38]

Wherein they received five thousand welcomes!

As a child watched them pass, Dorothy heard her say, "Mother wherefore doth she ride upon such lion?" To which her mother whispered in reply, "Hush child, 'tis long of thee to spur me with such questions!"[39]

The grand procession marched o'er the Palace drawbridge and halted at the gate where the Captain of the Guard and the Sergeant-At-Arms[40] saluted one another. The Captain then proclaimed the honored guests to all assembled there.

"Salutation and greeting to you all![41] Here is Dorothy of Kansas," announced the Captain sharply, "she who killed the Wicked Witch! In matters of great moment, she comes to have some conference with his Grace.[42] Withal, shall she feast with us this night,[43] as our honored guest, when vesper bells dost chime. But, for now, show her and all, anon, to such accommodations as ye hast prepared for their good comfort."[44]

The Sergeant-At-Arms then struck his staff upon the Palace threshold and boldly proclaimed, "Be't so! Proceed! Dorothy of Kansas, come into the court,[45] anon!"

The Palace vestibule, adorned with green arras,[46] stood upon green marble, thick inlaid with bright emeralds and patines of bright gold.[47] All entered, and all heard another whistle,[30] therewithal. A young maid, with green eyes and green hair, in an ivy green dress and white apron, stepped forward to greet Dorothy. "Kindly follow me," she said with a curtsy, "and I will bring thee to thy chamber."[48] Dorothy followed her through seven passages and up three flights of stairs until at last they came[49] to a small chamber on the west side of the Palace.

Kindly follow me and I will bring thee to thy chamber.

It was a lovely room, all in green, with a comfortable bed and chair, and a silver basin full of rose-water, bestrewed all o'er with flowers.[50] Against one wall were shelves of leather-bound volumes of books, with unfamiliar titles by unfamiliar authors. On another wall hung a small, intriguing painting of a grand balloon hovering above the city. And before her, where the sun was beginning to gild the western sky,[51] beautiful stained-glass windows manifested scenes of flowering gardens in midsummer[52] season. The filtered light from those same windows filled the chamber with countless shades of green. "I like this room," declared Dorothy, "and willingly could waste my time in it."[53]

"Thy bed awaits thee,"[54] said the maiden, "as doth a change of wardrobe[55] behind these mirrored doors. Withal, this bowl of fruit, sweetmeats[56] and bread and, so too, doth this pitcher of cool spring water, lightly flavored with a slice of lime. If ye dost desire anything a'tall, I prithee, ring this silver bell.[57] I will return when 'tis time for thee to attend the Captain's feast."

When the maid in green had left, and gently closed the door behind her, Dorothy washed her face and hands and then sampled each appealing dish for, i'sooth, she was famished,[58] and so was Toto too. Then, to spare the soft green velvet counterpane, Dorothy removed the silver slippers[59] for the first time since she donned them at the bidding of the Good Witch of the North. She felt a strange disquiet[60] in so doing, as if now separated from something vital, and she could not help but reflect upon her separation from her kin. She longed to put the slippers on again and so, despite relief for her sore labor,[61] she didst not rest o'er long upon the feather-bed.[62]

She next browsed the green silk and satin dresses in the wardrobe,[63] holding each one to herself and admiring her reflection[64] in the glass, before choosing one of silk, with an intricate brocade, which didst fit her perfectly. She then rang the silver bell.[57]

"Here, sweet miss, at your service,"[65] said the maid, upon re-entering the chamber. "I prithee," asked Dorothy, "might I have a basin in which to bathe Toto and so prepare him for the feast?"

"Marry!" replied the maid. "But I must bathe him for thee, to spare thy silken dress! For a single drop of water will spot it notably!" Then asked she, "I trust he will not mind me bathing him?"

"Nay, not a'tall," laughed Dorothy, "Toto loves his bath![66] But he must be bathed out of doors, for he will shake with vigor whene'er his bath is o'er!"

In time, Toto didst return, fresh and with a bright green ribbon 'bout his neck. Dorothy then asked, "Say, good miss, how fare my friends[67] since last we parted company?"

"All are well," answered she. "Master tailor hath mended the Scarecrow where needed and hath made him a doublet of changeable taffeta, for his mind is a very opal.[68] And master tinsmith hath polished the Tin Woodman 'til not a scruple[69] of rust nor tarnish remains. So too he filled his oilcan with his sweetest oil. Withal, he hath brightly polished his heavy axe and keenly sharpen'd it to its former might."[70]

"And what of the Lion?" asked Dorothy. "He hath never been within a city proper, nor yet within a house, to say nought of a palace, so grand as this. I fear he will find little comfort in these lovely rooms."

"Quite so," replied the maid, "and so he takes his ease along the lake that doth adjoin the Palace. He hath declined our offerings of food, preferring instead the fish that he himself hath caught! Withal, he swam in that same lake, he whom our master groomer then so carefully hath dress'd."[71]

"So too," she continued, "must I now brush thy hair, for anon I must return thee to the Captain."

Anon were Dorothy and Toto presented[16] to the Captain, whom they found conversing with the Scarecrow and Tin Woodman, for all were there awaiting her arrival.

"Do we wait upon the Lion?" asked Dorothy.

"Alas, he hath respectfully declined our invitation," replied the Captain. "He is apprehensive of enclosed spaces and prefers to remain this night among the trees by the palace lake. We may enter now."

The Captain then escorted all into the Great Hall and led Dorothy to the head of the table.

"O!" exclaimed Dorothy! "Certainly, this seat of honor must belong to thee, our host, or still more to the Great Oz himself. Anon will he then join us? I do so long to make his acquaintance."[72]

"The Great and Powerful Oz is e'er invited to these great affairs, held often in his honor, but ne'er doth he attend," replied the Captain.

"Shall I never meet this wizard?" lamented Dorothy.

"I' faith, thou shall, on the morrow," the Captain reassured her, "but this night we honor thee."

Then, to the Tin Woodman, he asked, "Dost thou ne'er eat a'tall? I regret I hast nought to offer thee."

"Nay," replied he, "for these tunes and madrigals are food for a weary soul! It hath been an age since last I heard such music, and I am starved for it! Marry, if music be the food of love, play on!"[73]

"And thee, miss? How dost thou like this tune?"[74]

"It gives a very echo to the seat where Love is throned,"[75] answered she.

"And what think you of our fair city?" asked the Captain then.

"'Tis wonderful, of course, but no more so than its people," answered Dorothy. "For what is the city but the people?"[76]

"Thou art full of pretty answers!"[77] laughed the Captain.

"And you sir," said the Captain to the Scarecrow. "What can I offer thee?"

"I' sooth," he replied, "this is my first stately dinner. Or any dinner a'tall, i' faith. I therefore crave of thee thy leave that I may[78] hear political discussion and that I may hear tongues tang arguments of state."[79]

"I am certain that thou shall!" laughed the Captain, once again. "Upon mine honor,[80] thy artless mind delights more than a witty fool!"[81]

The feast began, and the food was excellent. Dorothy, in defiance of good manners, slipped many a tender morsel under the Captain's table[82] to little Toto, who was as hungry as the sea and could digest as much.[83]

As the conversation flowed 'round the table, all were keen to learn wherefore Dorothy and her companions had come to the Emerald City. Their tales were the fruit to that great feast.[84] Yet none asked Dorothy, nor any, how the Wicked Witch had died. Nor did they ask how a scarecrow might have life and speech, or a man of tin, or even still a lion. Appearances notwithstanding, all believed Dorothy to be a witch of immense power and great transcendence,[85] for she had killed the Wicked Witch of the East, and none dared to ask impertinent questions, to inquire of her magic. Withal, all assumed Dorothy's companions were further manifestations of her art, and so all didst tread most carefully and some feared to speak a'tall.

I' sooth, in deeds of hospitality[20] and entertainment didst the Emerald City excel. And yet, when Dorothy asked wherefore the stone bridge was left in disrepair, and how long it had been so, all were quiet or evasive in their answers. "Surely the tradesmen who built this beautiful city are equal to the task of its repair," thought she. So too were all evasive when she asked why Oz was ne'er to be seen.

In time, Dorothy said to the Captain, and to all, "I could fain wish this feast might ever last,[86] yet give me now leave to leave ye.[87] I am most grateful for your deeds of hospitality,[20] but now must I retire for tomorrow I have audience, at last, before The Great and Powerful Oz."

In his official report to the Wizard, the Captain described Dorothy as the nonpareil of beauty[88] and, so too, reported that she doth speak masterly.[89] Withal, he found the Scarecrow to be political and cerebral and, so too, he reported the Tin Woodman's sentimental love of music. This above all:[90] he reported each reason given by each honored guest for seeking an audience with The Great and Powerful Oz.

But absent from the Captain's report was any intelligence regarding how the Wicked Witch of the East had died, and this angered and annoyed The Great Oz exceedingly, for it was this that he most desired to learn.

Thought Oz then, "I learn by this report they have more in them than mortal knowledge.[91] I burn in desire to question them further."[92]

Dorothy and Toto left the Great Hall accompanied by the Tin Woodman and the Scarecrow. "Before I sleep this night," said she to the

Scarecrow, "I would fain say goodnight to our friend the Lion, for I long to know that he is well. I prithee, guide me to the lake where he takes his ease."

As Dorothy took his arm,[93] the Scarecrow led her, and all, to where the Lion was resting in the moonlight by the lake. At their approach, the Lion lifted his head and spoke.[94] "How now?"[95] said he, "Did ye enjoy the feast?"

All said they did, and yet the Lion sensed there was something left unsaid. He said to Dorothy then, "Forgive me, but I fear something unsettles thy wits.[96] Pray tell me what it is."

"The Great and Powerful Oz didst not attend the feast," said Dorothy. "The Guardian said sooth when he said that Oz will not be seen!"

"Or," added the Scarecrow, "if he be, it's four to one he'll none of us!"[97]

"An he doth not, 'tis pity of our lives,"[98] replied the Lion, "yet I hast been informed The Great Oz will vouchsafe to see me to-morrow at sunrise, and alone. I fear I shall not sleep one wink this night."[99]

"Wherefore alone?" asked Dorothy.

"I know no answer,"[100] replied the Lion, "save to say The Great Oz may believe I am in thy service, for I carried thee through the streets. I do not know if I can muster even a bit of courage to face The Great and Powerful Oz alone."

"Perchance," said the Scarecrow to Dorothy, "the Wizard intends to question each of us alone and then compare our answers to his questions. 'Tis no surprise he should wish to learn all that may be learned from thy companions before he questions thee. For, like all in this great city, he is likely to be in awe of she who killed the Wicked Witch, and so yearns to know all that he can know of thee."

"Thou'rt i' the right,[101] of course," replied Dorothy, "though her demise surprised none more than me." Then, to the Lion, Dorothy said, "Put thyself into a 'havior of less fear.[102] I will give thee, and all, the advice the Good Witch of the North gave me; *when ye dost meet the Great and Powerful Oz, though in his stars he be above thee, be not afraid of greatness,[103] but simply tell thy tale and beseech him to assist thee.'"

"Toto and I must now haste me to my bed, the dear repose for limbs with travel tired,"[104] said Dorothy, "to get what sleep I may before the dawn doth break."

"By your leave,"[105] said the Scarecrow, "I shall stand watch outside thy door, for no sleep do I require."

"I thank thee," replied Dorothy, "Sleep shall dwell upon mine eyes[106] knowing thou art near."

"Nay," replied the Scarecrow, "'tis my honor to play the watchman ever for thy sake."[107]

"My chamber[108] hath a writing-desk," said the Tin Woodman then, "I believe I shall avail myself of it this night to pen the letter I have been composing in my mind these many months. Let us meet hither on the morrow, when the Lion hath returned from his audience with The Great and Powerful Oz."

"Marry," said Dorothy, "I shall say good night till it be morrow."[109]

In his chamber that night, whilst others slept or kept their watch, the Tin Woodman wrote a letter[110] to the Munchkin maid he loved.

My Dearest,

If this fall into thy hand, revolve![111] For at last are we free of the Wicked Witch and I am hither, in the Emerald City, the Palace guest of The Great and Powerful Oz himself, whom I pray will vouchsafe[112] me a heart, at long last!

I have not art to reckon my groans, but that I love thee best, oh, most best, believe it![113] I search for words that may express my love or thy dear merit,[114] yet my modern quill doth come too short![115] But the poet, with a worthier pen,[116] hath writ thus, which doth encompass all that I would say:

"Let me not to the marriage of true minds
Admit impediments. Love is not love
Which alters when it alteration finds,
Or bends with the remover to remove.
O no! it is an ever-fixed mark
That looks on tempests and is never shaken;
It is the star to every wand'ring bark,
Whose worth's unknown, although his height be taken.

Love's not Time's fool, though rosy lips and cheeks
Within his bending sickle's compass come;
Love alters not with his brief hours and weeks,
But bears it out even to the edge of doom.
If this be error and upon me prov'd,
I never writ, nor no man ever lov'd."[117]

"If I could write the beauty of your eyes
And in fresh numbers number all your graces,
The age to come would say 'This poet lies:
Such heavenly touches ne'er touch'd earthly faces.'"[118]

"Haply I think on thee, and then my state,
Like to the lark at break of day arising
From sullen earth, sings hymns at heaven's gate;
For thy sweet love remember'd such wealth brings
That then I scorn to change my state with kings."[119]

I think of thee by day, pray for thee by night, and find my greatest comfort in the memory of thy affection. [120]

Yours,
NC

The next morning, the Lion awoke from a restless sleep betimes, in that hour betwixt day and night, before the heavenly harness'd team began its golden progress in the east.[121] Nervously he awaited the Palace Guard, charged with his delivery before The Great and Powerful Oz.

The guards arrived and escorted the Lion into the Palace where they opened the heavy, ornately carved green doors that led to the Throne Room. They bid the Lion enter, 'though they did not enter with him. Beyond the doors a long passageway led to a large, circular room with a skylight overhead, lit by the first rays of the new day's morning sun. Around the chamber hung intricately woven arras[47] depicting scenes of the Emerald City as viewed from high above the city among the clouds, alternating with scenes of the sun, the moon, and the stars[122] in the night sky constellations.

In the center of the room, the Lion saw a large throne,[123] larger than any throne e'er sat upon by any human king, and hovering o'er it was an enormous head, absent body and limbs. There was no hair upon its head and its eyes were closed. On either side of the throne burned large torches of green fire, and the Lion could feel their heat even at his distance from the throne.

As the Lion gazed upon this sight in fear and wonder, he saw the head move slightly and then saw its eyes open and fix themselves upon him. At once, and instinctively, he deeply bowed and said, "Your Grace."

"Who art thou?" demanded the enormous head in a powerful voice, as the torches on either side flared brightly,[124] "and wherefore dost ye appear before The Great and Terrible Oz?"

Oz struck the Lion dumb with fear and yet, anon, he somehow found a bit of courage and told his tale, speaking in starts, distractedly.[125] The Wizard listened as the Lion spoke of his lonely and anxious life in the Eastern Forest, of being left behind to survive as best he could. Spoke he, withal, of the day not long before when he first met Dorothy and the others, and of how they escaped the Kalidah and so camest hither.[126]

"And so, dost ye see," said the Lion, "I hast come to ask thee to instill a fortitude from heaven[127] in my bosom,[128] and so elevate me to my rightful place in the forest, as King of Cats[129] and sovereign of all who dwell therein."

"And why should I do this for thee?" asked the Wizard.

"Because of all Wizards thou art the greatest, and thou alone hast the power to grant this, my request,"[130] answered the Lion.

"Tell me, sirrah, how didst Dorothy destroy the Wicked Witch of the East? Did she chant[131] some ancient incantation?[132] Or, perhaps, she plied her with some 'pothecary's drug?[133] Doth she, perchance, wield a stick[134] of prodigious power?" asked the Wizard then.

"I' sooth," replied the Lion, "she dropped a house on her."

"Preposterous!"[135] shouted the enormous head. "I warn thee, do not trifle with me!"[136]

"I do not," replied the Lion, "I do assure thee."[137]

"How then did she surmount our natural defenses to the north and to the east?" demanded the Wizard.

"Of what defenses dost ye speak?" asked the Lion in reply.

"I speak of the bulwark of the fallen bridge[138] and of the deadly poppy field, of course," replied the Wizard.

"Ah," said the Lion, who then spake of how the Scarecrow, and so too all, had urged him to attempt the leap across the rushing river, and of his triumph therewithal. And, so too, of how the sudden shower had saved Dorothy and Toto, and himself, from the deadly poppy scent.[139]

"How fortunate were ye," said the Wizard, "to hast thy Fates open their hands[140] to thee."

"And how didst Dorothy subdue such a mighty beast as stands before me now?" asked the Wizard. "Was it by the power of her enchanted slippers?"

"Nay, thou dost mistake.[141] I am not in her service, though I am at her service," said the Lion. "She listened as I told my tale and she loved me for the dangers I had pass'd. And I loved her, for she didst pity them. This is the only witchcraft she hath used,[142] and 'tis no art a'tall, save love. Though I be but a coward, to the death wouldst I defend her for the kindness she hath shown me."

With desire to turn their conversation, the Wizard said, superciliously, "I heard ye didst not attend the Captain's feast, 'though cordially invited."

"I heard the same of thee," replied the Lion.

"And I have heard thy request of me!" shouted the Wizard in anger! "Now hear mine of thee! I require the Wicked Witch of the West to be banished from this land![143] Thy request shall ne'er be granted until this hath been accomplished!"

"And how will ye accomplish this?" asked the Lion.

"Not I," replied the Wizard, "but thee."

The Lion looked from side to side and then behind, searching for whom the Wizard spoke. Then, startled, he exclaimed, "Nay! Ne'er could I e'er banish[143] a wicked witch from Oz!"

"Perhaps not," said the Wizard in a more mellow[144] tone, "but thou know'st one who can. Now leave me!" he shouted, as the green torches flared[124] once more!

The Lion returned to the lake to find the others eagerly awaiting his return, and e'en little Toto, the first to see his friend approaching, barked in glad excitement.

"Say, didst thou speak with him? Know'st thou his mind?"[145] asked Dorothy.

"Ay, ay, he told his mind upon mine ear. Beshrew his hand, I scarce could understand it,"[146] said the Lion.

"Spake he so doubtfully, thou couldst not feel his meaning?"[147] asked the Scarecrow.

"Nay, he struck so plainly I could too well feel his blows,[148] for I tremble yet," said the Lion. Then he said, regretfully, "Oz, The Great and Terrible, hath denied my request for a modicum of courage."

"Nay, nay, not denied," added the Lion hastily, "yet he suffers my request upon the exile of the Wicked Witch of the West from this land. Then, strangely, said he, that I didst know of one with power to banish[143] her. I would say this too: this Wizard hath not the humour of state[149] I once presumed of him!" said the Lion, emphatically.

The others looked at one another and knew not what to say.

At last, the Tin Woodman asked, "What manner of man[150] is he?"

"Of very ill manner,"[151] said the Lion, decisively. "Sir, he's rash and very sudden in choler."[152]

"Of what personage and years is he?"[153] asked Dorothy. "What kind o' man is he?"[154]

"Old, and yet without an age," said the Lion, "and he is not of mankind.[155] He is an apparition,[156] i' sooth a disembodied head, of enormous brow, without limbs or any visible support."

"Oh my!" said Dorothy, "The Good Witch of the North didst say she knew not if The Great and Powerful Oz was e'en a man, for she had ne'er seen him." Then she asked the Lion, "Who dost thou know with strength and power to banish[143] a wicked witch?"

"I know no answer,"[100] said the Lion.

As all pondered these tidings and wondered at their meaning, then didst Toto bark. Turning, they saw the Palace Guard approaching. The Guard addressed the Tin Woodman and said, "Salutations![157] The Great and Powerful Oz summons thee anon."

And so, anon, the Tin Woodman walked the same long passageway through which the Lion had passed at sunrise. The eyes of the enormous head fixed upon him as he approached the Throne Room for his feet, being made of tin, were not so silent as the Lion's padded paws.[158]

"Who art thou?" demanded the enormous head in a powerful voice, as the torches brightly flared[124] on either side, "and wherefore dost ye appear before The Great and Terrible Oz?"

The Tin Woodman told his tale, in most affecting terms, as the Wizard listened intently to all he had to say concerning Dorothy or the Wicked Witch of the East, in particular.

The Wizard asked him then, "Didst Dorothy press thee into service to secure the protection of thy axe in the perilous Great Forest? Or had she another reason?"

"Nay. When she heard of my lost love, she then said to me, "We must find for thee a heart." She didst not compel me but, the rather,[159] didst invite me to add my quest to hers and, so too, to the Scarecrow's. She doth not command my axe, though it is ever at her service, such is my gratitude and love for her."

"Amongst thy company," said the Wizard, "thou art unique. Not only art thou a man of tin without a heart[160] but, amongst thy fellowship, thou alone hast known two witches. Even now, ye stand before me under a witch's spell. Is it not so?"

"'Tis true, 'tis pity, and pity 'tis, 'tis true,"[161] he answered.

"And of the silver slippers?" asked the Wizard then. "What is their magic power?"

"I know no answer,"[100] replied the Tin Woodman, "nor dost any in Munchkinland, not e'en the Good Witch of the North herself, though she held no doubt of their enchantment, and power to protect."

"Why did the Good Witch of the North not take the silver slippers unto herself, to the increase of her power?" asked the Wizard. "Is Dorothy so powerful she durst not?"[162]

"Nay. The Good Witch of the North vouchsafed Dorothy the slippers, and encouraged her to wear them always, for protection, and she didst say they rightfully belonged to her, she who killed the Wicked Witch of the East."

"And how, precisely, did she kill that Wicked Witch?" asked the Wizard.

"She dropped from the heavens[163] and, in so doing, ended her," replied the Tin Woodman.

"That is not what the Lion said!" shouted the Wizard! "Ye would have me think she flies, and yet she journeyed from Munchkinland to the Emerald City on foot! One of ye dost lie!" said he, as the torches shot green flames[124] as high as the dome of that great room. "Or, perhaps, do ye both."

"I know not what the Lion said," replied the Tin Woodman meekly, "but she didst communicate in her own words to mine own ears[164] that she didst drop from the heavens."[163]

The Wizard paused as he studied the Tin Woodman. Then he said, "I pray, sirrah, tell me,[165] why didst thou not implore the Good Witch of the North unlock this spell and make of thee a man of flesh and blood once more?"[166]

"I' faith, the Munchkin maid I love didst beseech of her that very thing, but to no avail. For 'twas no use whilst that Wicked Witch yet lived, for her rough magic was ever the more potent.[167] Withal, the Good Witch said she could recall but a small portion of the spell to make me human once again. And this above all,[90] should I become a man once more, recall I have no heart; 't would be a certain death."

"Alas," continued the Tin Woodman, "though the Wicked Witch be dead, I yet must have a heart if ever I shall hold the bent of my affection[168] for the Munchkin maid I love and, still more, have any hope a'tall to be a man of flesh and blood[166] once more."

"As I stand before thee, I am like the painting of a sorrow, a face without a heart.[169] Wilt thou even now lend me a heart replete with thankfulness?"[170]

"Why should I do this for thee?" asked the Wizard.

"Because I ask it," answered the Tin Woodman, "and thou alone can grant my request."[171]

"As I didst tell the Lion," said the Wizard then, "no request will I grant until the Wicked Witch of the West be banished[143] from this land."

"The Lion said as much," replied the Tin Woodman, "but, I pray, sir, tell me of my heart, is it e'en possible?"[165]

"It is," answered the Wizard, "and all that I require of thee is that the Wicked Witch of the West be banishèd."[143]

"Mine own sad tale is proof that I am not the equal of a wicked witch," replied the Tin Woodman. "I'sooth, the rather, 'twas I who was banished[143] to the forest by the Wicked Witch of the East. Never could I ever banish the Wicked Witch of the West from this land."

"Perhaps not," replied the Wizard, "but thou know'st one who can. Now leave me!" shouted he, as the green torches flared[124] once more, "and send to me the Scarecrow! Anon!"

The Tin Woodman returned to the lakeside where his companions waited anxiously.

"How now![95] What news from him?"[172] asked Dorothy, with apprehension, upon his sad arrival.

"Alas, my stars shine darkly over me,"[173] answered he, "for ne'er will he bestow in me a heart, so long as e'er the Wicked Witch of the West be a denizen of Oz. And yet, he didst bestow one hope within mine ear,[146] for he didst say of my request, 'tis possible!' O joy!"

"This is hope, indeed!" exclaimed Dorothy! "Of thy time with him, what more can ye say?"

"Keen was he to hear all that I would say[174] of the Good Witch of the North," answered the Tin Woodman, "and, so too, of the Wicked Witch of the East."

"Wherefore?" asked Dorothy.

"I know no answer,"[100] replied he, "save to say he doth appear obsessed with the witches of this land."

"Was he not cross?" asked the Lion.

"Nay," answered the Tin Woodman, "save when I said the Wicked Witch of the East was killed when Dorothy dropped from the heavens. He said ye answered differently when asked how she didst die and then he became quite cross."

"I said much the same," replied the Lion, "why should he inveigh against[175] our honest testimony? In his choler[176] I find no sense, I do not understand it."[177]

"The more we learn of this Great Wizard, the less we understand, it seems," said the Scarecrow.

"Perchance ye will fare better," said the Tin Woodman to the Scarecrow, "for the Wizard doth bid thee stand before his throne, anon."

The Lion trembled, hearing these words, and said unto the Scarecrow, "Hast courage, for if I could find such fortitude[127] to stand before The Great and Terrible Oz then, most certain, ye can do as much."

"I fear him not,"[178] said the Scarecrow, "though I could wish his sovereign throne 'twas not supplied[179] on either side by brightly burning torches[124] of green fire."

Anon, then, stood the Scarecrow before the Throne of Oz.

"Who art thou?" demanded the enormous head in a powerful voice, as the torches brightly flared.[124] "And wherefore dost ye appear before The Great and Terrible Oz?"

"Your Grace," spoke the Scarecrow, as he lifted his arm[94] to shield his blue eyes from the fiercely burning fire, "I am but a humble scarecrow, the companion of she who killed the Wicked Witch of the East. I hast come to the Emerald City to beseech thee to bestow in me a brain, for none hast I."

"Why should I do this for thee?" asked the Wizard.

"Because thou art powerful and wise," answered the Scarecrow, "and no one else can help me."[180]

"What is thy substance?" asked the Wizard. "Whereof art thou made?"[181]

"I am but a scarecrow made of ordinary straw," replied the Scarecrow. "I was but lately made by two Munchkin brothers who didst hang me on a pole[182] above the corn, till Dorothy didst save me."

"We will not debate the question of thy straw,"[183] replied the Wizard, "but I pray, sir, tell me,[165] didst she, by her art, give thee life to enthrall thee that thou should be her bond-slave?"[184] asked the Wizard.

"Nay," replied the Scarecrow, "for life had I before we e'er didst meet. Yet I would fain be her servant, if she would but let me,[185] in my gratitude for my deliverance by her hand. But the rather,[159] she seeks for me a grander life, by her invitation to join her in her quest to meet thee, The Great and Powerful Oz, to beseech of thee a brain for my head of straws."

"*Cucullus non facit monachum*,"[186] said the Wizard then, to test this man of straw.

"In this Land of Oz, I am but five days old," replied the Scarecrow. "As strange unto thy land as to thy talk, who every word by all my wit being scanned, want wit in all one word to understand."[187]

He then continued, "'Tis true, '*the cowl makes not the monk*', but what's that to th' purpose?"[188]

"That's as much to say, 'ye wear not motley in thy brain',"[189] answered the Wizard.

"I hast no brain," said the Scarecrow.

"So thou hast said," replied the Wizard. "Yet one made but five days prior doth know the Latin tongue.[190] How can this be so?"[191]

"I know no answer,"[100] replied the Scarecrow.

Then thought the Wizard, but to himself, "The soul of this man is in his clothes."[192]

"I pray, sirrah, tell me,"[165] said the Wizard then, "how didst Dorothy kill the Wicked Witch of the East?"

"In the dead of night,[193] beneath her house, she crushed all life out of her," answered the Scarecrow.

The eyes of the great head closed, and its face grimaced in rage and frustration at this answer. When once again they opened, the eyes flashed with anger! "Will none speak truly of the demise of this most Wicked Witch? By so many means may one Witch die? Thou art a barren rascal[194] to beg my entertainment[195] whilst giving me the lie!"[196] cried the Wizard!

"But 'tis no lie," insisted the Scarecrow. "In my brief life, I have yet to tell a lie.[197] Marry, wherefore would I lie to thee when, by doing so, I would imperil that to which I most aspire?[198] I'sooth, in my gratitude for thy good service I would, in turn, do any service thou would ask of me, an it be within my power so to do."

"If ye would be of service," replied the Wizard, "then banish[143] from this land the Wicked Witch of the West! No brain will I bestow in thee till this hath been accomplished!"

"One as wise as thee," said the Scarecrow, "must know that it is not within my power to banish[143] that Wicked Witch."

"Perhaps not," replied the Wizard, "but thou know'st one who can! Now be gone! And send Dorothy to me! Anon!"

When he was once more with his friends, the Scarecrow said, "The Great and Terrible Oz doth seem determined that the Wicked Witch of the West be banishèd.[143] No brain will he bestow in me till this be done."

"When sorrows come, they come not single spies but in battalions,"[199] said Dorothy. "No courage for the Lion, no heart for the Tin Woodman, nor any brain for the Scarecrow. In sooth, too well I know why I am sad."[200]

"Let us for a moment," said the Scarecrow to Dorothy, "reflect on what we know of this Great Wizard. He doth labor under wrong imaginations,[201] the root of which is his belief that thou art but a witch thyself, for thou didst kill the Wicked Witch of the East. And not the Lion, nor the Tin Woodman, nor I be in thy service, yet he imagines each of us to be thy servant."

"Hungry is he[202] to learn how the Wicked Witch hath died," said the Lion, "yet when the truth of her demise is plainly told, he doubts truth to be a liar."[203]

"Withal," said the Tin Woodman to the others, "he suspects some evil,[204] where none is to be found, in the loving acts of kindness[205] Dorothy hath bestowed."

"He doth seem o'erly suspicious," observed the Scarecrow, "and suspicion always haunts the guilty mind."[206]

"His heart seems out of place,"[207] said the Tin Woodman.

"Perchance he harbors an unknown fear,"[208] said the Lion.

"Or perhaps," suggested Dorothy, "there is yet some secret[209] he holds dear. And, withal, I wonder, if he be the most powerful being in the land, is it not within his power to exile[210] the Wicked Witch of the West himself?"

"I trow he will see me now?" asked Dorothy of the Scarecrow.

"Marry," replied the Scarecrow, "he waits on thee anon."

"I hast now not any hope a'tall that he will send me safely back to Kansas," said Dorothy, "nor Toto too. But as the Good Witch of the North advised, I shall not fear his greatness,[103] nor shall I leave his presence till I have dropped the curtain on these foul imaginations,[211] and made whole the good name of my friends."

Turning then to the Lion, Dorothy said, "I prithee, kindly keep Toto under thy watchful eye[212] until I dost return."

The Wizard listened for Dorothy's approach, with a mix of eagerness and apprehension, but heard not her steps, which way they walked,[213] as she stepped along the passageway, for reason of the silver slippers, for they were as silent as falling snow in winter.

"Who art thou?" demanded the enormous head in a powerful voice, as the torches[124] flared once more, "and wherefore dost ye seek The Great and Terrible Oz?"

"I prithee," said she, "I am Dorothy, the Small and Meek. I hast come to thee for help."[214]

"I heard you were saucy at my gate, and I allowed your approach rather to wonder at you than to hear you. If you be not mad, be gone. If you have reason, be brief."[215]

"I entreat your Grace to pardon me," said Dorothy. "I know not by what power I am made bold, nor how it may concern my modesty, in such a presence here to plead my thoughts, but I beseech your Grace[216] vouchsafe to hear the purpose of my coming and suddenly resolve me in my suit."[217]

"Why should I do this for thee?" asked the Wizard, "For one so young and so untender?"[218]

"Because what is yours to bestow is not yours to reserve,"[219] said Dorothy, "for thou art strong and I am weak, and thou art a great wizard and I am only a little girl.[220] Withal, think me young but, I prithee, not untender.[218] For highly do I esteem my elders, and so do I seek safe return to Kansas to my elder kin, for their good welfare the more so than for mine own."

"Express thy darker purpose!"[221] cried the Great and Terrible Oz, as the torches flared![124] "Art thou not a witch thyself? Dost ye not seek to rule the Emerald City in my stead? To enslave the people of this city?"

"Sir," she answered, "I am by birth a farmer's daughter, my wit untrain'd in any kind of art."[222]

"Then say truly how thou didst kill the Wicked Witch of the East!" demanded the Wizard. "Tell me no lies[223] as didst thy false companions."

"Nay, i' sooth, all spoke truly," said Dorothy, "and I do promise to make all this matter even."[224]

Then did Dorothy tell her tale, how the tempest[225] carried her house to the heavens and how it then dropped it again upon the Wicked Witch of the East, crushing her in the dead of night.[193] And of the gifts vouchsafed her by the Good Witch of the North, for protection from the Wicked Witch of the West who, perforce, holds her responsible for her sister's death.

Thou art a great wizard, and I am only a little girl.

"What a plague means that witch to take the death of her sister thus?"[226] asked Dorothy. "I' sooth, I knew nought of the death of the Wicked Witch of the East, nor anything of her a'tall, till the Good Witch of the North spake of it to me. I' faith, of all in Munchkinland, was I the last to know of her demise."

"I see," said the Wizard. "How fortunate thy Fates opened their hands[140] to thee." Continuing, he asked, "I pray, miss, tell me,[174] how didst ye subdue a mighty lion if ye be not a witch?"

"I'sooth," replied Dorothy, "I but slapped his tender nose. 'Twas my good fortune he is but a pusillanimous lion."[227]

"Most fortunate indeed," agreed the Wizard. "Thou didst ride upon a tempest[225] across the heavenly firmament and lived to tell the tale. Thou then kilt a wicked witch, subdued a mighty lion, escaped the fierce Kalidah and, withal, the deadly poppy field, and leapt a rushing river."

"Fortune and I are friends indeed," said Dorothy, "I bear a charmed life."[228]

"Marry," concurred the Wizard. "'Tis 'nough to give one pause.[229] Such good fortune flows not from any font as is of this world. No witch art thou, thou sayest, but neither art thou plain."

Continuing he said, "Ye ask of me a favor, thy safe return to Kansas. Yet ye know not the cost to me to grant to thee this favor. Before I do, there is but one small favor I dost ask of thee."

"I pray, sir, tell me[165] what is it?" asked Dorothy.

"Banish[143] the Wicked Witch of the West from this land!" he shouted, as the torches flared[124] to emphasize his words!

"O sir!" protested Dorothy, "That I could never do! Thy request is so far from reason's yielding![230] I' sooth, 'tis a task more suited to thyself, a Great and Powerful Wizard!" said she, her reason thus making her defence.[231] "Indeed, I wonder, why hast thou not banished[143] her thyself, by thine own hand?"

At these words, the flames receded notably as The Great and Terrible Oz pondered, looked from side to side, then back to Dorothy and said, "Very well, if ye wouldst know the reason, 'tis simply this; the source of her dark power is unknown to me, for her art is far more ancient than mine own. It is a mystery[232] known to her alone. So too is the means of her destruction. In the absence of this knowledge, to challenge her wouldst be a folly[233] most unwise."

The Wizard continued and said, "If thou truly cannot banish[143] her, then do this for me instead; travel to the western lands and therewithal learn the source of her great power, to report then this knowledge unto mine ear."

"Again," objected Dorothy, "how can I, so small and meek,[214] do such a thing as this when this is knowledge she alone possesses?"

"I know no answer,"[100] replied the Wizard, "but of all the citizens of this great city, indeed of this great land, thou art the most likely to succeed in this, the task I lay before thee."

"How now?"[95] asked Dorothy.

"Thou art Fortune's friend,"[234] answered the Wizard. "Thou hast the silver slippers and the kiss of the Good Witch of the North upon thy brow, for protection from that Wicked Witch.[235] Ye hast already made a long journey in this land and overcome many obstacles. Indeed, through the Eastern Forest ye hast come, unharmed. And thou hast loyal friends who will help thee in this quest. Friends, withal, who stand to profit from thy success. And, of all the denizens of this land, thou alone hast kilt a wicked witch."

"Think too but of the Winkies, enslaved by that Wicked Witch," continued the Wizard, "and of the people of this city who could one day share their dismal fate, should her power grow. It well may lie within thy fortune to free the yellow Winkies, as thou didst free the Munchkins from their cruel oppression."

"I hast no words,"[236] said Dorothy.

"What is decreed must be; and be this so!"[237] said the Wizard, "Now leave me and return when you have fulfilled this noble quest."

Rejoining then her friends, Dorothy spoke of all that had transpired in her audience with The Great and Terrible Oz.

"Apparently," said the Scarecrow, upon hearing all she said, "our way lies due west."238

"Reserve thy state, and in thy best consideration check this hideous rashness!"239 exclaimed the Lion! "Were not the woods more free from peril than this envious Wizard's court?240 Or still too, western lands ruled by a Wicked Witch?"

"Take courage, good King of Cats, recall you hast nine lives!"129 admonished the Tin Woodman.

"Recall, withal, I have the gift of a coward," said the Lion, "by which gift I have them still, else I should quickly have the gift of a grave!"241

"O, peace, peace!"242 implored Dorothy. Then said she, but softly, "Dear Lion, I would not ask of thee to journey into the western lands, where we have many enemies in the Witch's court,243 but, i' faith, I must go."

"If that is so," replied the Lion, "come what may, I do adore thee so, that danger shall seem sport, and I will go."[244]

"But how are we to find this Witch's castle?" asked Dorothy of the others. "For the Captain of the Guard did say there is no yellow road to follow into the western lands, for none dost go that way."

"Perhaps," suggested the Lion, "we might follow the sun in its walk about the orb."[245]

"Nay," replied the Tin Woodman, "for I have seen cloudy skies and rainy days one upon another.[246] How then will we find our way in such inclement weather?"

"Tin Woodman," said the Scarecrow, "you must now build for us the raft which ye once proposed. The river we crossed that day will carry us into the western lands."

"Ay," agreed Dorothy. "What else may hap to time we must commit."[247] And so didst all concur.

Chapter XII

The Search for the Wicked Witch

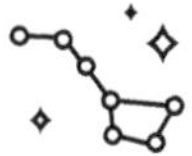

"Look to the heavens," said the Tin Woodman to the Lion, hopefully. "There under Ursa Major[1] burns a comet to be wondered at.[2] Perchance it doth portend[3] our better fortune in the west."

"Perhaps," said the Lion, "for 'tis a pretty sight and, withal, it notably points to the western lands, but I believe it is not in the stars to hold our destiny but in ourselves."[4]

"Our remedies oft in ourselves do lie, which we ascribe to heaven,"[5] agreed the Tin Woodman, "E'en so, when beggars die there are no comets seen.[6] We ourselves be beggars, hither in this land of Oz, and so it must follow, as the night the day,[7] 'tis not our timeless ends[8] this comet doth foretell but something more benign. Is not such better fortune adequate for thee?"

"As King of Cats," answered the Lion, "So hast I nine lives,[9] as thou once said to me. Perhaps ye dost esteem thy solitary life more than I dost one of mine."

"Perhaps," checked the Scarecrow then, "these quillities and quiddities[10] could wait upon the morrow?[11] Our work this day is not yet done!"

"Ay, marry,"[12] said the Lion. "Of course," concurred the Tin Woodman.

"Is the raft yet incomplete?" asked Dorothy.

"Nay," answered the Tin Woodman, "the raft stands at the ready and the smooth current is at help,[13] we lack only two poles to steer her by. And she doth need a name," added he, romantically.

"Excellent," said Dorothy. "And, I pray, sir, with such poles, ye shall find her yare.[14] Now let us sleep and launch at dawn's first light, for we must take the current when it serves, or lose our ventures.[15] Perchance, if my slumbers should be broken, a name for her will come to me in some sweet dream of home if, so far from home, my dreams into my deeds do pry."[16]

"Come thy ways,"[17] said the Tin Woodman to the Scarecrow, "thou that seest in the dark![18] Help me to find two saplings that may serve as poles to steer our watercraft."

"Ay," said the Scarecrow. "Perhaps there, where the female ivy so enrings the barky fingers of the elm."[19]

"Perhaps so," said the Tin Woodman.

Two days prior, when Dorothy and her companions were preparing to leave the Emerald City on their quest to the western lands, the maid in green presented Dorothy with her basket, freshly filled with all things good, and said to her, "The heavens give safety to your purposes."[20]

"I thank thee for thy care and honest pains,"[21] said Dorothy, sincerely, as she embraced the youthful maid, who dried her salt tears[22] on the hem of her white apron and then quickly left the chamber.[23]

Withal, the Captain of the Guard supplied still other needs: rope and tools to build the raft, a tent of olive green, and a canopy[24] to mount upon the raft for shelter from the elements,[25] and, so too, fishing lines and nets, to spare them catching trout by tickling.[26]

"Come, I'll convey ye through the city-gate,"[27] said the Captain to Dorothy and her companions.

In the city streets, all assembled to wave fare-thee-well[28] and to wish them such good fortune, as good luck would have it,[29] as the Palace Guard and the Marching Band escorted them as far as the Eastern Gate. Therewithal, the Guardian of the Gates solemnly advised all to lie low[30] in the western lands and to stay out of the Witch's view, lest she enslave them all, or lest they meet some darker fate.

The company then wound their way o'er the yellow bricks, arriving soon at the bridge of stone where the Lion made his famous leap. Therewithal, the Tin Woodman set about cutting logs with which to build the raft. To himself he thought, "This, my mean task, would be as heavy to me as odious, but the mistress which I serve quickens what's dead and makes my labors pleasures."[31] Then, before two days had passed, the raft was complete and provisioned, and was ready to be launched.

The river now had lost its former rage and smooth ran the water where the river was deep.32 Early in the morning, when the sun began to guild the eastern sky,33 didst the Scarecrow and Tin Woodman ply their poles to push the raft away from the riverbank, to join the current where, with gentle murmur, it didst glide.34

"Didst any name for our craft meddle with your dreams?"35 asked the Tin Woodman then of Dorothy.

"None a'tall," said Dorothy, "though I believe 'Westward Ho!'36 might serve."

"Apt, in good faith, very apt,"37 said the Tin Woodman, with a smile.

Dorothy said to the others, as they drifted gently along, "I told the Good Witch of the North I feared my journey to the Emerald City might prove no more than a wild-goose chase,38 and now my prophecy comes true. For how, i'faith, can anyone have any sense of the source of this Witch's power,39 knowledge known to her alone, when I am sure 'tis safer to avoid40 her than to approach her?"

"What may give thee sense of her great power,39 I know not," said the Scarecrow, as he slowly plied his pole to steer the craft.

"Nor I," said the Tin Woodman. "'Perchance thy silver slippers will prove an aid in such discovery."

"I should like to dip them in this cool water," said Dorothy, "but I fear me[41] I might lose a slipper in the current if I did, and I am loath to[42] take them off."

"I think it wise to keep them on," said the Scarecrow then, "the more so the more westerly we drift."

"Perhaps," suggested the Lion then, "the Wicked Witch hath slippers of her own, not unlike her sister's. If so, perhaps they are the source of her great power."[39]

"Perhaps," said the Scarecrow. "In any case, sir, we do desire to learn[43] all that may be learned of her, whilst we are in these lands. Perchance we may learn something of her habits and her history[44] and, withal, any hints of any weakness[45] that might, in time, call her power to account."[46]

"Thou'rt i' the right,[47] of course," replied Dorothy. "Perchance we may learn something of her instruments of darkness which, by and by, may tell us truths."[48]

"Marry," continued she, "if circumstances lead me, I will find where truth is hid, though it were hid indeed in the centre[49] of her castle."

"Strong reasons make strong actions,"[50] said the Scarecrow then, "and none have reasons stronger than our own."

For two days and for two nights the raft carried them westerly, and by many winding nooks they strayed.[51]

On the morning of the third day, after a night of rain, contagious fogs lay thick upon the river.[52] The Scarecrow and Tin Woodman, for reason of such heavy fog, were then most attentive[53] to their navigation, for here the river widened and, withal, became less deep, and their voyage was now bound in shallows and in miseries.[54]

Then, of a sudden,[55] the raft emerged from that same bank of fog into the glorious morning[56] sunlight. And therewithal, in their ample view,[57] loomed the castle of the Wicked Witch of the West!

"Fall to 't yarely, bestir, bestir!"[58] cried the Scarecrow to the Tin Woodman, "make for the riverbank anon, afore we art seen by yon castle!"

Anon didst the Scarecrow and Tin Woodman use the strength of all their state[59] to push the raft to the shaded shelter of the riverbank where nodding trees over-canopied[60] the river's edge. But in this they were too late. For sitting in her chair in a hall in the castle,[61] the Wicked Witch, in her one eye, had already spied them.

To add to their outrageous fortune,[62] in his haste to alter course,[63] the Scarecrow pushed so hard upon his pole that it stuck hard into the muddy river bottom and left him stranded in midstream, once more a scarecrow hoisted upon a pole, as the raft parted company, and as all called to him in their alarm.

'Twas not by chance, or nature's changing course untrimm'd,[64] that Wicked Witch didst spy them on the river. She had been expecting them, for sightings of their bold presence on the river,[65] the prior day, had reached her ear from crows bound to her in service.[66] She removed then her pointed hat and donned a Golden Cap of finer fashion,[67] with diamonds and red rubies all around. Then, in a foreign tongue,[68] and standing on one foot and then the other, she recited the chant[69] inscribed within the Golden Cap and so summoned the Winged Monkeys to herself. Anon didst they arrive.

"Bring to me that lion!" ordered the Wicked Witch to the leader of the Winged Monkeys. "'Tis a most dreadful thing![70] Evict the other strangers! Expel them from my land!"

Meanwhile, the raft ran aground[58] as it lodged against the riverbank and all hands abandoned ship. The Tin Woodman jumped ashore, then offered the handle of his axe to Dorothy to help her and Toto off the raft and up the riverbank. The Lion leapt after them and all then hastened along the riverbank back to where the Scarecrow hung upon his pole in the middle of the river's flow.

"Perhaps I could swim out to him," said the Lion in speculation, "and then return with him upon my back."

"Nay," said Dorothy, "for then would ye both be most provident in peril[71] and, perchance, the river would sweep the Scarecrow off thy back and carry him away!"

Then i' the very moment[72] they debated this idea didst Toto bark upwards at the sky. Looking to the heavens, all then saw approaching a line of flying creatures.

"By the pricking of my thumbs, something wicked this way comes…"[73] whispered Dorothy, as the others stood mutely by, amazed by what they saw.

Chapter XIII

The Winged Monkeys

"Hell is empty and all the devils are here!"[1] cried the Scarecrow, as he clung to his pole in the river.

Dorothy lifted Toto into her arms and whispered, "Angels and ministers of grace defend us!"[2]

"This is my fight!" cried the Tin Woodman, "Get ye behind me and I will meet them as they come!"[3]

As the first of the monkeys descended upon them,[4] the Tin Woodman swung his great axe[5] in a wide arc to slay it. But the winged monkey was nimble and stirring[6] and easily avoided the deadly stroke.[7] The Tin Woodman turn'd on the toe and down he fell,[8] as two monkeys seized his arms, and a third his weighty axe. They then lifted him from the ground, flying up and up, ever higher to the heavens.

And in th' very moment,[9] another monkey plucked the Scarecrow from his pole in the riverbed. In blind obedience to the Witch's order, he flew after those who bore the Tin Woodman away, ne'er asking nor e'en thinking, "What hath this scarecrow done to make him fly the land?"[10] Notably, their flight took them not to the nearby castle but, rather, farther west until nought of them could be seen in the western sky.

Still more monkeys landed 'round Dorothy and Toto and the Lion. At this, the Lion roared as he had ne'er roared before![11] Anon then didst the monkeys retreat to a safer stance. But then, of a sudden,[12] the Lion felt a noose 'bout his neck. Startled, he turned to see a monkey had lasso'd him. Soon others did the same and, anon, was the Lion bound,[13] as Dorothy, dismayed to see him thus restrained,[14] held Toto tightly to herself as he barked fiercely in her arms, to see their noble friend so dishonored.[15] Then, a multitude of Winged Monkeys, grasping each a line, together lifted the Lion into the air and carried him away to the Wicked Witch's castle.

By many ropes of strength was the Lion thus ensnared!

With the Lion thus removed,₁₆ the Winged Monkeys then encircled Dorothy and Toto and slowly moved e'er closer with intent to firmly seize them and fly west with them, after the Tin Woodman and the Scarecrow. But, of a sudden,₁₂ their leader checked his advancing steps and cried, "Forbear, forbear, I say!₁₇ She bears the kiss of the Good Witch of the North upon her brow!" Perplexed, the leader pondered what unsmooth course₁₈ he must follow next. "The Wicked Witch of the West doth command the removal[16] of these strangers," thought he, "but no harm must come to one so favored by the Good Witch of the North." At last, he ordered the Winged Monkeys to bring Dorothy to the Witch's castle, and to take every care for her especial safety.[19]

Far to the west, the Winged Monkeys carried the Scarecrow and Tin Woodman o'er the high tops of the mountain pines[20] of the vast Western Forest. When they had reached its center, they dropped them into the dense woods and then turned to fly back to the castle of the Wicked Witch of the West.

Meanwhile, the leader of the Winged Monkeys approached the Wicked Witch and reported the Lion was now caged within the castle walls. So too, said he, was the girl, and her small animal, who had been with the Lion on the raft.

"Why dost ye disobey me? Why was this girl not evicted as I didst command thee?" demanded the Wicked Witch.

"She bears the kiss of the Good Witch of the North upon her brow," said the leader, "she who made the Golden Cap ye wear. I dared not harm her, and I have done no harm."[21]

"Bring her before me!"[22] she cried to the Winkie guards! "I have no fear of kisses, nor of any tender witches! Nor am I afraid to do her harm!" With a wave of her hand she dismissed the leader of the Winged Monkeys, who quickly took his leave.[23]

Anon then didst Dorothy stand before the Wicked Witch, with Toto in her arms.

The Wicked Witch had expected to see the kiss of the Good Witch of the North upon Dorothy's brow, but it shocked her to see her sister's silver slippers on her feet. The sight struck her dumb with fear[24] but anon she surmised Dorothy knew not how to wield their awesome power.

"Give to me those silver slippers!" demanded the Wicked Witch. "They are of no use to thee!"

"Never, never, never, never, never!"[25] insisted Dorothy. "The Good Witch of the North vouchsafed them to me and bade me wear them always!"

"Accursèd, wretchèd child!"[26] cried the Wicked Witch. "Come not within the measure of my wrath!"[27]

Snarling, Toto then leapt from Dorothy's arms, ran to the Wicked Witch, and bit her on the leg![28] The Witch struck at him with her umbrella as Dorothy ran to him and lifted him to herself once more.

The Witch struck at him with her umbrella!

"Give to me those silver slippers or bear witness to[29] this animal's destruction!" threatened the Wicked Witch.

"If e'en the smallest harm doth come to little Toto ye shalt ne'er hast these slippers! I will destroy them myself before I see them on thy feet!" declared Dorothy.

"A plague o' thee!"[30] cried the Wicked Witch again. "Catch her from my sight!"[31] so ordered she the yellow Winkie guards. "Make of her a kitchen-maid![32] Let her scrub my floors on hands and knees, day upon day, till she doth render me those slippers, till she doth yield them up!"[33]

I' sooth, this interview with Dorothy left the Wicked Witch much out of quiet.[34] She had not known her sister's slippers had survived her sister's death, and now they were hither, almost within her grasp. Still less had she imagined they would grace the feet of she who kill'd her sister.[35] How could she separate the silver slippers from she who wore them? For Dorothy must be separated from the slippers before the Wicked Witch could risk any revenge[36] upon her, for fear of destroying the power of the slippers, withal.

Nor had she expected strangers in her realm before their sighting on the river one day prior. Wherefore camest they?[37] Who sent this danger from the east unto the west? Was it honor-crossed by those witches in the north and south?[38] Had she err'd in the removing of the strangers from her realm[39] whilst their vaulting ambition[40] was unknown to her?

"No matter," thought she then, "this girl's intent is neither here nor there.[41] If I but abide then, in good time, I shall have the silver slippers for myself, and then shall greatness be thrust upon me![42] E'en the Great and Powerful Oz himself must yield[43] to me then."

Yet the Wicked Witch err'd in her maltreatment of Dorothy and the Lion. Dorothy's duties as a kitchen-maid reminded her of the many times she helped her Auntie Em in their small kitchen back in Kansas, times she remembered fondly. And, anon, she made fast friends in the kitchen of the castle. Withal, Dorothy did not mind scrubbing castle floors. Thought she to herself, "I'm where I should be[44] to learn what I must learn. In time, my charwoman duties shall take me to every corner of this castle and, therewithal, who can say what I might learn? Then too, satisfaction always comes from a task that is well done, no matter what the circumstances."

Nor had the Witch any success a'tall in her efforts to tame the Lion. The Winkies feared his roar, and none dared to approach him. The Witch imagined she could starve the Lion and bend him to her will, but Dorothy foiled her in this by bringing the Lion meat and drink[45] from the kitchen after dark. Sitting outside his cage each night, Dorothy and the Lion found comfort in their society,[46] as they wondered what ill fate had befallen their friends, the Tin Woodman and the Scarecrow.

I' sooth, the Scarecrow and Tin Woodman also wondered what ill fate had befallen Dorothy and Toto and the Lion within the castle. As he was being carried away, the Scarecrow saw the Lion roped and bound, but no more of his fate than this did he know.

When the Winged Monkeys dropped them into the Western Forest, the Tin Woodman, clinging tightly to his heavy axe, fell through the branches of the pines to the place beneath.[47] The Scarecrow, being made of straw, found himself atop a tree, unable to climb down. In time, they found each other, 'though the Tin Woodman had to fell the tree that held the Scarecrow aloft before they were together once again.

"How far do you suppose we are from the Witch's castle?" asked the Tin Woodman of the Scarecrow.

"Let me see, let me see, let me see,"[48] said the Scarecrow to himself. "I estimate our speed was at least twenty knots due west, and our time of flight to be two hours plus. A distance, perhaps, of twenty leagues from where we last saw Dorothy and Toto and the Lion. A journey of several days walking day and night, in this dense wood, would bring us there, if we but knew the way."

"By day we could but step against the sun in its walk about the orb,"[49] said the Scarecrow.

"By night, the same, only then the moon, with the comet o'er our shoulder," replied the Tin Woodman.

"Or, failing that, Jupiter rising," said the Scarecrow, "for I can see its moons as clearly as a child with perfect vision. Yet these trees hide the heavens from our ample view.[50] How then do we proceed?"

"Thou art a blessed fellow[51] to have a woodsman for thy friend," answered the Tin Woodman. "Look here upon this tree. On the north side dost ye see this bit of moss? 'Tis true of every tree in this great forest. Notice, too, this spider's weave[52] on the south side of its trunk."

"Excellent!" exclaimed the Scarecrow. "Let us address our gait unto[53] the castle anon! Our noble quest, bestowed upon us by the Wizard, may now lie in ruins, but a new one doth now live, for ye and I must again find means to rescue Dorothy and the Lion, as we did that day in the deadly poppy field."

"Agreed," said the Tin Woodman, "'though I pray 'twill not rain this time, for no oilcan hast I."

Chapter XIV

The Rescue

"I' sooth, too well I know why I am sad,"[1] said Dorothy to little Toto, whose head was in her lap as she sat upon her cot in her tiny quarters, in the kitchen pantry. Her eyes brimmed with tears as she thought of her Auntie Em and Uncle Henry, and of the Lion's sad estate,[2] and so too of her missing friends, the Scarecrow and Tin Woodman. Yet, through her tears, she glimpsed a small field mouse beside a hole in the pantry wall, and its presence made her wanly smile.

"That little mouse hath a lean and hungry look,"[3] thought Dorothy to herself, as she offered it the last morsel of the biscuit from her meager supper. She smiled as the mouse picked it up in its tiny paws and nibbled it away.

"Oh, how cute is he?" said Dorothy to Toto, "Look, he's winding up the watch of his wit! By and by it will strike!4 I will be sworn5 he will speak to us anon!"

"Thank ye," said the little mouse then, in a tiny voice, as he finished nibbling the biscuit crumb.

"Didst thou speak,6 a'tall?" asked Dorothy, drying her eyes in disbelief, as Toto's ears pricked up.

"Marry, so I did," said the little mouse. "None in this castle are ever kind to mice. The Witch herself hath struck at me with her umbrella, ever in her hand."

"Now I will believe that there are unicorns,"[7] said Dorothy, to no one in particular. Then, to the mouse, she said, "She hath ne'er struck at me, though once she struck at little Toto. Though, i' sooth, she had just cause."[8]

"Wherefore weep thee then?"[9] asked the little mouse.

As the mouse listened patiently, Dorothy told her tale, ending with, "and so, dost ye see, the Wizard will not send me safely home until I learn the wherewithal[10] of the Witch's power."

"I know not every source of her malignant power,"[11] said the little mouse, "yet I can say how she calls forth the Winged Monkeys, for I hast seen it for myself.[12] An unlawful espial was I, seeing unseen,[13] in her private chamber, when she donned the Golden Cap, and caper'd,[14] and spake her little words, and so summoned forth the monkeys. And, anon, they came, for they must obey the wearer of the Golden Cap, by the magic found therein. Anon, I left her chamber when the monkeys didst arrive, for they dost love to plague wee little mice like me."[15]

"Thou art so kind to commend this secret unto mine ear!"[16] exclaimed Dorothy! "If ever I shall once more stand in his Great Presence, I shall do as much for the Great and Powerful Oz. Perchance it will mollify him, and perchance he will then finally send me safely home to Kansas and, withal, Toto too."

Toto, i' faith, had been watching this exchange betwixt[17] Dorothy and the mouse with increasing curiosity, looking first to Dorothy, and then back to the mouse, as each in turn didst speak. At home in Kansas, Toto devised grand sport[18] of chasing mice himself, yet even he could see that this behavior would not do hither in this Land of Oz, where little mice didst speak.

"I am pleased to be of service to one so generous, guiltless, and of free disposition,"[19] said the little mouse. "I am most grateful for thy kindness."

"I pray, little mouse, tell me,"[20] inquired Dorothy of him, "doth every mouse in these western lands speak as I hear thee?"

"Of course," answered the little mouse, "how could it be not so?"

"Indeed," replied Dorothy. "I wonder if I might beg of thee thy good entertainment[21] on a matter that is close to my heart?"

"How may I be of service?" asked the mouse.

"My dear friends,[22] the Scarecrow and Tin Woodman, are somewhere in the Western Forest, lost. I would fain have them know[23] I am in the Witch's castle, alive and unharmed, and so is Toto too, and, withal, the Lion. May I ask thee to pass a word[24] to any and all of thine acquaintance and relation and they, withal, to theirs until at last someone of thy distant kin finds them in those woods and tells them we art well?"

"Anon!" said the mouse as he disappeared into the wall.

And, in th' very moment,[25] far to the west, the Scarecrow and Tin Woodman were walking eastward, to gain the Witch's castle, 'though they were yet some leagues away.

"How far dost thou think we hast already come?" asked the Scarecrow of the Tin Woodman, "And how long before we hast some notion of locality, or when we might leave this forest?"

"I know no answer,"[26] said the Tin Woodman, "but I fear our journey thither may soon become so like an old tale,[27] told new."[28]

"I would fain know thy meaning,"[29] said the Scarecrow.

"I mean, but this," replied the Tin Woodman. "I have noted broken twigs and leaves o'er turned in this underbrush we are passing through, and 'tis my belief we are not alone in this part of the forest."

"Kalidah?" asked the Scarecrow.

"'Tis something of that nature, I do fear," replied the Tin Woodman, as they emerged from the underbrush into a clearing in the woods. "But, this time, we hast not the Lion to lead us on to safety."

"Or perhaps we do," said the Scarecrow. For then, from every side, stepped lions from the leafy underbrush into that same clearing!

The largest of the lions stepped forth to accost[30] them, saying, "Who art ye? And wherefore comest ye hither, before this royal pride?"[31]

"I am called simply Scarecrow," said the Scarecrow, "and this is my companion, the Tin Woodman. I' sooth, we are well met!"[32] exclaimed the Scarecrow, in his mounting excitement. "For we know another Lion, our true and honest friend, who will be full joyous[33] to make thy better acquaintance!"[34]

"Varlet, thou liest, thou liest, wicked varlet!"[35] roared the elder lion, as both the Scarecrow and Tin Woodman stepped back hastily and then fell upon the ground. "There *are* no other lions to be seen!"

Varlet, thou liest, thou liest, wicked varlet!

"Liars and trespassers!" said another lion. "And I didst hear them speak of Kalidah!" said a third. "They are espials[13] from the Eastern Forest, come to surveil this western realm to assist the Kalidah!"

"Nay! Nay!" cried the Tin Woodman, "Forbear these imputations![36] Do but hear our tale! The Winged Monkeys dropped us into this forest two days past, and our friend, the Lion, truly saved us from the Kalidah in the Eastern Forest! Saved he, withal, Dorothy, she who killed the Wicked Witch of the East!"

"I' sooth, did we see monkeys two days past, small in number, as they flew from west to east," said the elder lion. "Yet thy tale alone is high fantastical![37] What proof hast ye the eastern Wicked Witch be dead? Or that ye hast known a lion?" demanded the elder lion.

"If strong circumstances, which lead directly to the door of truth, will give you satisfaction, you may have it,"[36] answered the Scarecrow, "for here we are, in thy ample view,[38] deep inside this forest. Withal, we approached thee from the west, not the east. Do hear how we came to be hither, and then, in thy best consideration,[39] judge for thyself the truth of our sad tale."

As the elder lion pondered this response, a still more ancient lion limped into the clearing and implored, "My son, let us hear them speak of this,[40] give them leave[41] to tell us what they know of the Kalidah, and of this eastern lion yet unknown to us. For I was there that day, now many seasons past, when many of our pride wast killed by the Kalidah, and many more made lame."

Anon then, as the Scarecrow and Tin Woodman spoke of what they knew, a notable passion of wonder appeared in all who listened.[42] For they spoke of the Lion's lonely youth and how he, in temperate blood,[43] had saved them all that night as the Kalidah didst lie in ambush for their lives.[44] So too, how he leapt o'er a rushing river and, withal, saved Dorothy from the deadly poppy field.[45] And how the Lion was the first amongst them to stand before the Wizard, alone, and how he then joined Dorothy in her quest, bestowed upon her by the Great and Powerful Oz himself, to learn the source of the Witch's power. So too, how he had stood betwixt Dorothy and danger[17] as the Winged Monkeys circled and moved ever closer.

"Such courage and audacity[46] hath this Lion!" exclaimed the elder lion, and so said all! At this, the Scarecrow and Tin Woodman looked at one another, and then back to the pride.

"Marry," agreed the Scarecrow, "He is full so valiant,[47] for these brave acts dost proclaim[48] themselves. Yet, in his great humility, I hast ne'er heard him profess any claim to courage."

"Nor I," agreed the Tin Woodman.

"Tis as I thought," said the ancient lion. "This valiant Lion must, perforce, be my brother's son, he whom I hast mourned, in my sad remembrance.[49] E'en now, I would fain give my life for his, and so too would I had then, had I but known he lived. Thou hast made me giddy with these tidings!"[50]

Continuing, he said, "My son, thou hast a cousin to be cherished![51] Let joy be unconfin'd!"[52]

"Do but recall the danger yet before him," cautioned the Tin Woodman. "For as the Winged Monkeys carried us away, so too didst we note others had ensnared him with many ropes of strength. By many hands was the Lion thus subdued.[53] We must make haste to this Witch's castle to affect his sure release and, withal, that of Dorothy and Toto."

"How can this be done?" asked the elder lion then.

"We know no answer,"[26] said the Scarecrow, "it is a mystery.[54] Yet we can do nothing from hither, where we are nought but standing water.[55] In haste must we address our gait unto[56] the Witch's castle."

"We will bring ye there, anon, or so near as wisdom doth advise," said the elder lion. "And we will speak more of this as we journey thither."

As evening fell, the castle of the Wicked Witch came into view, through the fog and filthy air that hovered there, upon the untamed heath.[57] Said the elder lion then, "Thus near this castle, and no nearer, dost wisdom guide our valor, to act in safety,[58] for do not witches and evil spirits abide in such as this? Withal, e'en should ye venture forth, and, withal, gain entrance to this castle, how shall ye then find this Lion there within? Or she who killed the Wicked Witch of the East? I' faith, how can ye e'en find safe passage o'er this foggy heath,[57] when soon black night will take away all light?"[59]

As all, in silence, pondered these fair questions, so too didst all then hear a tiny voice, barely to be heard.

"Perchance I could be of help," said a little mouse, "for I bring tidings from Dorothy and Toto. I trow ye art the Scarecrow and Tin Woodman, her true friends, for whom I, and many of my kind, hast been searching."

Then, looking down, all didst see a mouse upon a stone, looking up at them.

"Marry!" said the Tin Woodman, bending down upon one knee,[60] "Indeed we are! What tidings dost thou bring?"

The mouse then spoke of Dorothy's occasion, what her estate was,[61] and, withal, whereat the Lion was being held captive inside the castle walls.

"I pray, mouse, tell me,"[20] asked the Scarecrow then, "how might one approach this castle yet unseen, and enter therewithal, and find our friend the Lion and, withal, Dorothy and Toto? For I see many straying streets, and the castle is the market-place where each one meets.[62] Yet all cannot be equal. I' sooth, only one can be the wisest choice of all."

"Indeed," replied the mouse, "dost ye see where tradesmen labor with the signs of their profession,[63] carpenters and masons? There, at present, is there a notable breach[64] in yonder castle wall. If ye enter there, when black night doth take away all light,[59] ye shall be not far from where the Lion is confined."

"I thank thee,"[65] said the Scarecrow to the little mouse, "we art in thy debt." The mouse made no reply but jumped down from the stone and scurried away.

"Well and good," remarked the elder lion, "but, anon, black night will fall upon the heath.[57] Nor shines the silver moon one half so bright[66] for hours yet. Alas, how will ye find thy way? For this heath is as a maze,[67] and none see in the dark."

"None save one," replied the Tin Woodman, as he put his hand upon the Scarecrow's shoulder. "Come thy ways,[68] Scarecrow! There is not a moment to lose!"[69]

Inside the castle walls, Dorothy and Toto were once more making their way to the Lion's cage with meat and drink[70] well hidden under rags in her scrubbing cart, which she pushed before her. If any Winkie e'er observed her movements about the castle with her cart, with Toto ever at her heel, none e'er spoke of it, nor of her evening visits with the Lion. For, throughout the castle then, 'twas fresh in murmur[71] that Dorothy was she who killed the Wicked Witch's sister, and the hearts of all who saw her were like a mingled yarn, with fear and hope together.[72]

Dorothy was glad at heart[73] to be with the Lion once again when she, at last, arrived at his dark cell. Toto, too, seemed comforted by these visits, and he slipped easily between the bars of the Lion's enclosure, to lie within his warm embrace.

As they talked that evening, through the bars,[74] Dorothy told the Lion once again of how the Wicked Witch, when first they met, had struck at little Toto with her umbrella, when he didst snarl and bite her on the leg.[75] But, she added, the Wicked Witch had yet to strike at her. Nor didst the Winged Monkeys harm her when once they saw the kiss of the Good Witch of the North upon her brow. "Why dost thou think this should be so?" asked Dorothy of the Lion.

"See, what a grace is seated on thy brow,"[76] answered the Lion. "I envy Toto's chance to bite that Wicked Witch. I pray someday to do as much, though it may be my final act."

Then, upon reflection, he said, "'Tis a curiosity, this umbrella she doth carry. Perchance it is an instrument of darkness,[77] of the sort ye once supposed, as we glided on the river. And yet no art o' magic do we see by this device. Perchance thy little friend, the mouse, doth know its secret use."

"Indeed, I asked him once," said Dorothy, "but no answer did he know,[26] save to say that once in his remembrance,[49] when the Wicked Witch was in her courtyard, it began to rain. Anon, the Witch raised her umbrella and quickly went inside. But there was nothing notable in that."

Before the Lion could reply, all heard footsteps along the passage[78] leading to the Lion's cage. "Alas," whispered the Lion, "we hast not kept to the hour! And now the guard approaches on his evening rounds! I hear him jangling his keys, to ward off evil spirits!"[79]

"Toto!" whispered Dorothy, "Come hither!" But Toto, in that moment, was chewing on a bone he found within the Lion's cage, and he willfully ignored her urgent plea.

Once more she called him forth, but again to no avail. Then, of a sudden,[80] was the guard at hand, gaping in surprise[81] at what he saw.

"Wherefore art thou₈₂ hither?" asked the guard, fearfully. "Hither, where the Wicked Witch hath said that none may come? She will blame me for this transgression! Come away, come away₈₃ with me, anon!"

Then, in th' very moment₂₅ he didst speak these words, came a lion's roar most terrifying, though it came not from the Lion's cage! Behind the guard, not far a'tall, stood the Scarecrow and Tin Woodman, and so too the elder lion from the Western Forest! In his fright, the guard dropped his keys and ran for his dear life!

"Oh!" cried Dorothy, as she ran to embrace them all. "How wonderful that ye art well! How wonderful that ye art truly hither! How wonderful that ye hast found another lion!"

"Marry," said the Tin Woodman, picking up the keys. "But let us hasten to free the Lion, for we are time's subjects, and time bids us begone.₈₄ I' sooth, we must begone, anon, before the Wicked Witch learns of our return!"

Dorothy then brought them to the Lion's cage, and anon was he set free. As he stepped out into the light, followed closely by little Toto, the Lion came nose to nose with the elder lion and 'twas as though he viewed his image in the glass.₈₅

"'Tis true, then," said the elder lion, "thou didst outlive the Kalidah attack."

"'Tis true, then," replied the Lion, "I am not alone."

"This happy meet must wait another hour," said the Scarecrow. "For if hither we are found, our stars will shine more darkly over us₈₆ than mere exile to the forest."

"Thou dost say sooth,"₈₇ said the Wicked Witch, who stood then where the guard had stood before! For she had been escorted there by that frightened guard, whose anxious tale explained the roar that she had heard, even from her private chamber.

"And you needn't fear for darkness," continued she, sardonically, "for there is light aplenty from this torch I bear!₈₈ It shall be thy timeless end!"₈₉ she cried, as she brought it near the Scarecrow!

"Nay!" shrieked Dorothy, as she reached for her pail of scrubbing water and tossed it at the flaming torch![88] Her aim was true, for she doused the torch, but so too was the Wicked Witch drenched from head to toe! Then were strange lamentations heard i' th' air, and strange screams of death![90] And in the age to come,[91] now and again, those screams would meddle with the dreams[92] of all who heard them in their sad misfortune.

"Thou wicked, wicked child!" cried the Wicked Witch. "See what thou hast done!" I' sooth, the Wicked Witch was melting! "Who would e'er believe a little girl like you could melt me and end my wicked deeds?[93] I am slain by a fair cruel maid!"[94] And in th' very moment,[25] did she melt entirely away!

I am slain by a fair cruel maid!

All stood in stunned silence, amazed by what they saw. All then tried to comprehend this truth, that this Wicked Witch was truly dead. At last, the guard said simply, "She is dead. She is gone."

Said the Scarecrow then to the guard, "Go to, thou art made, if thou desirest to be so.[95] By the hand of Dorothy of Kansas art thou free and, so too, art all the Winkies now free of this Wicked Witch! Tell all you see these joyful tidings!"[96]

Across the foggy heath,₅₇ the lion pride sat waiting for the elder lion to return. As they watched and waited, they saw a light break through a window in the castle,₉₇ and then another and another, till light beamed from every window. Anon was a bonfire lit in the village, and then another and another!₉₈ And, at first, the wisest beholder amongst them, that knew no more but seeing, could not say if the importance were joy or sorrow.₉₉

"What doth this portend?"₁₀₀ asked one lion of another.

"I know no answer,"₂₆ said the other. "Perhaps they search in earnest for something they have lost. Or perhaps some oracle hath been fulfilled.₉₈ Yet, in my heart's core, ay, in my heart of heart,₁₀₁ I believe this omen is full joyous,₃₃ for it doth seem a celebration, though what of I cannot say."

Chapter XV

The Discovery of Oz the Terrible

The celebration and rejoicing continued throughout the night and all the following day. The Winkie mayor declared a holiday,[1] a day of thanksgiving and independence, to be remembered always as the day the Wicked Witch was melted and their freedom manifested, and, withal, as a day when lions roamed the civil streets.[2] For the lions didst attend the grand feast of celebration and were honored for the part that they had played in the demise of the Wicked Witch.

Yet the Scarecrow noted something amiss in Dorothy's countenance and said to her, "Thy heart is full of something that doth take thy mind from feasting."[3]

"This feasting and rejoicing hath been wonderful," replied Dorothy, "but one can desire too much of a good thing,[4] as my Auntie Em is wont to say. I' sooth, we must return in haste to the Emerald City with these glad tidings and, therewithal, claim the promises vouchsafed us by the Great and Powerful Oz."

"Indeed," replied the Scarecrow, "I shall be glad to finally hast a brain. Yet I fear our journey back to the Wizard will be more arduous than our journey hither. For we cannot sail a raft against the river's flow. We must make its wand'ring[5] path our own, and walk its bank, back to the fallen bridge, and then on to the Emerald City. And, I fear, it shall take forever and a day."[6]

"I know," replied Dorothy, "but what remedy?[7] I see our path so lies,[8] and the sooner we depart, the sooner will we gain our destination. So too, we must bring proof of the demise of the Wicked Witch to the Great and Powerful Oz if we are to hast any hope a'tall that he will, at last, fulfill his promises."

"Perhaps her pointed hat would suffice," suggested the Tin Woodman, pointing to his own.

"Her hat must yet be in her private chamber," said Dorothy, "for she was not wearing it when she melted. Follow me, I know the way, for I didst stand within her danger[9] in that very chamber, and so didst Toto too."

Then, with Dorothy, did the Scarecrow and Tin Woodman, and the Lion and his cousin, withdraw to the Witch's private chamber,[10] as Toto led the way for, inexplicably, he seemed quite certain of their destination. Therewithal, they found her pointed hat. So too, were there potions, charms, and bottles of dark contents, arranged along her shelves, which all agreed were best left undisturbed.

And on one wall was there a cupboard, yet without a knob or handle by which to open it. Upon the door, in golden script, Dorothy read aloud:

Aperta et seras, quicumque pulsat!

"What doth this mean?" asked the elder lion.

"I know no answer," replied Dorothy.

"*Open locks, whoever knocks!*"[11] said the Scarecrow. "I believe that is the literal translation."

Dorothy looked at the Scarecrow, then at the others, and then back to the cupboard. She then knocked upon the cupboard door. Instantly it opened and there within was the Golden Cap!

"Thy friend hath amazed me[12] yet again," said the elder lion to his cousin. "Marry," replied the Lion, "yet he claims to hast no brain."

"I' sooth, I know what this must be," whispered Dorothy, as she turned it in her hands. "This is the Golden Cap the Wicked Witch used to summon and command the Wingèd Monkeys." And i' th' very moment[13] she spoke these words she felt compelled to touch the kiss upon her brow and to remember she who placed it there.

"This splendid cap will surely satisfy the Wizard that the Wicked Witch is dead," said the Tin Woodman. "Though 'twill be no use to him, for 'twill ne'er fit upon his enormous head!"

"True," said Dorothy. "So too, the little mouse didst say one must also caper[14] and recite a little spell, and he could ne'er do that, for no legs hath he! Nor could I, i'faith, for these are things I know not of. Still, 'tis a pretty thing," said Dorothy, as she put it on. Then, still stronger, thoughts of the Good Witch of the North sprang forth unbidden in her mind.

"'Tis strange to think the Winged Monkeys must, perforce, obey me if I but knew the magic held within this Golden Cap," said Dorothy. "For the little mouse didst say the magic to command them lies within."

"Then perhaps," suggested the Scarecrow, "you might look within the Cap."

Dorothy removed the cap and looked inside. And there, in golden script, she beheld these words:

Sta in sinistra pedem tuum,
Loqui, "Eppe, Peppe Kakke!"
Tum stans in dextro pede
Loqui, "Hillo, Hollo, Hello!"
Tum sta super pedes tuos et dices, "Zizzy, Zuzzy, Zik!"

"Scarecrow," asked Dorothy, "what is this charm, written within this Golden Cap?"

The Scarecrow then recited,

Standing on thy left foot speak, *"Ep-pe Pep-pe Kak-ke!"*
Then standing on thy right foot speak, *"Hil-lo, Hol-lo, Hel-lo!"*
Then standing on thy two feet speak, *"Ziz-zy, Zuz-zy, Zik!"*[15]

"By mine honor,"[16] said Dorothy, "if I comprehend the meaning of this charm, 'tis within my power to summon forth the Winged Monkeys and, withal, command them! I' sooth, could I command them, 'Anon! Fly me to Kansas!' And anon, they must obey! So too, fly ye to the Emerald City, therewithal to claim thy promises from the Great and Powerful Oz!"

"Nay!" said the Lion! "Recall how these Winged Monkeys didst bind me and didst cage me! So too, how they untreasured[17] us of the Scarecrow and Tin Woodman! Forbear, forbear, I say!"[18]

"O, peace, peace!"[19] said Dorothy. "The little mouse didst say the Winged Monkeys must obey the wearer of this Golden Cap. Their prior actions wast constrained by the bidding of the Wicked Witch herself. 'Twas not the freewill of these monkeys that led to our harsh treatment, but her own."

All then considered the truth of Dorothy's words, not least of whom was Dorothy herself.

"'Tis wrong," said she, upon reflection. "These monkeys are slaves, and this Golden Cap is the instrument of their servitude. Withal, this Wicked Witch used it to command the Winged Monkeys to enslave the Winkie people and, so too, mistreat us all. This Golden Cap must be destroyed."

"The hand that hath made you fair hath made you good,"[20] said the Tin Woodman, smiling down at her.

"Then let us vouchsafe this cap to the Winged Monkeys," said the Scarecrow, "to do with as they will. By such action they will know their freedom manifested."

"Thou'rt i' the right,[21] of course," said Dorothy, and so said all.

Donning then the Golden Cap, Dorothy recited the charm within, first standing upon her left foot, then upon her right, and then upon her two feet. Then, the purchase made, all waited to see if fruits would then ensue.[22]

Anon, all heard the shouts and exclamations of the revelers outside the castle walls, they who saw the Winged Monkeys approaching from the west.

"Who summons us?" asked the leader, arriving at the window of the Witch's private chamber, "and what is thy command?"

"I am Dorothy of Kansas," answered Dorothy, "whose acquaintance thou hast already made. But I hast no command of thee."

"I do not understand," replied the leader.

"The Wicked Witch is dead, and the Winkies are now free," said Dorothy. "So too should ye be free. Therefore, on behalf of all here present, I vouchsafe thee this Golden Cap, to do with as ye will."

The leader looked at Dorothy, then to all who stood behind her, and said, "For generation upon generation hast we been subject to this Golden Cap. 'Twas made by the Good Witch of the North, she whose kiss I see upon thy brow. 'Twas a wedding gift from the Good Witch of the North to a princess who once lived in this very castle, long ago, that by such gift she might ban us from her sight, and not without just cause,[23] for mischievous wast we."

Continuing he said, "Shall we truly be the masters of our fates,[24] as in that time so long ago? What shall we do, once our freewill is manifested?"

"I pray, rejoice in thy newfound freedom,[25] justice long denied, and embrace it wisely, always," answered Dorothy, as she espied her little friend, the mouse, peering out between the dark bottles of potions on the shelf.

"I do have one request of thee," said Dorothy, "by which mercy seasons justice.[26] Of thy freewill, I would have thee spare, from thy mischievous ways, the Winkies and the lions, and, especially, the field mice of these western lands."

"We will fain do this for thee," replied the leader. "But, so too, of our freewill, let us do thee one last entertainment. I prithee, what is thy heart's desire?"[27]

All looked at one another, and then back to the monkeys, as Dorothy said, "The Scarecrow and Tin Woodman and, so too, the Lion must return to the Emerald City, anon," answered Dorothy. "And Toto and I must return to Kansas, as quickly as ever ye canst fly us there."

"Alas," said the leader, "'Tis not within our power to fly ye back to Kansas. But we can fly ye to the Emerald City, with these others, before the sun doth set upon this day."

To this, all agreed, and, anon, all made their fond farewells to the Winkies and to the lions.

"Wilt thou not return with me to the Western Forest?" asked the elder lion of his cousin.

"'Tis my intent, in time, to join ye thither" answered the Lion. "But first I must see Dorothy safely back to the Emerald City and then, by the Wizard's art, safely back to Kansas. So too, hath the Wizard made promises to me, and I stand on sudden haste[28] to speak with him."

"'Tis meet so,"[29] replied his cousin, "honorable and meet and right, of course."

And then, anon, Dorothy and her companions found themselves, once more, being carried by the Winged Monkeys as they flew eastward to the Emerald City.

As they approached the city the setting sun silhouetted the Winged Monkeys, and the people trembled stiff with fear[30] at the sight. For it was well established in the city's folklore that, many years before, the Monkeys pursued the Great and Powerful Oz as he soared through the heavens. Anon was the Wizard informed of their approach by the Palace Guard, who then stood by, awaiting his orders.

But before any orders were forthcoming, the line of monkeys parted. Half went to the north and half went to the south, only to rejoin and land at the Eastern Gate, where Dorothy had first entered the Emerald City.

This time there was no need to ring the bell, nor to knock upon the gate, for the Guardian of the Gates had already opened the inner door and stood ready to unlock the outer gate. He too had seen the Winged Monkeys. Withal, he saw that Dorothy and her companions had returned from their quest into the west, by those same monkeys.

"I thank thee,"[31] said Dorothy to the leader of the Winged Monkeys, as she handed him the Golden Cap. "Be free now and forevermore." The leader nodded his respect and then all the monkeys rose together and flew over the city and the Wizard's Palace as they flew westward, against the twilight sky which yet did glimmer with some streaks of day.[32]

The Guardian of the Gates then hastened to unlock the outer gate and welcomed them back to the Emerald City. Bowing low, he asked of Dorothy, "Why did the Wicked Witch not enslave ye? Did ye not find her castle in the west?"

As the Guardian fitted them with green spectacles, Dorothy explained that the Wicked Witch of the West was melted and is no more.

"Who melted her?" asked the Guardian of the Gates.

"It was Dorothy," replied the Lion gravely.[33]

Word quickly spread throughout the city that the Wicked Witch of the West was dead, by Dorothy's own hand. And, so too, 'twas fresh in murmur[34] that the Winged Monkeys obeyed her beck[35] and call.

Once more, Dorothy rode through the streets of the Emerald City upon the Lion's back to the Palace Gate, escorted by the Captain of the Guard. The Scarecrow, carrying the pointed hat of the Wicked Witch of the West, and the Tin Woodman, carrying her umbrella, waved to those who cheered them on as they passed through the civil streets.

At the Palace Gate, the Captain of the Guard announced them once again and, once again, were they promptly admitted by the Sergeant-At-Arms and shown to their former chambers.

"A hundred thousand welcomes, miss," said the maid in green to Dorothy, when they were once more in her chamber. "I could weep and I could laugh! Welcome!"[36]

"I thank thee," smiled Dorothy, "I am heart-glad to once more be in the Emerald City, and in this lovely room." It comforted her to see all was as it was before. The lovely counterpane and reading chair, the silver basin[37] and leather-bound volumes on the little shelves, and the painting of the balloon hovering o'er the city; nothing was out of place. So too did she find dresses of her size yet hanging in the mirrored wardrobe.[38]

"I will return anon," said the green girl,[39] "with a warm supper for thee and with a meaty bone for Toto, and, so too, to draw thy evening bath." However, before returning as she promised, she stopped at the Tin Woodman's chamber and knocked upon his door. When he answered, she politely curtsied to him, and then took a letter from her apron pocket and handed it to him.

"Sir," she explained, "this letter arrived for thee from Munchkinland a few days after thy departure into the western lands." I' sooth, it was from the Munchkin maid he loved:

My Dearest,
Thy letter found its way into my heart, may mine now find its way to thine!

Doubt thou the stars are fire,
Doubt that the sun doth move,
Doubt truth to be a liar,
But never doubt I love.[40]

I pray the Wonderful Wizard of Oz hath bestowed a blessèd heart in thee, and that it overflows with joy! May it be so, and mayst thou return to me, anon!
Yours,
MM

The next morning, Dorothy and Toto and, so too, the Scarecrow and Tin Woodman, proceeded to the lake to await there, with the Lion, an invitation to stand before The Great and Powerful Oz.

The company spent their day at leisure, recounting their adventures[41] in the west, notably their time apart, and remembering those whose effectual aid proved decisive in the moment, the lions and the field mice and, withal, the Winged Monkeys, once the Wicked Witch was dead.

To pass the time, the Tin Woodman tossed a stick for Toto to fetch many, many times until poor Toto finally tired and took his rest beside the Lion.

Now and again were they approached, but not by the Palace Guard. I' faith, many from the city proper stopped by to wish them well and to bring them tender offerings of their gratitude and affection.

But no summons from The Great and Powerful Oz was forthcoming, that day or that evening. At last, when the full moon rose, they admitted to one another that something was amiss.

"How sweet the moonlight sleeps upon this bank,"[42] said Dorothy, "but why did the Wizard ne'er summon us before him all this day? In delay there lies no plenty.[43] Surely, he hath heard by now the Wicked Witch is dead."

"I know no answer," replied the Tin Woodman.

"Nor I," said the Scarecrow, "but to keep us waiting, though we embraced the quest he didst bestow upon us, most perilous, defies comprehension and, withal, it doth seem extremely rude."

"It makes no sense," concurred the Lion, "he should be full joyous[44] that the Wicked Witch is dead. I do not understand it."[45]

"Is't possible," asked Dorothy anxiously, "the Wizard hath forgot the promises he made? Or hath no resolve to honor them? Marry, God defend his Grace should say us nay![46] I cannot be so answer'd!"[47]

"An that be so, my weighty axe will soon recall his better angel to his duty!"[48] insisted the Tin Woodman. "I' sooth, my state is desperate for a heart!"[49]

"And I must hast my brain," said the Scarecrow.

"And I my bit of courage," said the Lion. "An he should say us nay,[46] then will I roll his head about the room as doth a kitten a ball of yarn!"[50]

"O, sweet friends!" said Dorothy. "Be patient for tonight! I will send the Wizard a note and request of him an audience, anon. If I do not gull him to agree, do not think I have wit enough to lie straight in my bed. I know I can do it.[51] For this night, to bed, and dream on the event. Farewell."[52]

The next morning, Dorothy passed a note to the young maid with the green eyes and green hair who, in turn, passed it to the Sergeant-At-Arms who, in turn, passed it to the Palace Guard who, in turn, delivered it to the Wizard's receptacle for official notes and mail:

"Your Grace,"[53]

"The Scarecrow, Tin Woodman, Lion, little Toto, and I have returned to the Emerald City, from our determinant voyage[54] *into the West, transported hither from the Witch's castle with no worse nor better guard than the Wingèd Monkeys.*[55] *The adventure thou bestowed upon us is now o'er, and its purpose is now moot, for the Wicked Witch of the West is dead. We now stand on sudden haste*[56] *to speak with Thee, and so dost we request an audience, anon."*

"Respectfully,"
"Dorothy of Kansas"

I' sooth, the Wizard knew all this already, yet this letter instantly turn'd rumors and reports into certainties. His suspicion that Dorothy was, herself, a witch, was now more acute than ever, despite her own account of her arrival in the Land of Oz, and the kiss of the Good Witch of the North upon her brow.

"I' sooth, perhaps they too are weird sisters,"[57] thought the Wizard of Dorothy and of the Good Witch of the North, "as wast those Wicked Witches, East and West, that Dorothy hath killed. So too, she doth command the Wingèd Monkeys, and why should they obey her if she be but a little girl from Kansas, and not a witch herself? Wherefore did they not that hour destroy her?"[58] Then too, 'twas true, the Wizard had himself encountered the Wingèd Monkeys many years before, in the western lands, and his fear of them yet meddled with his dreams.[59]

Indeed, the Wizard was most apprehensive to grant an audience to Dorothy and her companions. But there was nought else he could do, for the people of the Emerald City, with bated breath,[60] awaited tidings from such a conference, where matters of great moment[61] would surely be discussed. At last, and with reluctance, he passed word[62] for Dorothy, and all, to approach the Throne of Oz when the sun had reached its zenith.

At noon, precisely, the Palace Guard opened wide the heavy, ornately carved green doors. Dorothy and her companions entered the long passageway that led to the Throne Room with Toto, as ever, in the lead. Naturally, all expected to see the same enormous head as they had seen before, with torches[63] of green flame on either side. But, to their surprise, there was no one on the throne, and the torches were extinguished.

"Oz is not here," said Dorothy in her amazement. "Wherefore should he summon us and then not be hither to greet us?"

"Perhaps he is delayed," suggested the Lion, though none could then imagine how he might enter and then take his seat upon the throne.

The large, circular room was full of light, for the sun was directly over the skylight of the parabolic dome. While the room itself was unchanged, it felt as empty as an unfilled tomb[64] without the powerful presence of the Wizard. The same intricately woven arras hung all 'round the room, depicting scenes of the Emerald City, the night sky constellations, and depictions of astrology. Toto made himself at home in this new setting, sniffing all about the room. So much so, Dorothy worried he might, after his own fashion, salute the Throne of Oz.

"These arras are quite beautiful," observed the Tin Woodman, who had but little time to mark them on his first approach before the Wizard.[65] "Look there, where Toto wanders, I believe that one depicts the Vapians passing the equinoctial of Queubus!"[66]

Then, from high above, boomed a voice that said, "Lord, what fools these mortals be!"[67]

All then looked in all directions, but there was no one to be seen.

"Your Grace," said Dorothy then, "Say whither[68] thou be?"

"I am everywhere," replied the Wizard, "yet invisible[69] am I to mortal eyes. Be patient as I take my seat upon the Throne of Oz."

Indeed, then, the voice seemed to emanate from the throne itself.

"Wherefore seek ye an audience before Oz the Terrible? Wherefore dost ye tread upon my patience?"[70] he demanded.

"An it please your Worship,"[71] said Dorothy, "we bring proof of the demise of the Wicked Witch of the West."

Then did the Tin Woodman and the Scarecrow lay the Witch's pointed hat and her umbrella before the Throne of Oz.

"So, she is dead and gone, miss,"[72] said the Wizard solemnly. "Pray tell me, miss,[73] how was she killed?"

"I melted her," replied Dorothy. "Of a sudden,[73] was her cruel intent to set the Scarecrow all afire. Then, in th' very moment,[13] I, to spare him, threw water from a pail to douse the torch she held. But, withal, did the water douse her too, and then she melted quite away."

"I see," replied the Wizard. "Commendable, commendable. 'Tis a fresh piece of excellent witchcraft.[74] On behalf of the people of the Emerald City I dost thank thee. Give me now leave to leave ye,[75] there are important matters of state to which I must attend."

"But hold, what of thy promises?" cried the Scarecrow.

"What promises?" asked the Wizard.

"Thou promised me a brain!" replied the Scarecrow.

"Thou promised me a heart!" said the Tin Woodman.

"Thou promised me a modicum of courage!" said the Lion.

"And you promised to send me safely back to Kansas," said Dorothy, "and, withal, Toto too!"

"I' faith," replied the Wizard, "These are not debts I promised I would pay.[76] I said only that these requests would not be considered whilst the Wicked Witch of the West was not yet exiled from this land. She hath been killed, perhaps, but that is not the same as exiled.[77] Withal, thy task was to learn the source of her great power. Pray tell me, miss,[73] what is it?"

"I'sooth, I learn'd how she summon'd forth the Winged Monkeys, and command'd them, yet she melted afore I could learn more," answered Dorothy, just as Toto began barking at an arras hanging on the wall behind the throne. "Toto!" called Dorothy, "Come hither!"

But, taking the arras in his teeth, Toto pulled with full puissance.[78] At this, the ornate curtain fell and there, for all to see, stood a little man! He was lean and little, old and bald and, so too, was he chopped,[79] and he seemed quite concerned that Toto might bite him next.

The Tin Woodman rushed across the room, his axe raised high, and demanded, "Who art thou? Wherefore art thou hid behind this curtain?"[80]

"I, I am Oz the Terrible," stammered the little man, "ruler of the Emerald City."

"You!" exclaimed Dorothy! "But you are nothing but a man! A subtle, perjur'd, false, disloyal man![81] Explain thyself! Say sooth!"[82]

"Anon!" cried the Tin Woodman, shaking his axe. "Anon!"

"O, peace, peace,[83] don't hurt me," cried the little man. "I meant no harm! I will tell ye all, only spare me thy sharp axe!"

"Why, this monstrous fellow art[84] more cowardly than I," observed the pusillanimous[85] Lion. "E'en little Toto doth subdue him."

"Marry," agreed the Scarecrow, "but give the devil his due.[86] We wast the more deceived[87] by him, save but little Toto. Now give this fellow leave[75] to tell his tale."

"Sir," said the Scarecrow to the little man, "art thou a wizard, a'tall?"

"Nay, I am much afeared[88] I am just a common man," replied he.

"Thou art a humbug!" said the Lion. "A humbug without honor! And all of this is such a deal of skimble-skamble stuff!"[89]

"Exactly so! I am a humbug." said the little man. "'Tis true, 'tis pity, and pity 'tis 'tis true."[90]

"Oh," cried Dorothy, "this is terrible! Thou art indeed '*Oz the Terrible*'! God hath given thee one face, and thou makest thyself another![91] Now shall I ne'er embrace my kin again!"

"I see my reputation is at stake," said the little man, "my fame is shrewdly gor'd.[92] But this deception was most necessary, for the greater good. I hast strong reasons[93] for it."

"I would fain know[94] thy reasons," said the Scarecrow.

"The people of the Emerald City dost believe me to be a powerful wizard," he began. "Moreover, dost all in this land believe it. This belief, and nought else, hath kept the Emerald City and its people safe these many years, for the best safety lies in fear.[95] I' sooth, the Wicked Witch of the East, and the Wicked Witch of the West, didst leave the Emerald City in peace because they afeard me and for no other reason, save this alone."

"Yet now those weird sisters[57] are no more. Wherefore keep this counterfeit?"[96] asked Dorothy.

"I would yet protect these people, who dost cherish their great city and great wizard, and who hast been good to me. If the truth was known, who can say who might make free to attack this defenseless city? Marry, the truth would invite[97] their malevolent approach."

"But what of my brain?" asked the Scarecrow.

"And what of my heart?" asked the Tin Woodman.

"And what of my courage?" asked the Lion.

"And what of Kansas?" asked all three together, on behalf of Dorothy. "How shall Dorothy e'er cross the desert and find her way to Kansas once again?"

"Say sooth,"[82] said the Scarecrow, "for thou would hast given us the lie,[98] had not little Toto taken thee with the manner[99] and shown thou art a counterfeit!"[96]

"I may be no wizard," said the little man, "but so didst I speak truly when I said I can yet bestow a brain, a heart, and a bit of courage in ye for I am not without such skill. Though I am not naturally honest, I am sometimes so by chance."[100]

Then did he tell his tale.

"When I was a boy, 'twas my dream to run away in search of pageantry,"[101] he began, "but I was far too sensible and timid to do anything so rash.[102] Instead, I sought adventure in the many books I read. I became a scholar[103] and, as a man, a professor of Latin Studies at a prestigious university in the east. So too, I studied architecture and herbology and horology and, for a time, I was a silversmith and lapidarist. 'Twas ever in my nature, I am afeard, to have one foot in sea, and one foot on shore, to one thing constant never."[104]

"I grew tired of my life in academia," said the little man, "and ne'er had I forgotten my youthful wanderlust. So, one day, I left the university. I bought a horse and caravan and as a pedlar,[105] with all my hobbies packed, I traveled west, selling herbs and spices, elixirs, watches and silver boxes, bracelets and ribbons and lace, and countless hallowed trinkets.[106] In time, I found a company of players, and bound myself to them. From them I learned illusions, puppetry, and pageantry, and, withal, ventriloquism."

"When we arrived in Omaha," continued he, but here was the telling of his tale interrupted.[107]

"Omaha!" exclaimed Dorothy! "Why that's not far a'tall from Kansas!"

"Nay, marry, it's not," continued he. "We arrived in Omaha just as the State Fair commenced, a most impressive exhibition, with a great balloon at its center. To augment my meager income, I found entertainment[108] as a bold balloonist for, when I was young, boldness be my friend.[109] My duty was to ascend with those who wished to view the fairgrounds, and the city, from on high, and to entertain them at those lofty heights with tales of true adventure. So too didst I make free to show samples of my wares to my captive audience."

"'Twas not a'tall a dangerous pursuit, or so thought I, for the balloon was tethered firmly to the ground and, when aloft, all the troubles of the world were far below. I quite enjoyed it, and there was nought for me to do but tell my stories and to reassure my nervous passengers that all was safe and sound. Each morning, before the fairgrounds opened, alone would I ascend to test the surety of the tether and to draw attention to the fair, far and wide. But, one morning, as I ascended all alone, such a powerful gust of wind struck the balloon that the basket parted from the tether, and the tether fell away upon the place beneath.[110] And, in th' very moment,[13] did the balloon then rise higher and higher and sail away."

"My gracious," exclaimed Dorothy, "what followed then?"

"The balloon sailed and sailed, driven by prevailing winds, and, in time, it sailed o'er the Western Forest of this land. 'And the worse I may be yet', thought I, for the worst is not, so long as we can say, 'This is the worst.'[111] And, i' sooth, then was I pursued by the Wingèd Monkeys."

"I saw them approaching in a line, much as they did of late when they brought ye from the western lands," said the little man. "Greatly did I fear them and, so too, I didst not set my life above a pin's fee.[112] But then, when they had climbed almost to touch the basket, there came another burst of wind to carry me higher still, and so too onward and into the eastern lands."

"The monkeys fell away and, anon, the air bit shrewdly and 'twas very cold.[113] The balloon then descended, precipitously, till 'twas o'er this very place, though, in that time, there was no city, nor palace to be seen. Of its own accord, the balloon then settled hither, and the good people of this land declared me to be a wizard, for I had descended from the heavens."

"As mine own occasion was so far from mellow,[114] I made no protestation but, the rather, I charged[115] them vouchsafe me raiment, bed, and food.[116] In time, I ordered the construction of this Palace, with this Throne Room built to my exacting terms, to facilitate my grand illusions of both sight and sound. So too, this Emerald City didst I command them to build, for none had e'er conceived of such a city afore I didst arrive."

"And all would hast been a pleasant dream, but for those two Wicked Witches. For their powers wast not counterfeit,[96] and no defense had I against them, save only this belief that at the heart of this great city dwelt a great and terrible wizard."

"I dost perceive sooth in thy report,"[117] said Dorothy, "for I recall the painting in my chamber of that balloon of which ye speak. So too, dost I recall a tale my father told to comfort me, afore he left this world, of another such balloon that sailed o'er a rainbow,[118] to gain heaven's gate.[119] In my mind's eye,[120] dost I e'er see him thither."

"I dost believe," continued she, "there's a divinity that shapes our ends, rough-hew them how we will."[121]

"That is most certain,"[122] agreed the Tin Woodman.

"I' sooth," said Dorothy, "'tis not of chance that we are met together in this time and place. Therefore, let us go forth together whence we are to whither we wish to be."

"Sir," she asked him then, "canst thou truly bestow a brain, a heart, and a bit of courage in my friends?"

"Ay, I hast considered this and I believe I can," he replied. "I' faith, I dost speak in sober judgement."[123]

"Return hither on the morrow, at nine o'clock in the forenoon, and I will make all this matter even, as I hath promised ye."[124]

"And what of Dorothy?" asked the Scarecrow. "Can ye send her safely back to Kansas?"

"That is indeed the question that now occupies my mind," answered the little man. "I pray, give me till tomorrow to say how best to answer it."

Chapter XVI

The Magic Art of the Great Humbug

"Congratulate me," said the Scarecrow to his friends, as they walked together down the long passageway leading to the Throne Room, "for, anon, I shall hast a brain and be as other men!"[1]

"I hast always liked you as you were,"[2] replied Dorothy simply.

"Thou art kind to say as much," said the Scarecrow, "yet surely when my thoughts dost rise to lofty heights, so too must I rise then in thine esteem."

"Or in thine own esteem," worried Dorothy, but to herself. For she loved the Scarecrow, as he was, and she feared the Wizard's brain might bring about some change in him. Yet, resolved was she to see this through and to trust to the strength and kindness of his character.

Dorothy felt the same about the Lion's newfound courage. She loved the wisdom that e'er blossom'd from his ever-present fear, and she rejoiced each time he found, deep within himself, his bit of courage to surmount it, to do then whatever he must do. She hoped the Wizard's courage would not make him foolish with his strength, nor arrogant in his confidence.

But Dorothy harbor'd no worries a'tall about the Wizard's heart for the Tin Woodman, for there is no such thing as too much love. In this alone, one cannot desire too much of a good thing,[3] as her Auntie Em was wont to say.

In the Throne Room, the Wizard sat upon his throne, like patience on a monument,[4] awaiting their arrival. Thought he but to himself, "To be or not to be a humbug? That is the question.[5] I' faith, how can I help but be a humbug when people make me do things everyone knows cannot be done?[6] For no mortal man can truly bestow a brain, a heart, or courage." Yet, he knew he could please them by seeming to grant these things, and it was within his power to do this much, at least.

At last, he resolved he would try to persuade each, *"To thine own self be true."*[7] For, i' sooth, was the Scarecrow already indu'd with intellectual sense and soul.[8] Withal, the Tin Woodman was already rich in love-thoughts.[9] And, as the lions of the Western Forest proclaimed, the Lion was already as valiant as any lion[10] known to them.

"In sooth, I know not why I am so sad," thought the Wizard. "Yet it wearies me."[11] For he was tired of being a humbug, and he felt he was a player on a stage, and that his was a sad part.[12] "E'en so," thought he, "if by granting these requests I assist[13] these three to overcome some false notions in themselves then I shall do it. So shines a good deed in a weary world."[14]

When all were assembled before him, the Wizard welcomed them and then addressed the Scarecrow.

"Before I bestow in thee a brain," said the Wizard, "give me leave[15] to catechise[16] thee."

"Of course," replied the Scarecrow, "ask me what you will."[17]

"Art thou certain thou dost need a brain?" asked the Wizard. "For thou art wiser than thou art ware of."[18]

"How now?"[19] asked the Scarecrow.

"Was it not thee who perceived the Tin Woodman to be more than a mere sculpture?" asked the Wizard. "Was it not thee who told the Lion to flee the deadly poppy field with Dorothy and Toto? Was it not thee who conceived how to cross the rushing river? Or how to find the Witch's castle?"

"'Twas," answered the Scarecrow. "But what's that to th' purpose?"[20]

"Dost ye not note how swiftly thy knowledge hath increased since ye wast lately made?" asked the Wizard? "Marry, ye dost know much which ye hast never learnt! I 'sooth, ye know the Latin tongue! Is there any limit to what ye will know in time?"

"And yet," replied the Scarecrow, "I heard the Munchkin brothers say I hast no brain. What o' that?"[21]

"How easy is it for the proper false in our waxen hearts to set their forms,"[22] replied the Wizard. "I' faith, how easily we accept as sooth pernicious words! I' sooth, others speak such words to calm some fear about themselves."

"I would advise thee," continued the Wizard, "To thine own self be true."[7]

"Yet," replied the Scarecrow, "if I am honest with myself, I must admit they spoke truly[45] for, i' sooth, I hast no brain."

"Neither hast thou a liver, yet ye dost feel every human emotion," responded the Wizard. "Neither hast thou a heart, yet ye dost love thy friends. Thy excellent hearing and notable vision dost surpass that of other men. I' sooth, thou dost bear a mind that envy could not but call fair.[23] Ye hast no need of a brain!"

"Yet, e'en so," replied the Scarecrow, "I dost desire a brain, this above all."[7]

"Then, perhaps, when all's done,[24] we ought to let thy firm desire guide us," said the Wizard. "For thou art one who sees alike in darkness and in light. For thou alone, there is no darkness but ignorance.[25] Thy keen desire for a brain may, i' faith, be a point of wisdom.[26] Very well, a brain ye shall have!"

"Truly?" asked the Scarecrow. "What fitting brain wilt thou bestow within me?"

"A felicitous brain for a stuffed man,[27] such as thyself, would be a poultice of select'd herbs and spices. I' sooth, I hast prepared for thee a perfect potpourri of herbs and spices to fortify[28] thy intellect, improve thy memory, and to make thy judgement sober."[29]

"Such as?" inquired the Scarecrow.

"Sage, of course," answered the Wizard. "Withal, turmeric and gillyvors[30] and rosemary and rue.[31] Oh, mickle is the powerful grace that lies in herbs, plants, stones, and their true qualities!"[32]

"How now?"[18] asked the Scarecrow.

"'Tis well known mugwort is a mystical sage for lucid dreams," replied the Wizard. "So too is rosemary an herb sacred to remembrance, for it doth strengthen memory,[33] and guards against witches and dreams that dost unsettle. And rue, withal, doth yield protection from the evil eye and the element of fire. So too, is rue an "herb of grace" o' Sunday,[34] and so will help allay thy awkward stumbles. And then, turmeric is a natural defense against depression, and, of course, gillyvors[30] yield pleasant thoughts and happiness, to aid in thy acceptance and enjoyment of the life giv'n thee."

"Gracious me!" exclaimed the Scarecrow! "I can no other answer make but thanks, and thanks, and ever thanks!"[35]

"By your leave,"[36] said the Wizard then, "I must off with thy head[37] to proceed."

When it was o'er, and when once again the Scarecrow's head was back where it belonged, Dorothy asked him cautiously, "How dost thou feel? What dost thou think?"

"I think, I think," said the Scarecrow, as he searched for words to express precisely what he thought of his new brain, "I think I am the same as I have ever been. I' sooth, they made me a fool, and a fool I remain. Yet the Wonderful Wizard of Oz hath bestowed in me a brain! I feel grateful, I feel blessed! And I thank my stars I am happy!"[38]

"If that be so," said the Wizard, "then thou art indeed a wise man. For 'tis said, '*The fool doth think he is wise, but the wise man knows himself to be a fool.*'"[39]

"But I pray, sir, tell me,"[40] asked the Tin Woodman of the Scarecrow, "dost thou know now, by virtue of thy seasoned brain, all things that may be known?"

"Nay. I' sooth, I now perceive how much I hast still to learn," answered the Scarecrow. "And I stand on sudden haste[41] to learn it all!"

"Then ye must be a patron of mine own library,"[42] said the Wizard. "'Twill be a pleasure to open it to one who will appreciate it and comprehend its value. It hath volumes that I prize[42] by every great mind of this land and, withal, a few that I have penned myself. So too, it hath my journals of my time hither playing the Great and Powerful Wizard of Oz and, withal, my plans for the Emerald City."

"I thank thee,"[43] said the Scarecrow, in his great humility. "I am most grateful for thy kindness."

Turning then to the Tin Woodman, the Wizard said, "I pray, sir, tell me, where is fancy bred? In the heart or in the head?"[44]

"Surely in the heart," said he, "if I should speak truly."[45]

"And yet," observed the Wizard, "thy love for the Munchkin maid hath not faltered all this while thou hath been a man of tin, a beast without a heart.[46] Withal, thou hast come to love thy newfound friends. What o' that?"[21]

"'Tis true," answered the Tin Woodman. "I dost love them all."

"I' sooth, I believe thou dost love as much as any I hast e'er known," said the Wizard.

"So do I too,"[47] said Dorothy.

"Love looks not only with the heart but with the mind,"[48] said the Wizard. "And yet," he continued, "the heart hath reasons that reason cannot know.[49] For this, and other reasons, ye should have a heart, and ye shall have a heart. Withal, it must be a heart of gold,[50] for nothing less will do."

The Wizard then took from his waistcoat bosom pocket a heart-shaped watch of solid gold. "I hast loved this all my days," said he, as he gazed at it lovingly. "Of late, mine own heart hast been troubled by what shall become of this heart when I am gone. Now it shall be thine. I know no safer keeping for this heart of gold,[50] and so mine own happiness is manifested, side by side, with thine."

At this, the Tin Woodman was afeard to speak, lest he should speak in starts, distractedly,[51] and tears formed in his eyes, which Dorothy quickly dried and, withal, her own.

"Ye must not wear this heart upon thy sleeve for daws to peck at,"[52] said the Wizard. "The rather,[53] I will make a portal in thy bosom so that, from time to time, ye may wind this heart of gold[50] that it may always be a living, beating heart within thy breast."

When the Wizard had hung the golden watch within the Tin Woodman's bosom, and closed the portal door, he said to him, "Go to thy bosom, knock there, and ask thy heart what it doth know."[54]

The Tin Woodman did so, and then answered, "Thou hast lent me a heart replete with thankfulness.[55] What doth it know? Too well what love to others I dost owe!"[56]

"Quite so," replied the Wizard. "To thine own self be true, for thou canst not then be false to any man."[7]

Turning then to the Lion, the Wizard said, "I pray, sir, tell me,[40] wherefore dost ye seek courage from me when ye hast, time and time again, found courage within thyself?"

"I crave the sort of courage that knows no fear, that makes one forget he is afraid,"[57] said the Lion.

"Yet the best safety lies in fear,"[58] replied the Wizard. "So too is fear thy friend, and fear is the beginning of wisdom."[59]

"How now?"[19] asked the Lion.

"Denial of fear is but willful ignorance and over-confidence," replied the Wizard. "That way lies danger and arrogance, foolishness and rashness.[60] But from caution and reflection flows the wisdom to choose wisely."

"I pray, sir, tell me,"[40] continued the Wizard, "art thou more valiant since making the better acquaintance[61] of these, thy new friends, and embarking upon adventures with them?"

"I' faith, I am," answered the Lion, upon reflection. "Thou dost know some strain in me, that I know not myself.[62] Yet why should this be so?"

"Courage mounteth with occasion,"[63] answered the Wizard. "And each fear we face yields an increase in our courage if we will but embrace it. For experience be the food of courage."[64]

"I' sooth," said the Wizard, "hast thou not surmounted every fear within thy mighty breast since ye hast made new friends? Didst thou not keep thy fear in check to save those very friends as the Kalidah didst lie in wait? And, in captivity, did not thy brave demeanor bring comfort to poor Dorothy in her servitude? I' sooth, thou hast more courage than many who boast of theirs!"

"'Tis true," agreed the Scarecrow. "For courage is not the absence of fear, but the strength of character to surmount it. And thou hast this in plenty."[65]

"But shall I hast it always?" asked the Lion of the Wizard. "I fear my courage will diminish when I'm untreasured[66] of my friends once more," confessed the Lion.

"'Tis not so much courage ye lack, but confidence,"[65] said the Wizard, "Confidence in thy convictions. When ye wast but a foundling, survival was thy duty and the friend ye kept under thy own life's key[67] was fear, for fear was thy best aid to safety. But ways that served thee well in thy youth belong to that time, not to the here and now. In this moment, be true to thine own self.[7] In this moment, I bid thee search thy heart and mind to find thy present duty. For in thy present duty, thy true calling, will thee find the courage of thy convictions."

"If I would say sooth,"[68] replied the Lion to this advice, "I would say my noble purpose is not to serve myself but, the rather,[53] those within my care. I' sooth, hast I known this since that first night by the fire wherewithal Toto trusted his safety unto me. There too lies my heart's content, for I hast ne'er been so happy as in these recent days when I hast been of service to my friends."

"Then truly thou art a king," said the Wizard, "and a wise one, withal. For a wise king serves his subjects, not himself."

"Now," said the Wizard. "The people of this fair city dost believe I keep a great pot of courage in this Throne Room, which I keep covered with a golden plate to keep it from running over."[69]

"And do you?" asked Dorothy.

"Certainly not," replied the Wizard. "Yet I hast prepared especially for our friend, the Lion, this elixir," said the Wizard, as he poured it into a green-gold dish, beautifully carved,[70] and set it before the Lion.

"What is it?"[71] asked the Lion.

"That is a secret," replied the Wizard truthfully, "known to none, save me. But drink it and forevermore wilt thou hast the courage of thy convictions, the courage to search thy heart and mind to see what must be done, and then to do that very thing, come what may."[72]

The Lion hesitated but an instant, then he drank the potion.

"How now?"[19] asked Dorothy of the Lion. "Art thou now absent of all fear?"

"Nay," replied the Lion, "yet presume not that I am the thing I was![73] For I feel as one who hath been infused with a fortitude from heaven!"[74]

"Now what of Dorothy?" asked the Scarecrow of the Wizard. "How may she and Toto cross the desert and find their home in Kansas?"

"As doth a wingèd messenger of heaven,[75] she must fly," answered the Wizard. "From the Emerald City, she must ride on the curled clouds[76] with me, in my great balloon, for I hast it still, though so many years hast gone by."

"You will bring me to Kansas thyself?" exclaimed Dorothy!

"Ay," said the Wizard. "I shall follow mine own teaching[77] to the Lion. I hast searched my heart and mind and find I must take thee and Toto back to Kansas myself. Like the Lion, I hast lived my life hither in fear, but the time hath come when I must find mine own bit of courage, the courage to do what is right, to do what must be done."

"But what will become of the Emerald City without its Wizard?" she asked.

Turning then to the Scarecrow, the Wizard said, "I hast, with special soul, selected thee my absence to supply. My terror I dost lend thee, and with my love I dress thee, and dost hereby give thee deputation of all organs of mine own power, as Ruler of the Emerald City: what think you of it?"[78]

"Can I be of worth to undergo such ample grace and honor?"[79] asked the Scarecrow.

"Thy scope is as mine own," continued the Wizard, "so to enforce or qualify the laws as to thy soul seems good.[80] Withal, the Tin Woodman and the Lion will counsel thee and assist thee in this, thy great commission."

To this didst all agree, and the Wizard said, "I am glad of it, for uneasy lies the head that wears a crown,[81] and I tire of being the end-all and the be-all[82] of this land. Withal, there are a few relations of mine own I should like to see again."

"Oh," said Dorothy, "I am so happy!"

"Alas, my dear," cautioned the Wizard. "I cannot promise thee, anon will we find Kansas, for the balloon will take us where it will. But if we fly across the desert, and safely land beyond, then we should have no trouble finding Kansas thereafter."

"I understand," said Dorothy, "but every hope excites to this,[83] that Toto and I are going home at last!"

Chapter XVII

How The Balloon Was Launched

"I' sooth, I shall be frightened to soar so high above our heads, to the vaulty heaven,₁ in this great balloon," said Dorothy, "And so shall Toto too, I fear."

"Yet 'twould seem a far safer means to fly than in a spinning house atop a tempest,"₂ said the Scarecrow, "marry, a far safer means."

"Oh, be thou blessed for thy good comfort!"₃ exclaimed Dorothy!

"If I could give thee all my newfound courage," said the Lion, "I would do so ere my pulse twice beat."₄

"I know ye wouldst," said Dorothy, "and I love thee for it."

"My new heart tells me thy safety will be manifested," said the Tin Woodman. "Perchance ye shall sail past heaven's gate₅ and therewithal see thy loving parents, and wave to them, and blow them kisses through thy tears and smiles, and tell them thou art well."

"Oh," smiled Dorothy through her brimming tears, "that is such stuff as dreams are made on!₆ Thou art so kind to say as much!"

I' sooth, the Emerald City had not seen such excitement since Dorothy's first arrival and parade through the civil streets with the Scarecrow, Tin Woodman, the Lion, and Toto. The game was now afoot,₇ for the news had quickly spread that the Wizard was leaving the Emerald City in his great balloon, and that the Scarecrow was to rule the city in his absence. Excitement expanded with the balloon itself, which now stood fully inflated and bouncing lightly upon the ground, pulling at its tether.

A carnival atmosphere had indeed settled upon the city. Many children waved balloons attached to sticks, and concessionaires were selling food and drink to the assembled crowds and, withal, trinkets of the momentous occasion, as they had hastily prepared.

The time to leave had come and the Wizard climbed into the basket of the great balloon to address the people assembled there to watch him go. Before joining him, Dorothy embraced her friends one last time and then stooped to pick up Toto. But Toto was not there! For in that very moment,[8] Toto disappeared into the crowd, in pursuit of a cat he spied wandering among so many legs and rubbing each one as it moved along.

"Toto! Toto!" called Dorothy as she pushed into the crowd.

"Friends, yeomen,[9] countrymen, lend me your ears!"[10] began the Wizard. "With all ye hither as my witness, I decree the Wise Scarecrow,[11] by virtue of his superior intellect, Steward of the Emerald City, to rule in my stead until my return! Obey him as ye would me!" he commanded.

"Give me now leave to leave ye![12] In matters of great moment, I am bound to the heavens to hold conference[13] with a great brother Wizard,[14] where he bestrides the lazy-puffing clouds!"[15]

"Anon, thy mortal eyes will gaze upon me as I sail upon the bosom of the air,[15] 'til clouds do blot the heaven!"[16]

'Twas then the Wizard noticed Dorothy was not yet in the basket. "Dorothy! Anon! The balloon cannot wait a moment longer!" he called.

"Anon!" called Dorothy, as she made her way back to the balloon through the crowd, with Toto underarm. "Anon!" But just as she reached the basket, with the Wizard reaching out to her, all heard a crack, loud and sudden, as the plank tethering the balloon gave way!

Up and away flew the balloon, at liberty at last to fly, as a wanton's bird, freed at last of its silken thread![17] "Oh, come back, come back!" called Dorothy. "I want to go, too!"[18]

"I cannot!" called the Wizard back to her. And then to the crowds he waved and called, "Goodbye! Goodbye! Parting is such sweet sorrow![19] I leave you now with better company!"[20]

Then was the Wonderful Wizard of Oz departed, ne'er to be seen again. And, for many days, the people grieved o'er his loss, and they would not be comforted.[21]

Chapter XVIII

Away to the South

Nor would Dorothy be comforted. She was bereft of all words[1] and wept bitterly with disappointment when the balloon, of a sudden,[2] departed with the Wizard whilst leaving her behind. Her bitter tears, which now he did see,[3] saddened the Scarecrow and he longed to bring her hope to comfort her,[4] for the miserable have no other medicine, but only hope.[5] He summoned his companions to the Throne Room and said to them, "Friends, this grief that Dorothy hast shown doth add more grief to too much of mine own.[6] I prithee, let us once more strive to find a path to hope, as we hast done so oft before."

"Thou art so kind to say and do as much," said Dorothy. "When all's done,[7] perchance 'tis well I did not ascend in the great balloon with the Wizard. For, i' sooth, his fate remains unknown to us. Withal, what's done is done."[8]

"Wilt thou be gone?[9] Wilt thou stay no longer?"[10] asked the Tin Woodman. "Won't ye stay with us hither in the Emerald City? Or, perhaps, return with me to Munchkinland and, therewithal, abide?"

"I' faith, now and again, I have more care to stay than will to go,"[11] answered Dorothy. "But i' sooth, if I be true to mine own self,[12] 'tis both my duty and my heart's desire,[13] to return anon to my Aunt Em and Uncle Henry, if I but had the means."

"I' sooth, I share thy sentiment," said the Lion, "for mine own comfort is in the forest, and not amongst the buildings and the stone of this majestic city." Then, but to himself, the Lion thought, "Nothing she does or seems but smacks of something greater than herself, too noble for this place."[14]

"Perhaps I should indeed return to Munchkinland," said Dorothy sadly. "Not to abide, but to consult once more with the Good Witch of the North."

"Perhaps," replied the Tin Woodman. "Yet the Good Witch of the North said she knew not which way Kansas lies, nor how to cross the desert. Her sober judgement[15] and advice was to approach The Great and Powerful Oz, and this we hast already done."

The Lion then asked the Scarecrow, "Is there nothing in the Wizard's volumes that might help affect Dorothy's safe return to Kansas?"

The Scarecrow considered this question thoughtfully, then said, "I' sooth, we hast not considered the southern lands, the country of the Quadlings and of Glinda, the Good Witch of the South."

"'Tis true!" exclaimed Dorothy! "The Good Witch of the North didst say there was, withal, a Good Witch of the South! What dost thou know of her from the Wizard's volumes?"

"But little. 'Tis written she is beautiful, and, so too, that her eternal summer shall not fade.[16] Withal, her castle doth stand by the desert,"[17] said the Scarecrow. "So 'tis not absurd to think she may know how one might cross it. But nought else do I know of her, or of the Quadling people. For between the Emerald City and thither, the Wizard's map shows a forest, black in color. This forest is not wide, if we may believe his map, but few travel the road that leads from hither to the southern lands, and this Black Forest may be the reason for't."

"Is there no one in this city who might tell us more?" asked the Tin Woodman.

"Give me leave[18] to summon the Captain of the Guard," said the Scarecrow then. "I'll put the question to him."[19]

Anon was the Captain summoned and anon did he arrive. His approach was tentative and timid, for he had never been beyond the large green doors that opened to the passageway leading to the Throne Room. When asked what he knew of the Quadlings, or of the Good Witch of the South, he answered, "Glinda is murmured[20] to be the most beautiful of all the witches of this land. So too, the Quadlings say that she is good. But in my years as Captain of the Guard, few Quadlings hast e'er come to the Emerald City, and I know of none who hast travelled from the Emerald City to the southern lands and then returned. For some say the very stones and trees of the Black Forest are enchanted, and most do fear to enter therewithal. Marry, some believe, not I, the stones dost move, and the trees dost speak."

"It seems," said Dorothy to the others, "my only hope lies to the south. Toto and I must now travel therewithal to find Glinda, the Good Witch of the South. But I cannot ask ye to accompany me. For surely," said Dorothy to the Tin Woodman, "now that ye hast a heart of gold,[21] thy proper place is in Munchkinland with thy Munchkin maid."

"So too," she said to the Lion, "is it not time for thee to return to thy kin[22] in the Western Forest?"

"And with the people of the Emerald City yet grieving the loss of their Wizard, surely they must not be without their new ruler, as well," said Dorothy, decidedly, to the Scarecrow.

All answered that they should be most ungrateful[23] indeed to look to their own heart's desires[12] whilst Dorothy's went unanswered. "I should be a fool upon a pole, accosting[24] crows, if not for thee," said the Scarecrow. "And I should be nought but a sculpture, left to rust and die,[25] if not for thee," said the Tin Woodman. "And I should be a coward, alone in the Great Forest, pursued by the Kalidah, if not for thee," said the Lion.

"Nay," said all. "We will see thee safely to the country of the Quadlings, and to the Good Witch of the South, herself."

"I hast no fear of this Black Forest," said the Lion, "and I would fain prove so[26] to thee."

"So too shall mine axe be at thy service," said the Tin Woodman.

"And thou dost wear the silver slippers yet," said the Scarecrow, "and the kiss of the Good Witch of the North is yet seated on thy brow.[27] Perchance these will yet protect thee in this southern forest."

"Oh, ye art all so good to me!" cried Dorothy. "Very well, then come thy ways, we'll go along together."[28]

"Withal," said the Scarecrow, "the Captain of the Guard may govern in my absence in the south. As Steward of the Emerald City, I desire better acquaintance[29] with Glinda, this Good Witch of the South. I' faith, I believe I shall invite her to the Emerald City or, if she cannot come hither, then perhaps she will send an embassy[30] on her behalf. I believe this will bring hope and comfort to the people of both our cities."

"This is wisely done,"[31] said Dorothy.

"Indeed," replied the Scarecrow. "The Wizard's library hath several volumes of diplomacy. 'Tis a fascinating subject. Of note is the importance of good relations, and trust."

"On this subject," said the Scarecrow to the Lion, "I wish ye would agree to be the Emerald City's embassy[30] to the Winkies in the west, and to the lions of the Western Forest."

"Of course," replied the Lion, "'twould be mine honor.[32] So too, I long to see my kin." And, inwardly, the Lion smiled and sighed contently to be reminded that he had kin to miss, kin who loved him and regarded him full so valiant.[33]

"And wilt thou be our embassy[30] to Munchkinland?" asked the Scarecrow of the Tin Woodman.

"Certainly," he replied. "I am most eager to see Munchkinland again!" And all didst smile to hear him say as much.

Upon the morrow, when Dorothy had once more made a tearful parting with the pretty maid in green and kissed her goodbye and wished her health and happiness, the company made their way to the city's southern gate, accompanied by the Captain of the Guard.[34]

"Farewell," said the Captain, "Godspeed![35] May the heavens give safety to your purposes[36] and may ye be triumphant in your homecoming, rather than make unprofited return!"[37]

When they were but a league beyond the gate, they rested, and Dorothy indulged herself with one last look at the distant Emerald City. Too well she knew[38] that this should be her last glimpse of that majestic place and, with a full heart, she felt the poignancy of the moment.

To pass the time when they resumed their journey, the Scarecrow spoke of the Wizard's plans for the Emerald City, and for the Land of Oz beyond the city walls.

"Many of the Wizard's plans are industrial," said the Scarecrow. "Of course, improvements in the efficient operation of a city are always possible, but I should like to see an increase of commerce amongst the cities and the regions of this land. The river we sailed to reach the western lands is well and good, but a yellow road is needed to better link the Emerald City with the western regions. So too, should the fallen bridge be rebuilt. And the yellow road to Munchkinland is in a sad state of repair, here and there,$_{39}$ within the Eastern Forest."

"I may pledge the help of the Munchkin people in its repair," said the Tin Woodman confidently. "I feel it in my heart."

"Withal," said the Scarecrow, "I believe the time hath come for a university to be founded in the Land of Oz, with its seat in the Palace of the Emerald City. For, in sooth, 'tis clear to me the Palace may be put to better use. It should serve those whose labor built it and, so too, all the people of this land."

"I' sooth, I see the age to come$_{40}$ will be both prosperous and peaceful," said Dorothy, "now that the evil of this land hath been defeated. Oh, I shall be sorry not to see the coming of this age!"$_{41}$

The Lion had been listening to these ambitious$_{42}$ plans distractedly and said little in response. At last, Dorothy said to him, "Thy heart is full of something that doth take thy mind from us.$_{43}$ Pray, sir, tell me$_{44}$ what is it?"

"Oh, forgive my rudeness,"$_{45}$ he replied. "I will tell thee my drift.$_{46}$ I prithee, do but recall the Eastern Forest and the Kalidah. Not every evil hath been vanquished from this land."

"Speak to me as to thy thinkings,"$_{47}$ said Dorothy.

"We must prevent the ubiquitous consociation of the Kalidah throughout this land," said the Lion. "We must confine$_{48}$ them to their own territory where, in time, they will naturally decline in strength and number."

"Wherefore must we concern ourselves with this question$_{49}$ of the Kalidah?" asked the Scarecrow.

"The reason is but this: the yellow road through the Eastern Forest is not safe whilst the Kalidah make free to hunt$_{50}$ its length," said the Lion. "What point is there to the yellow road's repair, or withal the fallen bridge, if it be not safe to travel?"

"Ay, well said,"[51] replied the Scarecrow, "'tis a point of wisdom."[52]

"Indeed," said the Tin Woodman, and so said all. "Yet how can the Kalidah be cabined, cribbed, confined, or still bound in[53] to their own territory?"

"The Kalidah rely on stealth as they pursue their prey, like the fell and cruel[54] predators they are, and, withal, upon the element of surprise," answered the Lion. "I suggest we seek the entertainment[55] of the crows and of the field mice of the western lands, and of other creatures known to me in the Eastern Forest, as lawful espials who, seeing unseen,[56] spy and report the movements of the Kalidah. If we deny them stealthy pace,[57] then they will be afeard to venture forth to hunt[50] beyond the safe margins and the comfort of their lands, lest they find it is they, themselves, who hast become the prey."

"'Tis a simple plan," said the Scarecrow, "and therefore the more likely to succeed."

"I should like to believe," said the Lion softly, "that the lives of my mother and my father wast not spent in vain.[58] I should like to believe the Kalidah may be prevented from e'er beginning a fresh assault[59] upon my kin, or any else."

"I know ye wouldst," said Dorothy softly, in reply. "In this, I share thy hard adventure[60] and, so too, I miss my parents. But soon ye will be amongst thy kin, and so too I with mine, if Glinda proves to be all that we hope and pray she is."

"We might, withal, clear the trees and underbrush along the boundary of their realm," suggested the Tin Woodman, yet lost in his own thoughts, "to make the Kalidah wary of its crossing."

"And perhaps," added the Scarecrow thoughtfully, "the civil engineers of the Emerald City could rebuild the fallen bridge as a gateway with watchful towers, to be attended by the Captain's Guard, who would allow safe passage to none save friends of the Emerald City."

"Still more ambitious[41] plans didst I see in the Wizard's library," said the Scarecrow to the others. "Plans for making rivers run, fair and evenly, in channels new, to not wind with such deep[61] indent into the forest lands.

So too, plans to dam such rivers with levees to form wide waterways in the ancient purlieus[62] along the Kalidah's domain."

"Impressive," said the Lion. "If this wast done, 'twould cut the Kalidah from the best of all the land[63] and 'twould limit their entry points into the forest proper."

"Perhaps," suggested the Scarecrow to the Lion, "ye might consider a role, withal, as Minister of Defense? 'Long side thy role of embassy[30] to the western lands and lions?"

"Perhaps," replied the Lion, "now that I hast found my courage."

As the afternoon wore on, they came, at last, to where the yellow road disappeared as it entered, then curved away inside the dark Black Forest.

"Art thou afeard to venture forth into this Black Forest?" the Lion asked of Dorothy.

"I do confess 't,"[64] she answered, in honesty. "In Kansas there are no forests to be seen, or certainly none such as this."

"Be not afeard," said the Lion. "We'll pass through this forest in a twinkling[65] of thine eye."

"Perhaps so," she replied. Then, recalling her anxiety whilst in the Eastern Forest, she added, "E'en so, let us wait for the morrow and not attempt its passage when the hour grows so late. For soon 'twill be the very witching time of night, when churchyards yawn and hell itself breathes out contagion to this world."[66]

"Even so quickly may one catch the plague?"[67] asked the Tin Woodman.

"'Perhaps not," answered the Scarecrow, "but 'tis a point of wisdom[52] to take all such simple measures[68] as will keep the plague at bay. Only a fool would not do as much. Let us break our journey hither."

The companions passed a restless night, therewithal, in an open field, beside a meager fire, with the Scarecrow and Tin Woodman once more keeping watch. Then, on the morrow, with Dorothy on the Lion's back, they warily entered the Black Forest, as vigilant as a cat to steal cream.[69]

Chapter XIX

Attacked by the Fighting Trees

"No doubt," said Dorothy, "this forest hath been enchanted since before Noah was a sailor.[1] Oh, that one might know the end of this day's business ere it come! But it sufficeth that the day will end, and then the end is known. Come, ho! Away![2] Lead on!"

"What enchantments[3] might this forest hold?" asked the Tin Woodman of the Scarecrow, as they entered the Black Forest. "Was there nothing in the Wizard's library to speak to this concern?"

"Or can there yet be some weird sisters[4] we know nothing of?" asked the Lion. "Perhaps some foul witch, who with age and envy, hath grown into a hoop?"[5]

"I know no answer,"[6] said the Scarecrow, "save to say we heard the Wizard say, 'Oh, mickle is the powerful grace that lies in plants and stones, and their true qualities.'"[7]

"So too the Captain of the Guard said hither stones do move, and trees do speak,"[8] added the Tin Woodman.

I' sooth, hither the stones and trees did indeed seem strange and so too sinister and weird. This forest was unlike the forests to the east and west. No snapping twigs or rustles in the underbrush did they hear. Nor were birds seen or heard, nor calls of any kind. The rather,[9] a solemn silence sat heavy on this place, like a tomb,[10] and it was as silent as the grave.

"This forest hath no birds nor beasts of any kind," said the Lion. "I hear none, neither dost I smell their faintest scent."

In this did Toto quite agree, for 'twas his notable habit to follow the woodland scents whene'er he was in woodlands such as these. Yet no such notable motion did he make, for no trail was there to follow, not even to a fault.[11]

"If 'tis true that we are in great danger hither," said the Lion, "then the greater therefore should our courage be.[12] This forest is not natural, yet are we truly to believe that stones may move and trees may speak?"[8]

The company continued onward, steadily, expecting at every turn to encounter some novel danger. Yet no danger manifested. In time, their apprehension of the forest lessened, and so too did their gait.[13] Now their conversation turned naturally to Glinda, the Good Witch of the South, and to their hope that she might, at last, send Dorothy back to Kansas.

"Oh," said Dorothy, "I hope she is as kind as she is fair![14] And yet," she continued, "the Good Witch of the North was kind but, e'en so, she had not the means nor method to send me home to Kansas. Oh, what if the same proves true of Glinda? What if no persuasion can do good upon her?"[15]

"Dost ye suppose," asked the Tin Woodman of the others, "Glinda knows how broad this desert be? Perhaps I could take Dorothy o'er it myself, for I hast no need of water."

"Do but recall," said the Scarecrow, "Dorothy and Toto require water still and, withal, food and rest. Then too, whilst water may rust thy joints, desert sand would wear them away entirely. And ye know not which way Kansas lies."

"All this is true,"[16] sighed the Tin Woodman, as he leaned upon his axe and looked down at the yellow road before him. But then, looking up once more, he suddenly exclaimed, "But look! Yonder is the forest's end! Anon shall we leave this forest and enter therewithal the Country of the Quadlings!"

Then at th' very mention[17] of the Country of the Quadlings, of a sudden,[18] didst a boulder tumble down a bank and stop before them, in the very center of the road.

At this the company halted and the Lion exclaimed to the Tin Woodman, "How now! Thy prophecy comes true! Hither dost stones move about[8] to block our easy way!" said the Lion, half in jest. "Anon, we shall hear these very trees call out to us!"

In this the Lion was mistaken, for not a sound came from these trees. The rather,[9] the branches of one such tree silently bent down upon the Scarecrow, who stood behind the others on the road, and entwined about him! As Toto barked a warning, the branches lifted the Scarecrow from the road and flung him o'er the others, to where he toppled headlong down[19] before the stone that barred their way.

"Good gracious!" exclaimed Dorothy! "What rough magic[20] hereabouts doth dwell?[21] These trees will suck our breath or pinch us black and blue!"[22]

"Marry, they seem intent to fight us, and so to end our journey,"[23] said the Lion. "Out of this nettle, danger, must we pluck this flower, safety!"[24]

Then, of a sudden,[17] was Toto seized by a wanton branch and shaken till he howled![25]

"Toto!" shrieked Dorothy, in her dismay. "Toto! Oh! Poor Toto!"

"Fear not! I am quickly moved to strike!"[26] called the Tin Woodman, as he let his great axe fall[27] to sever the branch that held Toto in its grip. Then did the tree recoil and shake as if it wast in pain.

"Anon! Follow me to plainer ground!"[28] called the Tin Woodman to the others. All then hastened past the stone and ran to the forest's end, and so they 'scaped another brawl[29] with those combative trees. But as Dorothy looked behind, to the forest they had fled, she would be sworn[30] she saw the very stone they had sidled past was now slowly rolling after them!

"Oh, let us not tarry hither to be pushed along[31] by yon rolling restless stone!"[32] cried Dorothy. "I stand on sudden haste to reach this realm of the Quadlings! Oh, let us hence!"[33]

Chapter XX

The Country of the Quadlings

With the Black Forest now several hours distant, the travelers found the Country of the Quadlings increasingly beautiful and bucolic, much like the countryside 'round Munchkinland and the Emerald City.

Hither, the wilderness and untamed summer grass[1] gave way to green cornfields[2] and acres of rye.[3] So too were orchards to be seen on hillsides and in dales where strawberries grew out of season underneath the nettle. And those wholesome berries thrived and ripened best where neighbour'd by fruit of baser quality.[4]

In one such dell, near a farmhouse and a pretty bridge o'er a stream, the company paused to rest where wild strawberries grew along the bank. As Dorothy sampled them, Toto and the Lion drank of the cool water flowing in the stream.

As they took their ease, a woman emerged from the farmhouse and approached them, smiling as she came. "I prithee, pretty youth," said the woman to Dorothy, "let me be better acquainted with thee."[5]

Dorothy rose to her feet and curtsied to the woman, saying, "Good day, madam. I am Dorothy of Kansas, and these are my true friends, the Scarecrow, Tin Woodman, and the Lion, and this is little Toto."

"Oh! Indeed!" remarked the woman. "Forgive my curiosity, but I have never seen such friends as these! Won't ye see my orchard, wherewithal, in an arbor we may eat a last year's pippin of my own graffing?"[6] So too did she press Dorothy and Toto, and the Lion, to partake of meat and drink[7] and pie of her own making earlier that morning, so pleased was she to entertain such unexpected guests.

"Wherefore hast ye come into the Country of the Quadlings?" the woman asked of Dorothy.

"I' faith," answered Dorothy, "I hast come to see Glinda, the Good Witch of the South, for I am far from home, and I seek her help to return safely therewithal with little Toto. I pray, madam, tell me,[8] where may we find her castle?"

"Follow this road south," she answered, "as ye hast been, and ye cannot help but come to the castle gate. Therewithal the guards will admit ye, if Glinda will receive ye."

"Oh!" exclaimed Dorothy! "I pray she will! Tell me, is she truly as fair and good[9] as 'tis spake[10] of her?"

"Marry," replied the woman. Then, noting Dorothy's worried countenance, she asked, "But wherefore do you droop? Why look you sad?"[11]

"My melancholy is mine own and is indeed the sundry contemplation of my travels in this land, which, by often rumination, wraps me in a most compelling sadness.[12] For everywhere hast I sought, to no avail, the method of my safe return to Kansas," answered Dorothy.

"A traveler!" exclaimed the woman. "By my faith, thou hast full reason to be sad! For a traveler sees much but hath nothing, and so hath rich eyes but poor hands.[13] And, therefore, dost travelers long for home where they may be rich in love and place."

"Ay," said Dorothy, "By hard adventure,[14] in my travels hast I gained my experience."[15]

"And thy experience makes thee sad,"[16] said the woman.

"But, so too, hast I found love hither in this Land of Oz," said Dorothy, "for I hast made such friends as these, and I count myself in nothing else so happy as in a soul remembering my good friends.[17] So too then, dost ye see, should Glinda send me safely home, I must, perforce, then part from my friends hither and so there is yet another reason for my sadness."[18]

"Ay," replied the woman, "for this is also true. I' faith, both friends and family in this world are necessary for our lives to be complete."

Rested now, the travelers thanked the woman for her deeds of hospitality[19] and then they were on their way once more. Anon, the distant city came into view and then, not long thereafter, didst they arrive at the castle gate.

Hither the companions met not a Guardian of the Gate, as they had encountered at the Eastern Gate of the Emerald City, but three young girls dressed in the handsome red uniform of the Castle Guard, all trimmed with golden braid.[20]

As they approached the gate, Dorothy asked, "Who keeps the gate here, ho?"[21]

The center guard stepped forward and responded, "Wherefore hast ye come to the South Country?"[22]

"To see the Good Witch who rules hither," answered Dorothy. "She is the list of my voyage.[23] Will ye take us to see her?"[24]

"What shall I say ye are?"[25] asked the guard.

"I prithee," answered Dorothy, "Tell thou the Good Witch that Dorothy of Kansas doth attend her hither,[26] accompanied by the Scarecrow, Steward of the Emerald City, the Tin Woodman, Embassy to Munchkinland, and the Lion, Embassy to the Western Lands."

The guard nodded, then turn'd on her toe[27] and entered the castle, as the remaining guards smartly side-stepped toward one another to close the gap between them.

Moments later the guard returned and announced the travelers were to be admitted[28] anon!

Chapter XXI

Glinda, The Good Witch of the South

Inside the castle, the travelers were shown to separate quarters to rest and to prepare for their presentation before Glinda and her court.

At the hour she appointed them,[1] the guard who announced their arrival now escorted them to an ornate room where Glinda sat upon a Ruby Throne, well attended[2] by fair ladies dressed in red, and more of the Castle Guard, on either side. Dorothy curtsied before her as the Scarecrow, Tin Woodman, and the Lion all bowed in unison.

Glinda, i' faith, seemed both beautiful and young, and yet there was something in the expressure of her eye, forehead, and complexion[3] that suggested she was far older than she appeared.

"I prithee,"[4] said Glinda to all, "approach and let me know ye better. Word hath reached me hither in this Southern Land, of the death of those weird sisters[5] in the east and west, and withal, of the departure of The Great and Powerful Oz himself. Thou hast been busy in the Land of Oz," said Glinda to Dorothy, archly, as she smiled at her.

"Alas 'tis true, I have gone here and there,"[6] Dorothy replied.

"So too dost I know how camest thou hither, and wherefore[7] thou hast come to me," replied Glinda to Dorothy. "I' sooth, I hast longed to make thy better acquaintance,[8] and to see the kiss of the Good Witch of the North upon thy brow, for it hath been many years since last I saw her. And I see the silver slippers on thy feet. 'Tis fortunate that they were spared when thy house fell from the sky. For had they been destroyed, so too wouldst any hope of thy going home to Kansas be, withal."

"Forgive me," said Dorothy, "I would fain[9] know thy meaning."

"Indeed," smiled Glinda, "and I will explain, anon. But first, I prithee,[4] I would know thy friends."

"Oh! Of course!" exclaimed Dorothy! "Forgive my rudeness, in my excitement I hast forgotten my manners."

"These are my true friends, Scarecrow, Tin Woodman, and Lion, and this is little Toto," said Dorothy.

"I pray, sir, tell me,"[10] said Glinda to the Tin Woodman, "art thou content to be a man of tin?"

"I am," he answered, "for there is no help for it. Withal, my life is so much better than it was, and so my new heart is a heart replete with thankfulness.[11] For no longer am I a solitary statue rusting in the Eastern Forest. No longer am I a slave to the Wicked Witch of the East. So too, hast I made such good friends as these. And this above all,[12] the Munchkin maid loves me yet! And once Dorothy is safely home, so too will I return to mine own home, anon, in Munchkinland, to be with her!"

"Why is there no help for thine enchantment?" asked Glinda then.

"The Good Witch of the North knows not the words to end the spell of this enchantment, and so her ancient incantations are too weak,"[13] answered the Tin Woodman. "I' sooth, I would sooner be a man of flesh and blood,[14] now that I hast a heart again but, e'en so, I hast so much to be grateful for."

"I see," said Glinda. "I pray, sir, may I see the heart the Wizard placed within thy breast?"

The Tin Woodman showed Glinda his heart of gold[15] then returned it to his bosom. Glinda then remarked, 'Tis well thy sides are made of tin, so to bide the beating of so strong a passion as love doth give thy heart![16] But let me say soberly, 'tis a wonderful heart, and 'twill serve perfectly."

Then, to the surprise of all, Glinda approached the Tin Woodman and whispered in his ear. Stepping back, she smiled at him and said, "But ye must return to Munchkinland, for there the spell wast cast, and only there may it be broken."

"What fire is in mine ear?" exclaimed the Tin Woodman! "Can this be true?"[17]

"What is it?" asked Dorothy, for it was plain that something wonderful had happened. "Pray tell us!"

Glinda, i' faith, seemed both beautiful and young.

"I have heard the words that will dissolve the charm[18] under which I live!" exclaimed the Tin Woodman, in his amazement. "Glinda spake them in mine ear, and they art, oh, so simple! I must return to Munchkinland, anon, to find the Good Witch of the North!"

"Oh, I am so pleased for thee!" said Dorothy, gleefully and so said all!

"And thou," said Glinda, turning to the Scarecrow. "I am told thou art the Steward of the Emerald City. Is it even so?"[19]

"It is," he replied, "and in such capacity dost I extend to thee an invitation to visit the Emerald City as my guest, to advance the good relations and good fortunes of both our cities."

"Apt, in good faith, very apt,"[20] said Glinda. "Certainly, I shall be honored to come to the Emerald City. I hast not been in that part of this land since the Good Witch of the North and I wast last together, when we wast young, both in our years and so too in our art."

"Forgive me," said the Scarecrow then, "but, pray tell me, why should it be apt that I am now the Steward of the Emerald City? For not long ago I was but a fool raised upon a pole above a field of corn."

"'Tis by virtue of thy garb," she answered, "for there's magic in the web of it.[21] I' sooth, I recognized thy clothes in th' very moment[22] I first saw thee, though it hath been an age[23] since I last saw them."

"How now?"[24] asked the Scarecrow, "I would fain know[9] thy meaning."

"To explain," answered Glinda, "I must tell thee of another wizard."

"Was there another wizard?" asked the Scarecrow in his surprise.

"Indeed, there was," answered Glinda, "he whose clothes you wear. I find in thee some part of him lives on."

"In a time now gone from nearly all remembrance,"[25] she continued, "there lived a wizard, where the Emerald City now stands. Powerful was his magic, and so too was he kind and honest. Under his tutelage I was train'd in my art,[26] and so too was the Good Witch of the North. But as we grew in skill, so grew the jealously of his sisters, those same weird sisters[5] whom Dorothy didst end."

At this the companions all looked to one another, astonished, and then back to Glinda.

"Those sisters plotted our destruction, so loving-jealous[27] wast they of his affection for us. All appeal to their sober judgement[28] was in vain, for no persuasion would do good upon them.[29] At last, for our protection, in secret did he send us north and south, to hide us from the measure of their wrath."[30]

"Oh, beware of jealousy!" said the Tin Woodman. "It is the green-eyed monster which doth mock the meat it feeds on!"[31]

"My gracious!" said Dorothy! "Pray tell us, what followed then?"

"Those outraged sisters then made war upon their brother and pursued him through the Eastern Forest, as far as Munchkinland. At last, on the bank of the stream that flows through that fair country, did he meet his timeless end,[32] for in the struggle that then ensued he fell into the stream, and was melted."

"My gracious!" said Dorothy again! "Melted! As was the Wicked Witch of the West! The good wizard melted and yet his wicked sisters lived on and thrived?"

"Just so," replied Glinda. "For some rise by sin and some by virtue fall.[33] All that remained of him wast these clothes," said Glinda, gesturing to the Scarecrow's clothes, and, withal, to his hat. His sister, she who would become the Wicked Witch of the East, retrieved his boots from the stream and, by her art, she transformed them into the silver slippers we now see upon thy feet."

At this Dorothy gasped and looked down at the slippers, as did all.

"Into these slippers she poured all the magic she possessed, to concentrate her power thither and to meld her magic with her brother's. When she, she who would become the Wicked Witch of the West, realized what her sister had done, she demanded the slippers for herself. But her power was not then the equal of her sister's, and so the Wicked Witch of the East exiled[34] her to the Eastern Forest."

"Just as she did to me!" exclaimed the Tin Woodman!

"Just so," replied Glinda, for she knew the Tin Woodman's tale.

"How dost thou know of these happenings with this wizard and his sisters?" asked the Scarecrow. "Did ye witness them thyself, with thine own eyes?"

"Nay," answered Glinda, "for I was hither, in the South. But there were Munchkins who espied these happenings, from their hiding places in the greenery. 'Twas they who then retrieved the wizard's clothing and his hat from the stream. But what became of that garb was unknown to me until this day when mine eyes did see thee first,"[35] said Glinda to the Scarecrow.

"In time, the Good Witch of the North heard these tales from the Munchkins," she continued. "And, in time, I heard these tales from her, in a letter[36] I received from her, in the Latin tongue. 'Twas then that I cast spells and enchantments on the Black Forest stones and trees,[37] to discourage any who might attempt to journey hither to this Land of the Quadlings ."

Turning then to the Lion, Glinda said, "Sir, I would beg of thee thy good entertainment in a matter of great importance."

"I am at thy service," replied the Lion.

"When thou dost return to the western lands, I beg of thee to find the clothes worn by the Wicked Witch of the West when she melted, and then to burn them. For, if any should ever find them and don them then the evil in their weave may come to life once more."

"This is already done," replied the Lion. "For as my cousin and I stood near, did we see the Winkies burn those very clothes on the bonfires they made that night to celebrate her melting."

"Oh! Joy comes well in such a needy time!"[38] exclaimed Glinda then! "So shines a good deed in a naughty world!"[39]

"May I ask a question of thee?" asked the Lion then of Glinda.

"Of course," she answered.

"How came the Wicked Witch of the West to leave the Eastern Forest?" he asked. "And pray tell us how she came to possess the castle wherein I was held captive, if thou dost know the tale."

"I' faith, I do," she replied. "In those times, lions dwelt in the Eastern Forest, the former lions of your blood,[40] and 'twas they who drove her ever west, and to the north, to the country now called the Kalidah's domain. There she dwelt for many years and 'twas there she first transformed a tiger and a bear into a beast,$_{41}$ a Kalidah, whose purpose was to be a scourge upon the lions. For the lions, like her sister, exiled$_{34}$ her and rejected her."

"Too well$_{42}$ I know what scourge was laid upon$_{43}$ us," said the Lion. "'Tis well I knew not of her hand in the creation of the Kalidah whilst I was yet a captive in her castle."

"Indeed," replied Glinda. "Of course, 'twas truly not her castle. 'Twas the castle of a royal family, a king and queen and princess, who ruled the Winkie people. When it was time for the princess to be wed, the Good Witch of the North sent her the Golden Cap as a wedding gift that she might expel the Winged Monkeys from her sight, for she didst fear them greatly."

"But to the sorrow of the Winkie people, that weird sister,$_5$ in her counterfeit,$_{44}$ made free to attend the royal wedding, uninvited. By her dark art of bottled potions did she poison$_{45}$ the princess and, so too, all her family. She then took possession of the Golden Cap and used its power o'er the Winged Monkeys to enslave the Winkie people. 'Twas in that very moment$_{22}$ that she became the Wicked Witch of the West."

"Dark times followed," continued Glinda, "for her sister, in the East, had already enslaved the Munchkin people. And 'though the Wicked Witch of the West now possessed a castle, and so too slaves of her own, her jealousy$_{31}$ and resentment of her sister never faded, nor did her envy$_{46}$ of the silver slippers. I' faith, she vowed she would someday hast them for herself."

"I' sooth," said Dorothy then, "she demanded them of me. Yet I told her she would never have them, for the Good Witch of the North bade me wear them always. I told her I would destroy the slippers myself if any harm e'er came to little Toto."

"I would hast thee know, my dear, 'twas only by thy resolute$_{47}$ courage in that very moment$_{22}$ that all hither in this land hast their liberty. For if the magic in these slippers had been added to her own then all in this land must, perforce, hast been subject to her will forever after."

Dorothy smiled wanly to hear Glinda speak this sooth.[48] Then she asked, "But what of the center lands? Why did those witches spare the people who lived where the Emerald City now stands?"

"I' faith," Glinda answered, "those who dwelt in the center lands stood within the danger[49] of those witches from two sides. And that country's fate[50] might have been a tragic fate, withal, but for the coming of the Wizard in his balloon. As good luck would have it,[51] the Wizard 'scaped the Winged Monkeys that the Wicked Witch of the West sent in pursuit of him, and his balloon then landed safely where the Emerald City now stands. The people therewithal believed the wizard of old had returned to them, at last. They embraced him and welcomed his return, and they willingly obeyed his commands to build the Emerald City."

"So too didst his sisters believe their brother had returned," continued Glinda. "I' sooth, they believed he was now more powerful than before, and they perceived the steady rise of the majestic Emerald City to be the measure of his increasing power. And ergo, they afeard to challenge him anew. But in my sober judgement,[28] I was doubtful that this new wizard was truly he of old. Therefore, I let stand the enchantments I had placed upon the trees and stones[37] of the Black Forest and, for these many years, hath our safety been manifested, hither in these southern lands."

"But now," said the Scarecrow, "a new age[52] is coming! For, by Dorothy's hand[53] art those weird sisters[5] ended. So too, art the Munchkins and the Winkies now free."

"And there is mirth in heaven when earthly things, made even, atone together,"[54] said Glinda. "All this is true."[55]

"Yet 'tis also true the time hath come for us to thank Dorothy for her good entertainment,"[56] said Glinda as she smiled at her, "and for us to say, 'fare thee well at once.'[57] For 'tis time for Dorothy to go home."

"Oh!" exclaimed Dorothy! "Wilt thou take me to Kansas thyself? Just as the Wizard meant to do?"

"Nay," smiled Glinda, "for I hast not the means to take thee back myself. But ye wear the silver slippers, and therein lies the power to affect thy safe return to Kansas. I' sooth, thou hast had the power to go home e'er since the Good Witch of the North first vouchsafed[58] these slippers to thee."

"Why did she not tell me so herself?" asked Dorothy.

"I believe," answered Glinda, "she hath forgotten much of the power of these slippers, just as she hath forgotten the words to end the Tin Woodman's sad enchantment. For she grows old, and she hath not my eternal summer,[59] more's the pity."[60]

"But how can these slippers take me safely home to Kansas?" asked Dorothy.

"'Tis simplicity itself," smiled Glinda. "Simply say where ye would be and then click thy heels three times together, and the silver slippers will see thee safely hence."

"And Toto too?" asked Dorothy.

"Ay," smiled Glinda. "Toto too."

"When you depart for Kansas, then sorrow wilt abide and happiness will take his leave,"[61] said the Lion.

"I hast full cause of weeping, but my heart shall break into a hundred thousand flaws should I allow myself to cry at this sad parting,"[62] said the Tin Woodman. Though, i' sooth, he cried.

"In Kansas wilt thou grow up and, so too, grow old," said the Scarecrow, "but to me, fair friend, you never can be old. As when first thine eye I eyed and wink'd, such wilt thou ever be for me."[63]

"Oh, and I shall miss ye all, withal," said Dorothy, "for ye hast been as brothers to me. I' sooth, I hast never known a sibling before, for I am all the daughters of my father's house, and all the brothers too."[64]

"And whether we shall meet again I know not," said Dorothy. "Therefore, our everlasting farewell take. Forever and forever farewell, friends. If we do meet again, why, we shall smile. If not, why then this parting was well made."[65]

"And now," said Glinda to Dorothy as she kissed her forehead, "art thou ready to go home?"

Dorothy hugged and kissed her friends one last time, then took Toto up into her arms and answered simply, "I am."

Chapter XXII

Home Again

"Slippers, take me home to Aunt Em!"[1] exclaimed Dorothy, as she thrice clicked her heels together!

Instantly she was whirling through the air, drinking the air before her as it whistled past her ears. Then, before her pulse twice beat,[2] she stopped so suddenly that she toppled down headlong[3] upon the grassy plain. 'Twas then she knew she was no longer in the castle of the Good Witch of the South.

Dorothy stood up and found she was in her stocking-feet. For the silver slippers, with their nimble soles, had fallen off her feet in her dance[4] through the air, and now they were lost forever.

"Good gracious!" she cried, as she looked about her. For she was once more on the Kansas prairie and, before her, not far away, was the new farmhouse Uncle Henry had built after the tempest had carried her away in the old one.[5]

Uncle Henry was milking the cows in the barnyard,₆ and Aunt Em had just come out of the house to water the cabbages.₇ Toto saw them and instantly raced ahead, barking excitedly all the while.₈

Hearing Toto's familiar bark, Aunt Em stopped abruptly on the step and Uncle Henry ceased milking and stood up and turned. Both shaded their eyes against the afternoon sun and looked in his direction.

And there on the prairie, just beyond the barnyard fence, they saw a little girl running towards them!

"Dorothy!" cried Aunt Em as she dropped her watering can and ran to meet her.

"My darling child!" she cried, folding the little girl in her arms and covering her face with kisses.₉ "Whence cometh thou?"₁₀

When Dorothy had caught her breath, she gasped, "From the Land of Oz! And here is Toto, too. And oh, Aunt Em! I'm so glad to be at home again!"₁₁

The End

Epilogue

Good plays prove the better by the help of good epilogues.₁ I hope the same proves true regarding modern fairy tales like *O Wonderful, Wonderful Wizard of Oz*.₂ L. Frank Baum, in the introduction to his famous book wrote this, *"The Wonderful Wizard of Oz was written solely to please children of today. It aspires to be a modernized fairy tale, in which the wonderment and joy are retained, and the heartache and nightmares are left out. – Chicago, April, 1900."*₃

One hundred and twenty years later, this is an aspiration I share, for I wrote this rendition of Baum's book solely to please my grandchildren and, so too, their children, in the years to come. I hope they have as much fun reading it as I had writing it!

*The Wonderful Wizard of Oz*₃ is a story about a Kansas farm girl and her little dog who are swept away to an unknown land. By her wits, kindness, courage, and morality she collects new friends, defeats the evil she encounters, determines what must be done and has the courage to do it, and, through it all, longs to return home to those she loves and who love her.

I know another farm girl who is much like Dorothy. In her I see the same talent for making friends, the same innate kindness and courage, and the same determination to stand against cruelty and injustice. Whether it be standing up to those who would dare to be unkind to her friends, or whether it be to rescue animals in need, Ivy, like Dorothy, is one who helps others. It is who she is.

Vermont is not Kansas. We have forests, for example. But, just as Kansas is home for Dorothy, so Vermont is home for Ivy. Perhaps someday adventures will take Ivy away from us for a time, to some undiscover'd country₄, or perhaps to college, where she will find she has more brains and heart and courage, than ever she imagined, so long as she remembers, *"To thine own self be true."*₅ Like Dorothy, Ivy will help the people she encounters, people who will become her lifelong friends. Perhaps she will bring a little dog along with her. I could see her doing that. Or at least a pair of silver slippers.

On her journey, however far away it leads her, the lessons she learned at home, and the advice and values passed down to her, will serve her well. So too will the knowledge and experience she gains from the hard adventures[6] on her journey.

And I predict, through it all, she will not forget her roots, nor the beauty of Vermont, nor those at home she loves. For as the Quadling woman said to Dorothy in her orchard, *"I' faith, both friends and family in this world are necessary for our lives to be complete."*[7]

And when, at last, she comes home once more she will smile and say, "Oh! I'm so glad to be at home again!"[8]

Love,

Grandad,

Christmas 2020

Endnotes

O Wonderful, Wonderful Wizard of Oz

1. As You Like It, 3.2.173, *O wonderful, wonderful, and most wonderful, wonderful!*

Chapter I. The Tempest

1. The Tempest

2. Henry IV, Part I, 1.1.25-26, *Over whose acres walked those blessèd feet which fourteen hundred years ago*

3. As You Like It, 2.4.92, *I pray thee, if it stand with honesty, buy thou the cottage,*

4. Titus Andronicus, 2.4.13, *Who is this? My niece, that flies away so fast!*

5. Twelfth Night, 1.2.36, *That died some twelvemonth since,*

6. Twelfth Night, 1.2.385, *for whose dear love, they say*

7. Hamlet, 1.2.184, *In my mind's eye, Horatio.*

8. King Henry VI, Part 3, 3.1.57, *Say, what art thou that talk'st of kings and queens?*

9. Hamlet, 1.3.78, *This above all: to thine own self be true,*

10. Twelfth Night, 1.2.25, *A noble duke, in nature as in name.*

11. Twelfth Night, 1.2.17, *So long as I could see.*

12. Twelfth Night, 2.3.55, *But shall we make the welkin dance indeed?*

13. The Tempest, 4.1.86, *Tell me, heavenly bow, If Venus or her son, as thou dost know,*

14. Twelfth Night, 1.1.41, *and fill'd her sweet perfections with one self king!*

15. King John, 4.2.13-14, *To smooth the ice, or add another hue unto the rainbow,*

16. Julius Caesar, 1.3.11-13, *Either there is civil strife in heaven, or else the world, too saucy with the gods, incenses them to send destruction*

17. The Tempest, 1.2.256, *To run upon the sharp wind of the north,*

18. Julius Caesar, 1.3.5-8, *I have seen tempests when the scolding winds have rived the knotty oaks,*

19. Julius Caesar, 1.3.47, *Who'ever knew the heavens menace so?*

20. Tempest, 1.1.23, *If you cannot, give thanks you have lived so long*

21. Tempest, 1.1.49, *All lost! To prayers! To prayers! All lost!*

22. Romeo and Juliet, 3.1.65, *No, 'tis not so deep as a well nor so wide as a church-door, but 'tis enough.*

23. As You Like It, 2.4.84, *and at our sheepcote now, by reason of his absence, there is nothing.*

24. Romeo and Juliet, 3.1.3, *And if we meet we shall not 'scape a brawl,*

25. Twelfth Night, 1.5.46, *As there is no true cuckhold but calamity, so beauty's a flower.*

26. Hamlet, 1.5.153, *Come on, you hear this fellow in the cellarage.*

27. The Winter's Tale, 5.3.170, *A prayer upon her grave.*

28. The Merchant of Venice, 1.2.41, *I am much afeard my lady his mother played false*

29. Twelfth Night, 2.5.288, *no woman's heart so big, to hold so much,*

30. The Winter's Tale, 2.2.78-79, *upon mine honor, I will stand betwixt you and danger.*

31. Twelfth Night, 1.1.35-36, *O, she that hath a heart of that fine frame to pay this debt of love but to a brother.*

32. Twelfth Night, 2.4.114-115, *What dost thou know? Too well what love women to men may owe:*

33. King Lear, 3.2.46-48, *such bursts of horrid thunder, such groans of roaring wind and rain, as none can e'er remember to have heard.*

34. Twelfth Night, 2.4.12, *and play the tune the while.*

35. Richard II, 2.1.300, *To horse, to horse! Urge doubts to them that fear.*

36. Twelfth Night, 1.3.39, *turn o' the toe like a parish-top.*

Chapter II. The Undiscover'd Country

1. Hamlet, 3.1.80, *The undiscover'd country from whose bourn no traveller returns,*

2. Hamlet, 2.2.313, *this brave o'erhanging firmament*

3. Twelfth Night, *1.5.257-258, You should not rest between the elements of air and earth,*

4. The Tempest, 1.2.309, *"Awake, dear heart, awake! Thou hast slept well. Awake!"*

5. Twelfth Night, 1.1.42, *Away before me to sweet beds of flowers:*

6. Twelfth Night, 2.5.58, *how he jets under his advanced plumes!*

7. A Midsummer Night's Dream, 2.1.254-258,

> *I know a bank where the wild thyme blows,*
> *Where oxlips and the nodding violet grows,*
> *Quite over-canopied with luscious woodbine,*
> *With sweet musk-roses and with eglantine:*

8. Twelfth Night, 1.1.4-5, *That strain again! it had a dying fall: O, it came o'er my ear like the sweet sound that breathes upon a bank of violets,*

9. Twelfth Night, 1.5.270, *With an invisible and subtle stealth to creep in at mine eyes.*

10. Twelfth Night, 1.3.48, *Good Mistress Accost, I desire better acquaintance.*

11. The Tempest, 1.2.509-512, *O you wonder! If you be maid or no?*

12. The Tempest, 1.2.509-512, *No wonder, sir. But certainly a maid.*

13. Twelfth Night, 1.3.52, *You mistake, knight;*

14. Twelfth Night, 1.1.15, *so full of shapes is fancy that it alone is high fantastical.*

15. Hamlet, 2.2.220-221, *Though this be madness, yet there is method in 't.*

16. King Henry VI Part II, 4.10.40-41, *and if I do not leave you all dead as a doornail,*

17. Twelfth Night, 2.5.47, *O, peace, peace!*

18. Twelfth Night, 2.4.58, *Come away, come away, death,*

19. Twelfth Night, 2.1.40, *upon the least occasion more mine eyes will tell tales of me.*

20. Twelfth Night, 1.5.160, *Whence came you, sir?*

21. Romeo and Juliet, 2.2.66, *How camest thou hither, tell me, and wherefore?*

22. Twelfth Night, 1.5.161, *I can say little more than I have studied, and that question's out of my part.*

23. A Midsummer Night's Dream, 5.1.7, *Doth glance from heaven to Earth, from Earth to heaven.*

24. As You Like It, 2.1.12, *Sweet are the uses of adversity.*

25. The Tempest, 1.2.267-268, *For mischiefs manifold and sorceries terrible to enter human hearing,*

26. The Tempest, 1.2.274, *And in her most unmitigable rage,*

27. Romeo and Juliet, 4.2.18, *To beg your pardon.*

28. Twelfth Night, 1.2.58, *Thou shall present me as an eunuch to him:*

29. As You Like It, 3.5.77, *'For who'ver lov'd that lov'd not at first sight?' Christopher Marlow, Hero and Leander, 182*

30. As You Like It, 2.7.8, *He saves my labor by his own approach.*

31. Twelfth Night, 1.5.73, *but he will not pass his word for two pence that you are no fool.*

32. Twelfth Night, 2.1.13, *You must know of me then, Antonio, my name is Sebastian,*

33. Twelfth Night, 2.3.99, *Is it even so?*

34. Twelfth Night, 1.3.32, *By this hand,*

35. Twelfth Night, 1.5.262, *What is your parentage?*

36. Romeo and Juliet, 4.2.19, *Pardon, I beseech you!*

37. Henry VI Part 2, 3.1.50-51, *forgive my rudeness,*

38. Othello, 1.3.135, *Then, in th' very moment,*

39. Sonnet 33, *my sun one early morn did shine,*

40. Twelfth Night, 2.5.49, *and after a demure travel of regard,*

41. King Lear, 2.4.149, *that you'll vouchsafe me raiment, bed, and food.*

42. Twelfth Night, 1.5.11, *He shall see none to fear.*

43. Much Ado About Nothing, 3.4.48, *but God send everyone their heart's desire.*

44. King Lear, 1.1.221, *I know no answer.*

45. Julius Caesar, 1.2.279, *But those that understood him smiled at one another and shook their heads. But, for mine own part, it was Greek to me.*

46. The Winter's Tale, 5.1.184-185, *Welcome hither, as is the spring to the earth.*

47. Twelfth Night, 1.2.44-45, *Till I had made mine own occasion mellow, what my estate is!*

48. Othello, 3.4.80, *Fetch me the handkerchief – my mind misgives.*

49. Taming of the Shrew, Induction.1.104, *And call him "madam," do him obeisance.*

50. Hamlet, 2.2.237, *there is nothing either good or bad, but thinking makes it so.*

51. Twelfth Night, 2.1.1, *Nor will you not that I go with you?*

52. Twelfth Night, 2.5.128-129, *In my stars I am above thee; but be not afraid of greatness:*

53. Twelfth Night, 1.4.21, *Sure, my noble lord, if she be so abandon'd to her sorrow as it is spoke, she never will admit me.*

54. Romeo and Juliet, 2.4.34, *Nay, if our wits run the wild-goose chase, I am done,*

55. Twelfth Night, 1.4.21-22, *Be clamorous and leap all civil bounds rather than make unprofited return.*

56. Twelfth Night 2.1.29, *Pardon me, sir, your bad entertainment.*

57. Twelfth Night, 1.5.18, *You are resolute, then?*

58. Twelfth Night, 2.1.39, *The gentleness of all the gods go with thee.*

59. Twelfth Night, 2.1.35, *Fare thee well at once.*

60. Twelfth Night, 2.5.1, *Come thy ways,*

61. Twelfth Night, 2.1.39, *I am bound to the Count Orsino's court: farewell.*

62. Henry IV, Part I, 2.4.261, *Faith, and I'll send him packing.*

Chapter III. How Dorothy Didst Render Scarecrow Free

1. A Midsummer Night's Dream, 1.1.168, *And in the wood, a league without the town-*

2. Merry Wives of Windsor, 3.1.28-30, *There comes my master, Master Shallow, and another gentleman, from Frogmore, over the stile, this way.*

3. As You Like It, 5.3.16, *That o'er the green cornfield did pass in springtime,*

4. Romeo and Juliet, 2.2.25, *See how she leans her cheek upon her hand.*

5. Twelfth Night, 2.4.110, *But let concealment, like a worm i' the bud, feed on her damask cheek.*

6. Twelfth Night, 1.5.240, *'Tis beauty truly blent, whose red and white Nature's own sweet and cunning hand laid on:*

7. Twelfth Night, 1.5.72, *Sir Toby will be sworn I am no fox,*

8. A Midsummer Night's Dream, 5.1.18-22,

> *Such tricks hath strong imagination,*
> *That if it would but apprehend some joy,*
> *It comprehends some bringer of that joy.*
> *Or in the night, imagining some fear,*
> *How easy is a bush supposed a bear!*

9. Twelfth Night, 2.4.1, *Now, good morrow, friends.*

10. Twelfth Night, 2.1.25, *I could not with such estimable wonder overfar believe that,*

11. Twelfth Night, 2.1.12, *therefore it charges me in manners the rather to express myself.*

12. Twelfth Night, 2.4.125-126, *And with a green and yellow melancholy she sat like patience on a monument,*

13. King Henry VI Part II, 4.10.86, *Leaving thy trunk for crows to feed upon.*

14. Hamlet, 1.5.168-169, *There are more things in heaven and earth, Horatio, than are dreamt of in your philosophy.*

15. Twelfth Night, 1.5.4-5, *he that is well hanged in this world needs to fear no colours.*

16. Tempest, 1.2.26-27, *The direful spectacle of the wreck, which touched the very virtue of compassion in thee,*

17. Twelfth Night, 2.4.62, *A thousand, thousand sighs to save,*

18. Twelfth Night, 2.1.31-32, *If you will not murder me for my love, let me be your servant.*

19. King Lear, 1.1.111, *So young, and so untender?*

20. The Tempest, 1.2.140, *My tale provokes that question.*

21. The Tempest, 2.2.56, *Hast thou not dropped from heaven?*

22. Twelfth Night, 2.4.58, *Come away, come away, death,*

23. Romeo and Juliet, 3.1.64, *Courage, man. The hurt cannot be much.*

24. King Henry VI Part II, 4.10.40-41, *and if I do not leave you all dead as a doornail,*

25. Twelfth Night, 2.4.6, *More than light airs and recollected terms*

26. The Tempest, 1.2.106, *Your tale, sir, would cure deafness.*

27. Twelfth Night, 1.5.215, *Lady, you are the cruel'st she alive if you will lead these graces to the grave and leave the world no copy.*

28. Hamlet, 3.1.66, *Ay, there's the rub.*

29. The Tempest, 1.4.267, *For mischiefs manifold*

30. The Tempest, 1.2.138, *Wherefore did they not that hour destroy us?*

31. The Tempest, 1.2.141, *Dear, they durst not.*

32. Twelfth Night, 1.5.160, *Whence came you, sir?*

33. Twelfth Night, 2.1.7, *Let me yet know of you whither you are bound.*

34. Twelfth Night, 2.1.8-9, *No, sooth, sir: my determinate voyage is mere extravagancy.*

35. As You Like It, 1.2.246, *Hereafter, in a better world than this,*

36. As You Like It, 1.1.4, *and there begins my sadness.*

37. Romeo and Juliet, 2.2.5, *Arise, fair sun, and kill the envious moon, who is already pale and sick with grief.*

38. Comedy of Errors, 3.2.75, *I am an ass, I am a woman's man, and besides myself.*

39. Twelfth Night, 1.1.34, *in her sad remembrance.*

40. Twelfth Night, 2.3.99, *Is it even so?*

41. King Lear, 1.1.221, *I know no answer.*

42. Twelfth Night, 1.5.76-77, *with an ordinary fool that has no more brain than a stone.*

43. Twelfth Night, 2.5.132, *Thy Fates open their hands.*

44. The Merry Wives of Windsor, 3.5.80, *As good luck would have it,*

45. Twelfth Night, 2.1.29, *Pardon me, sir, your bad entertainment.*

46. The Tempest, 1.2.55-56, *'Tis far off; and rather like a dream than an assurance*

47. Henry V, 4.6.17, *My soul will keep yours company on the way to heaven.*

48. As You Like It, 3.2.234, *I thank you too for your society.*

Chapter IV. The Road Through the Forest

1. As You Like It, 2.4.11, *Well, this is the Forest of Arden.*

2. Othello, 1.3.135, *Then, in th' very moment,*

3. Twelfth Night, 2.4.46-48, *The spinsters and the knitters in the sun and the free maids that weave their thread with bones do use to chant it:*

4. Twelfth Night, 2.3.108, *Thou'rt i' the right.*

5. Hamlet, 1.3.72, *For the apparel oft proclaims the man,*

6. Twelfth Night, 2.3.47, *What's to come is still unsure;*

7. King Lear, 1.1.221, *I know no answer.*

8. Hamlet, 3.3.62-63, *There the action lies in his true nature,*

9. As You Like It, 4.2.190, *- I pray you, will you take him by the arm?*

10. The Merchant of Venice, 1.1.15, *Believe me, sir, had I such venture forth,*

11. As You Like It, 2.4.9, *I pray, bear with me; I cannot go no further.*

12. As You Like It, 2.4.84, *and at our sheepcote now, by reason of his absence, there is nothing*

Chapter V. Another Part of the Forest – The Emancipation of the Tin Woodman

1. As You Like It, 2.4.11, *Well, this is the Forest of Arden.*

2. Romeo and Juliet, 2.2.189, *That I shall say good night till it be morrow.*

3. Twelfth Night, 1.1.34, *in her sad remembrance.*

4. The Tempest, 1.2.25, *More to know did never meddle with my thoughts.*

5. A Midsummer Night's Dream, 4.1.204-205, *I have had a most rare vision!*

6. Twelfth Night, 2.4.1, *Now, good morrow, friends.*

7. Twelfth Night, 2.5.142-143, *cast thy humble slough and appear fresh.*

8. The Taming of the Shrew, 1.1.117-118, *I pray, sir, tell me is it possible that love should of a sudden take such hold?*

9. Twelfth Night, 2.5.14-15, *He has been yonder i' the sun practicing behavior to his shadow this half hour:*

10. Twelfth Night, 2.5.121-122, *The cur is excellent at faults.*

11. The Two Gentlemen of Verona, 4.3.37-38, *…when didst thou see me heave up my leg and make water against a gentlewoman's farthingale?*

12. The Tempest, 1.2.86, *The ivy which had hid my princely trunk,*

13. As You Like It, 3.5.74, *Where, in the purlieus of this forest stands a sheepcote fenced about with Olive trees?*

14. Romeo and Juliet, 3.1.61, *What, art thou hurt?*

15. Twelfth Night, 2.5.83, *By your leave, wax.*

16. The Taming of the Shrew, 5.2.159, *To watch the night in storms, the day in cold,*

17. Othello, 1.3.135, *Then, in th' very moment,*

18. 3 Henry VI, 5.5.5, *Bring forth the gallant, let us hear him speak*

19. Romeo and Juliet, 2.2.33-34, *Wherefore art thou Romeo?*

20. Twelfth Night, 1.2.56, *I prithee – and I'll pay thee bounteously -*

21. Shakespeare's Roman Worlds, page 117, *this pitiful and miserable estate*

22. Twelfth Night, 1.2.36, *That died some twelvemonth since,*

23. Twelfth Night, 1.2.31, *For but a month ago I went from hence,*

24. Twelfth Night, 1.4.14, *Therefore, good youth, address thy gait unto her;*

25. Twelfth Night, 2.1.8-9, *my determinate voyage is mere extravagancy.*

26. Twelfth Night, 2.5.2, *if I lose a scruple of this sport,*

27. Twelfth Night, 2.3.99, *Is it even so?*

28. Henry VI, Part II, 1.1.10, *and humbly now upon my bended knee,*

29. Twelfth Night, 2.4.114-115, *What dost thou know? Too well what love women to men may owe:*

30. The Tempest, 1.2.1-2, *If by your art, my dearest father, you have put the wild waters in this roar, allay them.*

31. Twelfth Night, 1.3.32, *By this hand,*

32. Romeo and Juliet, 3.2.125, *All slain, all dead. Romeo is banishèd.*

33. Much Ado About Nothing, 2.3.185-186, *It seems her affections have their full bent. Love me? Why, it must be requited!*

34. Twelfth Night, 2.5.23-24, *Besides, she uses me with a more exalted respect than anyone else that follows her.*

35. Romeo and Juliet, 3.3.13-14, *For exile hath more terror in his look, much more than death.*

36. Twelfth Night, 2.1.23-24, *But, come what may, I do adore thee so,*

37. Twelfth Night, 2.4.39, *Or thy affection cannot hold the bent;*

38. Twelfth Night, 2.3.75, *Beshrew me, the knight's in admirable fooling.*

39. Hamlet, 1.5.22, *To ears of flesh and blood.*

40. Sonnet 116, 3-4, *Love is not love which alters when it alteration finds.*

41. As You Like It, 2.7.137, *I thank you; and be blessed for your good comfort.*

42. Twelfth Night, 1.2.39-40, *for whose dear love, they say, she hath abjured the company and sight of men.*

43. Twelfth Night, 2.3.160, *I was adored once too.*

44. Twelfth Night, 1.2.20-21, *Whereto thy speech serves for authority the like of him.*

45. A Midsummer Night's Dream, 1.1.134, *The course of true love never did run smooth.*

46. Hamlet, 2.2.333, *Is 't possible?*

47. The Hidden Hand, Ch VII, *With caution judge of probability. Things deemed unlikely, e'en impossible, experience oft hath proved to be true.*

48. Twelfth Night, 1.5.108-109, *as if thy eldest son should be a fool, whose skull Jove cram with brains,*

49. Twelfth Night, 1.2.65, *Only shape thou thy silence to my wit.*

Chapter VI. Yet Another Part of the Forest – The Pusillanimous Lion

1. As You Like It, 2.4.11, *Well, this is the Forest of Arden.*

2. Henry IV Part 2, 4.3.84-86, *left the liver white and pale, which is the badge of pusillanimity and cowardice;*

3. The Tempest, 3.1.54-55, *I would not wish any companion in the world but you.*

4. Henry V, 3.7.111-112, *There is flattery in friendship.*

5. All's Well That Ends Well, 2.3.5-6, *we submit ourselves to an unknown fear*

6. King Lear, 1.1.221, *I know no answer.*

7. Twelfth Night, 1.1.34, *in her sad remembrance.*

8. Hamlet, 1.5.22, *To ears of flesh and blood.*

9. Romeo and Juliet, 5.3.322, Epilogue, *The sun, for sorrow, will not show his head.*

10. Coriolanus, 3.3.163, *There is a world elsewhere.*

11. Romeo and Juliet, 3.2.22-24, *take him and cut him out in little stars, and he will make the face of heaven so fine that all the world will be in love with night!*

12. A Midsummer Night's Dream, 5.1.287, *My soul is in the sky.*

13. Romeo and Juliet, 3.3.16, *Be patient, for the world is broad and wide.*

14. The Tempest, 4.1.146-147, *We are such stuff as dreams are made on*

15. Twelfth Night, 2.3.108, *Thou'rt i' the right.*

16. Twelfth Night, 2.5.136-137, *Ay, an you had any eye behind you, you might see more detraction at your heels than fortunes before you.*

17. King Lear, 3.4.151, *His wits begin t' unsettle.*

18. Twelfth Night, 2.3.122-123, *Since the youth of the Count's was today with thy lady, she is much out of quiet.*

19. King Lear, 3.2.48, *as none can e'er remember to have heard.*

20. Twelfth Night, 1.3.51, *Is that the meaning of "accost"?*

21. Twelfth Night, 2.4.12, *and play the tune the while.*

22. Othello, 1.3.135, *Then, in th' very moment,*

23. A Midsummer Night's Dream, 3.2.335, *And though she be but little, she is fierce!*

24. Twelfth Night, 1.5.166-167, *And yet, by the very fangs of malice, I swear, I am not that I play.*

25. Hamlet, 2.2.534, *Gives me the lie I' th' throat*

26. Twelfth Night, 2.3.118-120, *to challenge him the field and then to break promise with him and make a fool of him.*

27. Hamlet, 2.2.100-101, *That he is mad, 'tis true, 'tis pity, and pity 'tis 'tis true – a foolish figure*

28. Hamlet, 2.1.27, *My Lord, that would dishonor him.*

29. Twelfth Night, 1.3.32, *By this hand,*

30. King Lear, 4.1.36-37, *As flies to wanton boys are we to th' gods, they kill us for their sport.*

31. Twelfth Night, 1.5.240-241, *In your denial I would find no sense; I would not understand it.*

32. Romeo and Juliet, 3.1.47, *Good King of Cats, nothing but one of your nine lives,*

33. King Richard II, 3.2.179, *How can you say to me, I am king?*

34. King Richard III, 1.4.78-79, *Princes have but their titles for their glories, an outward honor for an inward toil,*

35. Twelfth Night, 1.5.147, *one would think his mother's milk were scarce out of him.*

36. The Winter's Tale, 1.2.85-87, *we knew not the doctrine of ill-doing, nor dream'd that any did.*

37. As You Like It, 2.4.39-40, *Alas, poor shepherd, searching of thy wound, I have by hard adventure found mine own.*

38. Twelfth Night, 2.5.136-137, *put thyself into the trick of singularity:*

39. Henry IV, Part 1, 3.3.131, *I fear thee as I fear the roaring of a lion's whelp.*

40. The Taming of the Shrew, 1.1.117-118, *I pray, sir, tell me is it possible that love should of a sudden take such hold?*

41. As You Like It, 3.5.5, *Falls not the axe upon the humbled neck*

42. Twelfth Night, 1.5.260, *In voices well divulged, free, learn'd, and valiant;*

43. Napoleon Bonaparte, *Courage is like love; it must have hope for nourishment.*

44. Twelfth Night, 1.5.202, *In Orsino's bosom.*

45. Henry IV, Part 1, 2.4.240-244, *I am as valiant as Hercules, but beware instinct.*

46. Hamlet, 3.1.90-91, *Nymph, in thy orisons be all my sins remember'd.*

47. King Richard III, 1.4.125, *Faith, some certain dregs of conscience are yet within me.*

48. Hamlet, 3.1.84, *Thus conscience does make cowards of us all;*

49. The Winter's Tale, 1.2.90-91, *with stronger blood, we should have answer'd heaven boldly, 'not guilty';*

50. The Merchant of Venice, 4.1.174-175, *The quality of mercy is not strain'd. It droppeth as the gentle rain from heaven upon the place beneath.*

51. Sonnet 43, 1, Elizabeth Barrett Browning, *How do I love thee? Let me count the ways.*

52. The Wonderful Wizard of Oz, Ch VI, *for my life is simply unbearable without a bit of courage.*

53. Sonnet 73, 6-7, *As after sunset fadeth in the west, which by and by black night doth take away*

54. Twelfth Night, 1.2.61, *I thank thee. Lead me on.*

Chapter VII. Yet Another Night in the Forest

1. As You Like It, 2.4.11, *Well, this is the Forest of Arden.*

2. Sonnet 73, 5, *In me thou see'st the twilight of such day*

3. Macbeth, 3.4.143-144, *Stepped in so far that, should I wade no more, returning were as tedious as go o'er.*

4. Hamlet, 2.2.85, *Go to your rest. At night we'll feast together.*

5. The Tempest, 1.2, *He does make our fire, fetch in our wood,*

6. Ecclesiastes, 3.5, *There's a time to scatter stones and a time to gather stones together.*

7. Hamlet, 2.2.122, *I would fain prove so.*

8. As You Like It, 3.2.27, *A great cause of the night is lack of the sun;*

9. Sonnet 73, 11, *In me thou see'st the glowing of such fire*

10. Twelfth Night, 2.2.4, *You might have saved me my pains to have taken it away yourself.*

11. Twelfth Night, 2.4.6, *More than light airs and recollected terms*

12. Measure for Measure, 4.3.91, *you shall find your safety manifested.*

13. The Winter's Tale, 5.2.14-15, *a notable passion of wonder appeared in them;*

14. In Memoriam A.H.H., XXVII, 15-16, Tennyson, *'Tis better to have loved and lost, than never to have loved at all.*

15. As You Like It, 3.2.14-16, *In respect that it is solitary, I like it very well; but in respect that it is private, it is a very vile life.*

16. Hamlet, 3.1.82-83, *and makes us rather bear those ills we have, than to fly to others that we know not of?*

17. Twelfth Night, 2.4.17-18, *Unstaid and skittish in all motions else save in the constant image of the creature that is beloved.*

18. Henry IV Part 2, 2.1.174, *till they come to Berwick, from whence they came*

19. Twelfth Night, 1.2.40, *Not three hours' travel from this very place.*

20. Twelfth Night, 2.5.153, *I thank my stars I am happy!*

21. Twelfth Night, 2.5.47, *And then to have the humour of state,*

22. Twelfth Night, 2.5.48, *and after a demure travel of regard,*

23. Twelfth Night, 1.3.48, *Good Mistress Accost, I desire better acquaintance.*

24. Julius Caesar, 2.2.37, *What say the augurers?*

25. King Lear 1.1.221, *I know no answer.*

26. The Tempest, 4.1.147-148, *and our little life is rounded with a sleep*

27. The Passionate Pilgrim, XXI, 34, *Faithful friends are hard to find;*

28. Julius Caesar, 2.2.18, *A lioness hath whelped in the streets.*

29. Twelfth Night, 2.1.8-9, *No, sooth, sir: my determinate voyage is mere extravagancy.*

30. Twelfth Night, 2.5.150-151, *I do not now fool myself, to let imagination jade me, for every reason excites to this, that my lady loves me.*

31. Twelfth Night, 2.5.145, *Daylight discovers not more, this is open.*

32. Twelfth Night, 1.5.77, *Look you now, he's out of his guard already.*

33. As You Like It, 2.7.137, *I thank you; and be blessed for your good comfort.*

34. Hamlet, 2.2.220-221, *Though this be madness, yet there is method in 't.*

35. Twelfth Night, 1.5.11, *And that may you be bold to say in your foolery.*

36. Romeo and Juliet, 1.5.43, *Oh, she doth teach the torches to burn bright!*

37. Macbeth, 5.5.19, *To-morrow, and to-morrow, and to-morrow,*

38. Romeo and Juliet, 3.1.3, *And if we meet we shall not 'scape a brawl,*

39. Twelfth Night, 3.1.119-120, *If one should be a prey, how much better to fall before the lion than the wolf!*

40. Henry V, 4.3.310-321, *If it be a sin to covet honour, I am the most offending soul alive.*

41. Hamlet, 1.5.168-169, *There are more things in heaven and earth, Horatio, than are dreamt of in your philosophy.*

42. Twelfth Night, 2.3.108, *Thou'rt i' the right.*

43. Henry IV Part 1, 5.4.120-121, *The better part of valor is discretion, in the which better part I have saved my life.*

44. Twelfth Night, 1.5.270, *With an invisible and subtle stealth to creep in at mine eyes.*

45. Romeo and Juliet, 3.5.19, *I'll say yon grey is not the morning's eye.*

46. Twelfth Night, 2.2.20, *The cunning of her passion invites me in this churlish messenger.*

47. As You Like It, 3.2.284, *I pray you, what is 't o'clock?*

48. As You Like It, 3.2.259, *There's no clock in the forest.*

49. Romeo and Juliet, 2.2.188, *'Tis almost morning. I would have thee gone.*

50. Twelfth Night, 1.4.24, *Say I do speak with her, my lord, what then?*

51. The Tempest, 4.1.148-150, *These our actors, as I foretold you, were all spirits, and are melted into air, into thin air.*

52. Twelfth Night, 5.5.67, *Nay, patience, or we break the sinews of our plot!*

Chapter VIII. The Deadly Poppy Field

1. Orthello, 3.3.340, *Not poppy, nor mandragora, nor all the drowsy syrups of the world, shall ever medicine thee to that sweet sleep which thou owedst yesterday.*

2. Romeo and Juliet, 3.5.7-8, *Look! What envious streaks do lace the severing clouds in yonder east!*

3. Twelfth Night, 2.4.12, *Methought it did relieve my passion much.*

4. Twelfth Night, 2.3.55, *But shall we make the welkin dance indeed?*

5. The Taming of the Shrew, 1.1.117-118, *I pray, sir, tell me is it possible that love should of a sudden take such hold?*

6. A Midsummer Night's Dream, 3.1.64, *I pray thee, gentle mortal, sing again.*

7. Twelfth Night, 2.3.99, *This is much credit to you.*

8. A Midsummer Night's Dream, 2.2.51, *Through the forest have I gone.*

9. Romeo and Juliet, 3.5.235, *Marry, I will, and this is wisely done.*

10. The Tempest, 1.2.401-402, *The fringèd curtains of thine eye advance and say what thou seest yond.*

11. King Lear, 4.6.1, *When shall we come to th' top of that same hill?*

12. Twelfth Night, 2.5.21-24, *I have heard herself come thus near that, should she fancy, it should be one of my complexion.*

13. Romeo and Juliet, 2.3.92, *Oh, let us hence. I stand on sudden haste.*

14. Henry VIII, 1.1.158-159, *to climb steep hills requires slow pace at first:*

15. Romeo and Juliet, 2.3.93, *Wisely and slow. They stumble that run fast.*

16. Julius Caesar, 2.1.335-336, *Bid me run, and I will strive with things impossible.*

17. Twelfth Night, 1.2.21-22, *Ay, madam, well. For I was bred and born not three hours' travel from this very place.*

18. Troilus and Cressida, 3.3.181, *One touch of nature makes the whole world kin.*

19. Twelfth Night, 2.4.7, *Of these most brisk and giddy-paced times:*

20. Twelfth Night, 2.3.80-82, *My masters, are you mad? Or what are you? Have you no wit, manners, nor honesty but to gabble like tinkers at this time of night?*

21. Sonnet 27, 7, *And keep my drooping eyelids open wide,*

22. Hamlet, 3.1.65, *To sleep: perchance to dream:*

23. Twelfth Night, 1.1.6, *That breathes upon a bank of violets,*

24. Twelfth Night, 1.1.7, *Stealing and giving odour! Enough; no more:*

25. Twelfth Night, 1.1.8, *'Tis not so sweet now as it was before.*

26. Twelfth Night, 1.1.39, *Away before me to sweet beds of flowers.*

27. Romeo and Juliet, 1.5.135, *My grave is like to be my wedding bed.*
28. Twelfth Night, 2.5.146, *I will wash off gross acquaintance.*
29. The Tempest, 4.1.86, *Tell me, heavenly bow, If Venus or her son, as thou dost know,*
30. Twelfth Night, 2.5.13, *Get you all three into the boxtree.*
31. Venus and Adonis, 304-305, *And whe'r he run or fly they know not whether; For through his mane and tail the high wind sings,*

Chapter IX. The River

1. As You Like It, 3.2.26, *the property of rain is to wet.*
2. Twelfth Night, 2.5.144, *cast thy humble slough and appear fresh.*
3. Richard II, 3.3.43, *And lay the summer's dust with showers of blood.*
4. Twelfth Night, 1.4.13, *Therefore, good youth, address thy gait unto her;*
5. Henry V, 3.3.1, *Once more unto the breach, dear friends, once more;*
6. Twelfth Night 2.5.103, *Nay, but first, let me see, let me see, let me see.*
7. Two Gentlemen of Verona, 2.1.131, *How now, sir? Are you reasoning with yourself?*
8. Romeo and Juliet, 3.1.65, *No, 'tis not so deep as a well nor so wide as a church-door, but 'tis enough.*
9. Richard III, 1.2.62, *Provokes this deluge most unnatural.*
10. Romeo and Juliet, 3.5.40, *The day is broke!*
11. Twelfth Night, 2.2.34, *Pardon me, sir, your bad entertainment.*
12. Hamlet, 2.2.303, *What a piece of work is man, how noble in reason,*
13. Romeo and Juliet, 4.2.18, *To beg your pardon.*
14. Twelfth Night, 2.4.6, *More than light airs and recollected terms*
15. Measure for Measure, 1.4.84-86, *Our doubts are traitors and make us lose the good we oft might win by fearing to attempt.*
16. Twelfth Night, 2.5.6, *I would exult, man.*
17. As You Like It, 2.3.283-284, *I'll tell you who time ambles withal, who time trots withal, who time gallops withal, and who he stands still withal.*
18. King Henry VIII, 5.1.171, *You take a precipice for no leap of danger, and woo your own destruction.*
19. Twelfth Night, 1.5.79, *I marvel your ladyship takes delight in such a barren rascal.*

Chapter X. The Guardian of the Gates

1. Twelfth Night, 2.2.2, *Even now, sir; on a moderate pace I have since arrived but hither.*
2. Macbeth, 2.1.39-40, *Go bid thy mistress, when my drink is ready, she strike upon the bell.*
3. Macbeth, 2.1.61, *I go, and it is done. The bell invites me.*

4. Macbeth, 3.1.158, *Like sweet bells jangled, out of tune and harsh;*

5. Macbeth, 5.1.45, *There's a knocking at the gate.*

6. Macbeth, 2.3.1, *Here's a knocking indeed! If a man were porter of hell-gate, he should have old turning the key.*

7. Macbeth, 2.3.8-9, *Knock, knock! Who's there, in th' other devil's name?"*

8. The Merry Wives Of Windsor, 1.1.170, *Why, sir, for my part I say the gentleman had drunk himself out of his five senses.*

9. Venus and Adonis, 304, *And whe'r he run or fly they know not whether;*

10. Hamlet, 1.1.54-55, *Before my God, I might not this believe without the sensible and true avouch of mine own eyes.*

11. Twelfth Night, 1.5.51-52, *Cucullus non facit monachum – that's as much to say as I wear not motley in my brain.*

12. Twelfth Night, 2.2.21-22, *The cunning of her passion invites me in this churlish messenger.*

13. Timon of Athens, 4.2.30, *We have seen better days.*

14. As You Like It, 3.2.254, *I do not like her name.*

15. As You Like It, 3.2.255, *There was no thought of pleasing you when she was christened.*

16. Twelfth Night, 2.5.46, *O, peace, peace!*

17. Twelfth Night, 1.4.21-22, *Be clamorous and leap all civil bounds rather than make unprofited return.*

18. The Taming of the Shrew, 1.2.5, *Here, sirrah, Grumio. Knock, I say.*

19. Twelfth Night, 1.5.137-138, *he says, he'll stand at your door like a Sheriff's Post and be the supporter to a bench, but he will speak with you.*

20. Twelfth Night, 1.4.15-17, *Here my fixed foot shall grow 'til I have audience!*

21. Twelfth Night, 1.5.7, *He shall see none to fear.*

22. Twelfth Night, 1.5.11, *and that may you be bold to say in your foolery.*

23. As You Like It, 4.3.34-35, *Patience herself would startle at this and play the swaggerer.*

24. Twelfth Night, 2.5.51, *O, peace, peace, peace! Now, now.*

25. Twelfth Night, 1.2.60, *Thou shall present me as an eunuch to him.*

26. Twelfth Night, 2.3.148, *My purpose is, indeed, a horse of that color.*

27. Twelfth Night, 1.2.61, *I thank thee. Lead me on.*

Chapter XI. The Emerald City and The Great and Powerful Oz

1. Taming of the Shrew, 4.5.72, *Who will of thy arrival be full joyous.*

2. King Henry V, 1.1.1, Scene I. London. *An ante-chamber in the King's palace.*

3. Richard II, 3.3.74, *We are amazed; and thus long have we stood*

4. Antony and Cleopatra, 5.1.15-16, *The barge she sat in, like a burnish'd throne, burned on the water:*

5. Macbeth, 5.1.1, *I have two nights watched with you but can perceive no truth in your report.*

6. Twelfth Night, 1.5.73, *but he will not pass his word for two pence that you are no fool.*

7. The Merchant of Venice, 5.1.38-39, *ceremoniously let us prepare some welcome for the mistress of the house*

8. Othello, 2.1.238-239, *The Lieutenant tonight watches on the court of guard.*

9. The History of Troilus and Cressida, 4.5.5-6, *Beat loud the tambourines, let the trumpets blow, that this great soldier may his welcome know.*

10. The Tempest, 5.1.110-111, *And to thee and thy company I bid a hearty welcome.*

11. Henry VIII, 1.4.1-2, *Ladies, a general welcome from his grace salutes ye all;*

12. Twelfth Night, 1.2.49, *I prithee- and I'll pay thee bounteously-*

13. Romeo and Juliet, 2.3.92, *Oh, let us hence. I stand on sudden haste.*

14. Twelfth Night, 2.5,42-43, *cast thy humble slough and appear fresh!*

15. The Comedy of Errors, 1.2.16, *For with long travel am I stiff and weary.*

16. Twelfth Night, 1.2.60, *Thou shall present me as an eunuch to him.*

17. Richard III, 3.7.59, *He doth entreat your Grace, my noble lord, to visit him tomorrow or next day.*

18. Sonnet 18, 9, *But thy eternal summer shall not fade,*

19. Twelfth Night, 2.3.93, *Farewell, dear heart, since I must needs be gone.*

20. As You Like It, 2.4.75-77, *My master is of churlish disposition, and little recks to find the way to heaven by doing deeds of hospitality.*

21. Romeo and Juliet, 1.2.20-23, *This night I hold an old accustom'd feast, whereto I have invited many a guest, such as I love; and you among the store, one more, most welcome, makes my number more.*

22. Othello, 1.3.135, *Then, in th' very moment,*

23. The Tempest, 3.3.65, *some of the courtiers draw their swords*

24. Twelfth Night, 1.1.4, *That strain again, it had a dying fall.*

25. Twelfth Night, 1,2.29, *And then 'twas fresh in murmur-*

26. Twelfth Night, 1.2.30, *-as, you know, what great ones do the less will prattle of-*

27. Twelfth Night, 1.5.92, *'Tis a fair young man, and well attended.*

28. Twelfth Night, 2.2.8, *And one thing more,*

29. Sonnet 148, *Lest eyes well-seeing thy foul faults should find.*

30. The Tempest, 1.1.5, *Take in the topsail – Tend to th' master's whistle – Blow till thou burst thy wind, if room enough!*

31. The Taming of the Shrew, Induction, 1.20, *Sirrah, go see what trumpet 'tis that sounds.*

32. Julius Caesar, 1.1.28, *Why dost thou lead these men about the streets?*

33. The Two Gentlemen of Verona, 2.5.3, *thou shalt have five thousand welcomes.*

34. Henry IV, Part I, 1.2.94, *Thou hast astonish'd me with thy high terms.*

35. Hamlet, 5.1.71, *Or of a courtier, which could say, "Good morrow, sweet lord!"*

36. Twelfth Night, 1.5.79, *I marvel your ladyship takes delight in such a barren rascal.*

37. Antony and Cleopatra, 5.1.15-16, *The round world should have shook lions into civil streets and citizens to their dens.*

38. Venus and Adonis, 59, *Even so she kissed his brow, his cheek, his chin,*

39. Love's Labor's Lost, 2.1.119, *'Tis 'long of you that spur me with such questions.*

40. Macbeth, 1.2.4-6, *This is the sergeant, who like a good and hardy soldier fought 'gainst my captivity.*

41. As You Like It, 5.3.38, *Salutation and greeting to you all!*

42. Richard III, 3.7.68, *In deep designs, and matters of great moment, are come to have some conference with his grace.*

43. Hamlet, 2.2.85, *Go to your rest. At night we'll feast together.*

44. As You Like It, 2.7.137, *I thank you; and be blessed for your good comfort.*

45. Henry VIII, 2.4.7-8, *Be't so. Proceed. Say, Henry King of England, come into the court.*

46. Hamlet, 2.2.155, *Be you and I behind an arras then,*

47. The Merchant of Venice, 5.1.57, *Is thick inlaid with patines of bright gold:*

48. Romeo and Juliet, 3.3.147, *Ascend her chamber, hence, and comfort her.*

49. The Wonderful Wizard of Oz, XI, Pg 89, *…through seven passages and up three flights of stairs until at last they came to a room at the front of the Palace.*

50. The Taming of the Shrew, Induction, 1.50, *Let one attend him with a silver basin full of rose-water and bestrewed with flowers.*

51. Two Gentlemen of Verona, 5.1.1, *The sun begins to gild the western sky;*

52. A Midsummer Night's Dream

53. As You Like It, 2.4.91, *I like this place, and willingly could waste my time in it.*

54. Macbeth, 5.1.45, *To bed, to bed.*

55. Twelfth Night, 2.5.35, *The Lady of the Strachy did marry the yeoman of the wardrobe.*

56. Romeo and Juliet, 1.4.77, *Because their breaths with sweetmeats tainted are.*

57. Macbeth, 2.3.55, *Ring the bell.*

58. The Merchant of Venice, 2.2.86, *I am famished in his service.*

59. The Taming of the Shrew, 4.1.87, *Where are my slippers?*

60. The Taming of the Shrew, 4.1.104-105, *be not so disquiet, the meat was well*

61. Macbeth, 2.2.37-38, *Sleep that knits the raveled sleave of care, the death of each day's life, sore labor's bath,*

62. The Merchant of Venice, 2.2.120, *to be in peril of my life with the edge of a feather-bed*

63. Sonnet 52, *Or as the wardrobe which the robe doth hide,*

64. Julius Caesar, 1.2.69-70, *you cannot see yourself so well as by reflection*

65. Hamlet, 3.2.45, *Here, sweet lord, at your service.*

66. Sonnet 153, *the help of bath desired, and thither hied*

67. The Tempest, 5.1.7-8, *Say, my spirit, how fares the king and 's followers?*

68. Twelfth Night, 2.4.72-74, *the tailor make thy doublet of changeable taffeta, for thy mind is a very opal.*

69. Twelfth Night, 2.5.8, *If I lose a scruple of this sport, let me be boiled to death with melancholy.*

70. Sonnet 56, *To-morrow sharpen'd in his former might:*

71. Richard II, 5.5.81, *That horse that I so carefully have dress'd.*

72. Twelfth Night, 1.3.48, *I desire better acquaintance.*

73. Twelfth Night, 1.1.1, *If music be the food of love, play on;*

74. Twelfth Night, 2.4.18, *How dost thou like this tune?*

75. Twelfth Night, 2.4.19-20, *It gives a very echo to the seat where Love is throned.*

76. Coriolanus, 3.1.244, *What is the city but the people?*

77. As You Like It, 3.2.259, *You are full of pretty answers.*

78. Twelfth Night, 2.1.4, *Therefore I shall crave of you your leave that I may bear my evils alone.*

79. Twelfth Night, 2.5.135, *Let thy tongue tang arguments of state.*

80. Twelfth Night, 1.5.105, *Upon mine honour, he's half drunk.*

81. Twelfth Night, 1.5.32, *Better a witty fool than a foolish wit.*

82. The Two Gentlemen of Verona, 4.4.17, *like dogs, under the duke's table*

83. Twelfth Night, 2.4.98-99, *But mine is all as hungry as the sea, and can digest as much.*

84. Hamlet, 2.2.52, *My news shall be the fruit to that great feast.*

85. All's Well That Ends Well, 2.3.35, *great power, great transcendence*

86. Venus and Adonis, 447, *Would they not wish the feast might ever last,*

87. Twelfth Night, 2.4.70, *Give me now leave to leave thee.*

88. Twelfth Night, 1.5.228, *though you were crowned the nonpareil of beauty.*

89. Twelfth Night, 2.4.20, *Thou dost speak masterly.*

90. Hamlet, 1.3.78, *This above all: to thine own self be true,*

91. Macbeth, 1.5.2-3, *I have learned by the perfectest report they have more in them than mortal knowledge.*

92. Macbeth, 1.5.3-5, *When I burned in desire to question them further, they made themselves air, into which they vanished.*

93. As You Like It, 4.2.190, *- I pray you, will you take him by the arm?*

94. Hamlet, 1.2.215, *Yet once methought, it lifted up its head and did address itself to motion, like as it would speak.*

95. Twelfth Night, 1.5.268, *How now?*

96. King Lear, 3.4.151, *His wits begin t' unsettle.*

97 Twelfth Night, 1.5.70, *Your niece will not be seen; or, if she be, it's four to one she'll none of me:*

98 Twelfth Night, 2.2.10, *An we do not, it is pity of our lives.*

99 Cymbaline, 3.4.109, *I have not slept one wink.*

100. King Lear, 1.1.221, *I know no answer.*

101. Twelfth Night, 2.3.108, *Thou'rt i' the right.*

102. Cymbaline, 3.4.9-10, *put thyself into a havior of less fear*

103. Twelfth Night, 2.5.128-129, *In my stars I am above thee; but be not afraid of greatness:*

104. Sonnet 27, *Weary with toil, I haste me to my bed, the dear repose for limbs with travel tired;*

105. Twelfth Night, 2.5.83, *By your leave, wax.*

106. Romeo and Juliet, 2.2.189, *Sleep dwell upon thine eyes,*

107. Sonnet 61, *To play the watchman ever for thy sake:*

108. Twelfth Night, 1.1.32-33, *and water once a day her chamber round with eye-offending brine:*

109. Romeo and Juliet, 2.2.189, *That I shall say good night till it be morrow.*

110. Twelfth Night, 5.1.278, *Has here writ a letter to you.*

111. Twelfth Night, 2.5.130, *If this fall into thy hand, revolve.*

112. King Lear, 2.4.149, *that you'll vouchsafe me raiment, bed, and food.*

113. Hamlet, 2.2.126-128, *I have not art to reckon my groans, but that I love thee best, oh, most best, believe it!*

114. Sonnet 108, *That may express my love or thy dear merit?*

115. Sonnet 83, *How far a modern quill doth come too short,*

116. Sonnet 79, *thy lovely argument deserves the travail of a worthier pen*

117. Sonnet 116, *Let me not to the marriage of true minds admit impediments…*

118. Sonnet 17, *If I could write the beauty of your eyes…*

119. Sonnet 29, *Haply I think on thee, and then my state…*

120. Little Women, Chapter 1, *Give them all of my dear love and a kiss. Tell them I think of them by day, pray for them by night, and find my best comfort in their affection at all times.*

121. Henry IV Part 1, 3.1.221, *As is the difference betwixt day and night the hour before the heavenly-harness'd team begins his golden progress in the east.*

122. King Lear, 1.2.120, *We make guilty of our disasters the sun, the moon, and stars,*

123. Measure for Measure, 5.1.314-315, *and let the devil be sometime honour'd for his burning throne!*

124. Romeo and Juliet, 1.5.43, *Oh, she doth teach the torches to burn bright!*

125. Twelfth Night, 2.2.19, *For she did speak in starts, distractedly.*

126. The Tempest, 2.2.49, *How didst thou 'scape? How camest thou hither?*

127. The Tempest, 1.2.182, *Thou didst smile, infused with a fortitude from heaven.*

128. Twelfth Night, 1.5.202, *In his bosom? In what chapter of his bosom?*

129. Romeo and Juliet, 3.1.47, *Good King of Cats, nothing but one of your nine lives,*

130. The Wonderful Wizard of Oz, Ch XI, *Because of all Wizards you are the greatest, and alone have power to grant my request.*

131. Twelfth Night, 2.4.46-48, *The spinsters and the knitters in the sun and the free maids that weave their thread with bones do use to chant it:*

132. Henry VI, Part I, 5.3.29, *My ancient incantations are too weak,*

133. Romeo and Juliet, 5.3.129-130, *O true apothecary, Thy drugs are quick.*

134. The Tempest, 1.2.474-475, *For I can here disarm thee with this stick and make thy weapon drop.*

135. The Taming of the Shrew, 3.1.10, *Preposterous ass, that never read so far to know the cause why music was ordained.*

136. Hamlet, 2.1.113, *I feared he did but trifle and meant to wreck thee.*

137. The Tempest, 2.2.57, *I do assure thee.*

138. Henry VI, Part I, 1.4.29, *And, I, here, at the bulwark of the bridge.*

139. Orthello, 3.3.340, *Not poppy, nor mandragora, nor all the drowsy syrups of the world, shall ever medicine thee to that sweet sleep which thou owedst yesterday.*

140. Twelfth Night, 2.5.132, *Thy Fates open their hands.*

141. Twelfth Night, 1.3.49, *You mistake, knight.*

142. King Lear, 4.7.169-171, *She loved me for the dangers I pass'd, and I loved her that she did pity them. This is the only witchcraft I have used:*

143. Romeo and Juliet, 3.2.125, *All slain, all dead. Romeo is banishèd.*

144. Twelfth Night, 1.2.44-45, *Till I had made mine own occasion mellow, what my estate is!*

145. The Comedy of Errors, 2.1.46-47, *Say didst thou speak with him? Know'st thou his mind?"*

146. The Comedy of Errors, 2.1.48-49, *Ay, ay, he told his mind upon my ear. Beshrew his hand, I scarce could understand it.*

147. The Comedy of Errors, 2.1.50, *Spake he so doubtfully, thou couldst not feel his meaning?*

148. The Comedy of Errors, 2.1.51, *Nay, he struck so plainly I could too well feel his blows,*

149. Twelfth Night, 2.5.47, *And then to have the humour of state*

150. Twelfth Night, 1.5.139, *What manner of man?*

151. Twelfth Night, 1.5.140, *Of very ill manner. He'll speak with you, will you or no.*

152. Othello, 2.1.201, *Sir, he's rash and very sudden in choler,*

153. Twelfth Night, 1.5.141, *Of what personage and years is he?*

154. Twelfth Night, 1.5.137, *What kind o' man is he?*

155. Twelfth Night, 1.5.138, *Why, of mankind.*

156. Hamlet, 1.1.34, *That if again this apparition come,*

157. As You Like It, 5.3.38, *Salutation and greeting to you all!*

158. Sonnet 19, 1, *Devouring Time, blunt thou the lion's paws*

159. Twelfth Night, 2.1.11, *Therefore it charges me in manners the rather to express myself.*

160. Julius Caesar, 2.2.42, *Caesar should be a beast without a heart* ·

161. Hamlet, 2.2.100-101, *That he is mad, 'tis true, 'tis pity, and pity 'tis 'tis true – a foolish figure*

162. The Tempest, 1.2.141, *Dear, they durst not.*

163. The Tempest, 2.2.56, *Hast thou not dropped from heaven?*

164. All's Well That Ends Well, 1.3.100-101, *alone she was, and did communicate to herself her own words to her own ears*

165. The Taming of the Shrew, 1.1.117-118, *I pray, sir, tell me is it possible that love should of a sudden take such hold?*

166. Hamlet, 1.5.22, *To ears of flesh and blood.*

167. The Tempest, 5.1.51, *By my so potent are. But this rough magic I here abjure*

168. Twelfth Night, 2.4.39, *Or thy affection cannot hold the bent;*

169. Hamlet, 4.7.105-106, *Or are you like the painting of a sorrow, a face without a heart?*

170. Henry VI, Part II, 1.1.19-20, *O Lord, that lends me life, lend me a heart replete with thankfulness!*

171. The Wonderful Wizard of Oz, Ch XI, *Because I ask it, and you alone can grant my request.*

172. Twelfth Night, 1.1.22, *"How now! What news from her?"*

173. Twelfth Night, 2.1.12, *My stars shine darkly over me:*

174. Much Ado About Nothing, 2.3.142, *I pray you tell Benedick of it and hear what he will say.*

175. The Rape of Lucrece, 1321, *No man inveigh against the withered flower,*

176. Othello, 2.1.201, *Sir, he's rash and very sudden in choler,*

177. Twelfth Night, 1.5.240-241, *In your denial I would find no sense; I would not understand it.*

178. Julius Caesar, 1.2.198, *But I fear him not.*

179. Twelfth Night, 1.1.39-40, *when liver, brain, and heart, these sovereign thrones, are all supplied*

180. The Wonderful Wizard of Oz, Ch XI, *Because you are wise and powerful, and no one else can help me.*

181. Sonnet 53, 1, *What is your substance, whereof are you made,*

182. Twelfth Night, 1.5., *Thou wilt be hanged for thy long absence.*

183. Hamlet, 4.4.25, *Will not debate the question of this straw.*

184. Twelfth Night, 2.5.174, *Shall I play my freedom at tray-trip, and become thy bond-slave?*

185. Twelfth Night, 2.1.31-32, *If you will not murder me for my love, let me be your servant.*

186. Twelfth Night, 1.5.51, *Cucullus non facit monachum, "the cowl makes not the monk"*

187. The Comedy of Errors, 2.2.141-143, *In Ephesus I am but two hours old. As strange unto your town as to your talk, who every word by all my wit being scanned, want wit in all one word to understand.*

188. Twelfth Night, 1.3.19, *What's that to th' purpose?*

189. Twelfth Night, 1.5.52-53, *- that's as much to say, I wear not motley in my brain.*

190. Twelfth Night, 1.3.82-84, *I would I had bestowed that time in the tongues that I have in fencing, dancing, and bear-baiting.*

191. Twelfth Night, 2.3.99, *Is it even so?*

192. All's Well That Ends Well, 2.5.42, *The soul of this man is his clothes.*

193. Twelfth Night, 1.4.249, *even in the dead of night,*

194. Twelfth Night, 1.5.75, *I marvel your ladyship takes delight in such a barren rascal*

195. Twelfth Night, 2.1.29, *Pardon me, sir, your bad entertainment.*

196. The Winter's Tale, 4.4.818, *therefore they do not give us the lie.*

197. Romeo and Juliet, 1.1.52, *You lie.*

198. The Two Gentlemen of Verona, 3.1.155-156, *Wilt thou aspire to guide the heavenly car and with thy daring folly burn the world?*

199. Hamlet, 4.5.73-75 *When sorrows come, they come not single spies but in battalions.*

200. The Merchant of Venice, 1.1.1, *In sooth, I know not why I am so sad:*

201. King Lear, 4.6.268-269, *And woes by wrong imaginations lose the knowledge of themselves.*

202. Julius Caesar, 1.2.194, *Yond Cassius has a lean and hungry look.*

203. Hamlet, 2.2.118, *Doubt truth to be a liar,*

204. Julius Caesar, 3.2.81-82, *The evil that men do lives after them; the good is oft interred with their bones.*

205. The Taming of the Shrew, 4.2.43-44, *Kindness in women, not their beauteous looks, shall win my love,*

206. King Henry VI, Part III, *5.6.11, Suspicion always haunts the guilty mind;*

207. Julius Caesar, 3.2.105, *My heart is in the coffin there with Caesar, and I must pause till it come back to me.*

208. All's Well That Ends Well, 2.3.5-6, *we submit ourselves to an unknown fear*

209. Julius Caesar, 2.1.300, *If this were true, then I should know this secret.*

210. Romeo and Juliet, 3.3.13-15, *For exile hath more terror in his look, much more than death. Do not say "banishment."*

211. Hamlet, 3.2.76, *And my imaginations are as foul as Vulcan's stithy.*

212. Timon of Athens, 4.3.350, *thou hadst some means to keep a dog.*

213. Macbeth, 2.1.57, *Hear not my steps, which way they walk,*

214. The Wonderful Wizard of Oz, Ch XI, *I am Dorothy, the Small and Meek. I have come to you for help.*

215. Twelfth Night, 1.5.177-179, *I heard you were saucy at my gates and allowed your approach rather to wonder at you than to hear you. If you be not mad, be gone. If you have reason, be brief.*

216. A MidSummer Night's Dream, 1.1.63-66, *I know not by what power I am made bold, nor how it may concern my modesty, in such a presence here to plead my thoughts, but I beseech your grace that I may know the worst that may befall me in this case,*

217. Love's Labor's Lost, 2.1.112, *Vouchsafe to read the purpose of my coming and suddenly resolve me in my suit.*

218. King Lear, 1.1.111, *So young, and so untender?*

219. Twelfth Night, 1.5.171-172, *what is yours to bestow is not yours to reserve*

220. The Wonderful Wizard of Oz, Ch XI, *Because you are strong and I am weak; because you are a Great Wizard and I am only a little girl.*

221. King Lear, 1.1.34, *Meantime, we shall express our darker purpose.*

222. Henry IV, Part I, 1.2.73-74, *Dauphin, I am by birth a shepherd's daughter, my wit untrain'd in any kind of art.*

223. The Tempest, 1.2.248-249, *Remember I have done thee worthy service, told thee no lies*

224. As You Like It, 5.4.21, *I have promised to make all this matter even.*

225. The Tempest

226. Twelfth Night, 3.1.1, *What a plague means my niece to take the death of her brother thus?*

227. Henry IV Part 2, 4.3.84-86, *left the liver white and pale, which is the badge of pusillanimity and cowardice;*

228. MacBeth, 5.8.15, *I bear a charmèd life.*

229. Hamlet, 3.1.67-69, *For in that sleep of death what dreams may come when we have shuffled off this mortal coil, must give us pause;*

230. Love's Labor's Lost, 2.1.154-155, *Dear Princess, were not his requests so far from reason's yielding,*

231. Sonnet 89, 4, *Against thy reasons making no defence,*

232. Measure for Measure, 4.2.41, *Sir, it is a mystery.*

233. Twelfth Night, 1.5.70, *God send you, sir, a speedy infirmity, for the better increasing of your folly!*

234. Romeo and Juliet, 3.1.98, *Oh, I am Fortune's fool!*

235. Twelfth Night, 5.1.235, *My father had a mole upon his brow.*

236. Macbeth, 5.8.8, *I have no words.*

237. Twelfth Night, 1.5.286, *What is decreed must be; and be this so!*

238. Twelfth Night, 3.1.138, *There lies your way, due west.*

239. King Lear 1.1.159-160, *Reserve thy state, and in thy best consideration check this hideous rashness.*

240. As You Like It, 2.1.12, *Are not these woods more free from peril than the envious court?*

241. Twelfth Night, 3.1.28-30, *and but that he hath the gift of a coward to allay the gust he hath in quarreling, 'tis thought among the prudent he would quickly have the gift of a grave.*

242. Twelfth Night, 2.5.46, *O, peace, peace!*

243. Twelfth Night, 2.1.40, *I have many enemies in Orsino's court,*

244. Twelfth Night, 2.1.42-43, *I do adore thee so, that danger shall seem sport, and I will go.*

245. Twelfth Night, 3.1.39, *Foolery, sir, does walk about the orb like the sun,*

246. Hamlet, 4.7.159-160, *One woe doth tread upon another's heel, so fast they follow.*

247. Twelfth Night, 1.2.57, *What else may hap to time I will commit.*

Chapter XII. The Search for the Wicked Witch

1. King Lear, 1.2.134, *my nativity was under Ursa Major*

2. Henry IV, Part I, Act 3, *By being seldom seen, I could not stir but like a comet I was wondered at.*

3. King Lear, 1.2.110, *These late eclipses in the sun and moon portend no good to us*

4. Julius Caesar, 1.3.140-142, *The fault, dear Brutus, is not in our stars, but in ourselves,*

5. All's Well That Ends Well, 1.1.218-219, *Our remedies oft in ourselves do lie, which we ascribe to heaven:*

6. Julius Caesar, 2.2.30, *When beggars die there are no comets seen.*

7. Hamlet, 1.3.79, *it must follow, as the night the day,*

8. Romeo and Juliet, 5.3.181, *Poison, I see, hath been his timeless end.*

9. Romeo and Juliet, 3.1.47, *Good King of Cats, nothing but one of your nine lives,*

10. Hamlet, 5.1.98-99, *Where be his quiddities now, his quillities, his cases, his tenures, and his tricks?*

11. Twelfth Night, 2.4.1, *Now, good morrow, friends.*

12. Hamlet, 5.1.21, *Ay, marry, is 't.*

13. Hamlet, 4.3.46, *The bark is ready and the wind at help,*

14. Measure for Measure, 4.2.56, *I do desire to learn, sir; and I hope, if you have occasion to use me for your own turn, you shall find me yare;*

15. Julius Caesar, 4.3.229, *And we must take the current when it serves, or lose our ventures.*

16. Sonnet 61, 3-6, *Dost thou desire my slumbers should be broken, while shadows like to thee do mock my sight? Is it thy spirit that thou send'st from thee so far from home into my deeds to pry,*

17. Twelfth Night, 2.5.1, *Come thy ways,*

18. The Tempest, 1.2.49-51, *What seest thou else in the dark backward and abysm of time?*

19. A Midsummer Night's Dream, 4.1.26. *The female ivy so enrings the barky fingers of the elm.*

20. Measure for Measure, 1.1.79, *The heavens give safety to your purposes.*

21. Much Ado About Nothing, 5.1.298, *I thank thee for thy care and honest pains.*

22. A Midsummer Night's Dream, 2.2.65, *How came her eyes so bright? Not with salt tears.*

23. Macbeth, 1.7.29, *Why have you left the chamber?*

24. Twelfth Night, 1.1.40, *Love thoughts lie rich when canopied with bowers.*

25. Twelfth Night, 1.5.249, *Between the elements of air and earth,*

26. Twelfth Night, 2.5.19, *for here comes the trout that must be caught with tickling.*

27. The Two Gentlemen of Verona, 3.1.252, *Come, I'll convey thee through the city-gate.*

28. Antony and Cleopatra, 3.2.39, *Farewell, my dearest sister, fare thee well.*

29. The Merry Wives of Windsor, 3.5.80, *As good luck would have it,*

30. Much Ado About Nothing, 5.1.51-52, *If he could right himself with quarreling, some of us would lie low*

31. The Tempest, 3.1.4-6, *This my mean task would be as heavy to me as odious, but the mistress which I serve quickens what's dead and makes my labors pleasures.*

32. King Henry IV Part II, 3.2.51, *Smooth runs the water where the brook is deep;*

33. The Two Gentlemen of Verona, 5.1.1, *The sun begins to gild the western sky;*

34. The Two Gentleman of Verona, 2.7.25, *the current with gentle murmur glides.*

35. The Tempest, 1.2.25, *More to know did never meddle with my thoughts*

36. Twelfth Night, 3.1.139, *Then westward ho!*

37. Twelfth Night, 1.5.24, *Apt, in good faith, very apt.*

38. Romeo and Juliet, 2.4.34, *Nay, if our wits run the wild-goose chase, I am done,*

39. Hamlet, 4.3.61, *As my great power thereof may give thee sense*

40. The Winter's Tale, 1.2.504, *I know not; but I am sure 'tis safer to avoid what's grown than question how 'tis born.*

41. Twelfth Night, 3.1.116, *So I did abuse myself, my servant, and, I fear me, you:*

42. Twelfth Night, 3.1.24, *I am loath to prove reason with them.*

43. Measure for Measure, 4.2.56, *I do desire to learn, sir; and I hope, if you have occasion to use me for your own turn, you shall find me yare;*

44. Twelfth Night, 2.4.108, *And what's her history?*

45. The Winter's Tale, 3.2.1-2, *it is but weakness to bear the matter thus; mere weakness*

46. Macbeth, 5.1.34, *What need we to fear who knows it, when none can call our power to account?*

47. Twelfth Night, 2.3.108, *Thou'rt i' the right.*

48. Macbeth, 1.3.123, *The instruments of darkness tell us truths.*

49. Hamlet, 2.2.159-161, *If circumstances lead me, I will find where truth is hid, though it were hid indeed in the centre*

50. King John, 3.4.186, *Strong reasons make strong actions.*

51. The Two Gentleman of Verona, 2.7.31, *by many winding nooks he strays*

52. A Midsummer Night's Dream, 2.1.89-93, *Therefore the winds, piping to us in vain, as in revenge, have sucked up from the sea contagious fogs, which falling in the land have every pelting river made so proud that they have overborne their continents.*

53. The Tempest, 1.2.38, *Obey and be attentive.*

54. Julius Caesar, 4.3.249-250, *Omitted, all the voyage of their life is bound in shallows and in miseries.*

55. The Taming of the Shrew, 1.1.117-118, *I pray, sir, tell me is it possible that love should of a sudden take such hold?*

56. Sonnet 33, 1, *Full many a glorious morning have I seen*

57. Twelfth Night, *1.1.28-29, the element itself, till seven years' heat, shall not behold her face in ample view*

58. The Tempest, 1.1.3, *Fall to 't yarely, or we run ourselves aground. Bestir, bestir.*

59. Sonnet 96, 13, *If thou wouldst use the strength of all thy state!*

60. A Midsummer Night's Dream, 2.1.254-258,

> *I know a bank where the wild thyme blows,*
> *Where oxlips and the nodding violet grows,*
> *Quite over-canopied with luscious woodbine,*
> *With sweet musk-roses and with eglantine:*

61. Hamlet, 3.2, *A hall in the castle.*

62. Hamlet, 3.1.59, *The slings and arrows of outrageous fortune,*

63. A Midsummer Night's Dream, *1.1.134, The course of true love never did run smooth.*

64. Sonnet 18, 8, *By chance, or nature's changing course untrimm'd:*

65. Henry IV, Part I, 1.3.16, *O sir, your presence is too bold and peremptory,*

66. The Tempest, 1.2.248-249, *Remember I have done thee worthy service, told thee no lies*

67. Much Ado About Nothing, 1.1.66-67, *he wears his faith but as the fashion of his hat;*

68. Twelfth Night, 1.3.82-84, *I would I had bestowed that time in the tongues that I have in fencing, dancing, and bear-baiting.*

69. Twelfth Night, 2.4.46-48, *The spinsters and the knitters in the sun and the free maids that weave their thread with bones do use to chant it:*

70. A Midsummer Night's Dream, 3.1.28-29, *A lion among ladies is a most dreadful thing.*

71. Twelfth Night, 1.2.11, *most provident in peril,*

72. Othello, 1.3.135, *Then, in th' very moment,*

73. Macbeth, 4.1.44-45, *By the pricking of my thumbs, something wicked this way comes.*

Chapter XIII. The Winged Monkeys

1. The Tempest, 1.2.216, *Hell is empty and all the devils are here.*

2. Macbeth, 7.1.5, *Angels and ministers of grace defend us!*

3. The Wonderful Wizard of Oz, Ch 3, Pg 103, *"This is my fight," said the Woodman, "so get behind me and I will meet them as they come."*

4. Romeo and Juliet, 5.3.32, *why I descend into this bed of death*

5. Hamlet, 4.5.179, *And where the offense is, let the great ax fall.*

6. Love's Labor's Lost, 5.2.18, *had she been light, like you, of such a merry, nimble, stirring spirit,*

7. Richard III, 1.2.182, *I lay it naked to the deadly stroke and humbly beg the death upon my knee.*

8. Love's Labor's Lost, 5.2.119, *The fourth turn'd on the toe, and down he fell.*

9. Othello, 1.3.135, *Then, in th' very moment,*

10. Macbeth, 4.2.1, *What had he done to make him fly the land?*

11. A Midsummer's Night Dream, 5.1.249, *Well roared, Lion!*

12. The Taming of the Shrew, 1.1.117-118, *I pray, sir, tell me is it possible that love should of a sudden take such hold?*

13. A Comedy of Errors, 4.4.107, *O bind him, bind him! Let him not come near me.*

14. King Lear, 2.2.138, *should have him thus restrained.*

15. Hamlet, 2.1.20-21, *marry, none so rank as may dishonor him;*

16. Sonnet 116, 4, *Or bends with the remover to remove.*

17. The Two Gentlemen of Verona, 5.4.125, *Forbear, forbear, I say!*

18. A Midsummer Night's Dream, 1.1.134, *The course of true love never did run smooth.*

19. Hamlet, 4.3.40, *this deed, for thine especial safety*

20. The Merchant of Venice, 4.1.76-77, *You may as well forbid the mountain pines to wag their high tops*

21. Macbeth, 4.2.79, *I have done no harm.*

22. King John, 4.2.174, *Bring them before me*

23. Twelfth Night, 2.4.70, *Give me now leave to leave thee*

24. King John, 4.2.243, *Deep shame had struck me dumb,*

25. King Lear, 5.3.325, *Never, never, never, never, never.*

26. Romeo and Juliet, 4.5.44, *Accursed, unhappy, wretched, hateful day!*

27. The Two Gentlemen of Verona, 5.4.131, *Come not within the measure of my wrath.*

28. 3 King Henry, IV, 5.6.77, *That I should snarl and bite and play the dog.*

29. The Tempest, 3.1.80, *O heaven, O earth, bear witness to this sound*

30. Romeo and Juliet, 3.1.59, *A plague o' both your houses!*

31. Romeo and Juliet, 4.5.49, *cruel death hath catched it from my sight!*

32. The Comedy of Errors, 4.4.67, *Did not her kitchen-maid rail, taunt, and scorn me?*

33. Measure for Measure, 2.4.194, *On twenty bloody blocks, he'ld yield them up,*

34. Twelfth Night, 2.3.122-123, *Since the youth of the Count's was today with thy lady, she is much out of quiet.*

35. Love's Labor's Lost, 5.2.15, *You'll ne'er be friends with him; a' kill'd your sister.*

36. Hamlet, 4.7.29, *But my revenge will come.*

37. Romeo and Juliet, 2.2.66, *How camest thou hither, tell me, and wherefore?*

38. Henry IV, Part 1, 1.3.194-195, *Send danger from the east unto the west, so honor cross it from the north to south,*

39. Sir Thomas More, 2.4.54, *Marry, the removing of the strangers, which cannot choose but much advantage*

40. Macbeth, 1.7.25-26, *I have no spur to prick the sides of my intent, but only vaulting ambition*

41. Othello, 4.3.44, *'Tis neither here nor there.*

42. Twelfth Night, 2.5.128, *Some are born great, some achieve greatness, and some have greatness thrust upon 'em.*

43. Henry VI, Part III, 3.2.55, *But Hercules himself must yield to odds;*

44. Romeo and Juliet, 5.3.160, *I do remember well where I should be*

45. As You Like It, 5.1.10, *It is meat and drink to me to see a clown.*

46. As You Like It, 3.2.234, *I thank you too for your society.*

47. The Merchant of Venice, 4.1.174-175, *The quality of mercy is not strain'd. It droppeth as the gentle rain from heaven upon the place beneath.*

48. Twelfth Night 2.5.103, *Nay, but first, let me see, let me see, let me see.*

49. Twelfth Night, 3.1.39, *Foolery, sir, does walk about the orb like the sun,*

50. Twelfth Night, 1.1.28-29, *the element itself, till seven years' heat, shall not behold her face in ample view*

51. Henry IV, Part II, 2.2.65, *and thou art a blessed fellow to think as every man thinks.*

52. Midsummer Night's Dream, 2.2.14, *Weaving spiders, come not here.*

53. Twelfth Night, 1.4.14, *Therefore, good youth, address thy gait unto her;*

Chapter XIV. The Rescue

1. The Merchant of Venice, 1.1.1, *In sooth, I know not why I am so sad:*

2. Twelfth Night, 1.2.44-45, *Till I had made mine own occasion mellow, what my estate is!*

3. Julius Caesar, 1.2.194, *Yond Cassius has a lean and hungry look*

4. The Tempest, 2.1.14, *Look he's winding up the watch of his wit. By and by it will strike.*

5. Twelfth Night, 1.5.72, *Sir Toby will be sworn I am no fox,*

6. The Comedy of Errors, 2.1.46-47, *Say didst thou speak with him? Know'st thou his mind?"*

7. The Tempest, 3.3.24-25, *Now I will believe that there are unicorns,*

8. The Winter's Tale, 5.1.73, *She had just cause.*

9. Romeo and Juliet, 3.2.107, *Wherefore weep I then?*

10. Henry VIII, 1.3.76, *He may, my lord; has wherewithal:*

11. The Two Gentlemen of Verona, 3.1.237-238, *No more, unless the next word that thou speak'st have some malignant power upon my life!*

12. Hamlet, 4.7.81, *I've seen myself, and served against, the French,*

13. Hamlet, 3.1.34, *Her father and myself (lawful espials) will bestow ourselves that, seeing unseen,*

14. Love's Labor's Lost, 5.2.118, *The third he caper'd, and cried, 'All goes well;'*

15. The Wonderful Wizard of Oz, Ch XIV, *The Winged Monkeys, Pg 123, They must obey the wearer of the Cap. They are full of mischief and think it great fun to plague us.*

16. Henry VIII, 5.1.21, *And durst commend a secret to your ear*

17. The Winter's Tale, 2.2.78-79, *upon mine honor, I will stand betwixt you and danger*

18. Richard III, 3.4.1-2, *What sport shall we devise here in this garden, to drive away the heavy thought of care?*

19. Twelfth Night, 5.1.86, *To be generous, guiltless, and of free disposition*

20. The Taming of the Shrew, 1.1.117-118, *I pray, sir, tell me is it possible that love should of a sudden take such hold?*

21. Twelfth Night 2.1.29, *Pardon me, sir, your bad entertainment.*

22. Henry V, 3.3.1, *Once more unto the breach, dear friends, once more;*

23. Much Ado About Nothing, 3.5.25, *I would fain know what you have to say.*

24. Twelfth Night, 1.5.73, *he will not pass his word for two pence that you are no fool.*

25. Othello, 1.3.135, *Then, in th' very moment*

26. King Lear, 1.1.221, *I know no answer.*

27. The Winter's Tale, 5.2.32-34, *this news which is called true is so like an old tale,*

28. King John, 4.2.18, *This act is as an ancient tale new told,*

29. Hamlet, 2.2.122, *I would fain prove so.*

30. Twelfth Night, 1.3.51, *Is that the meaning of "accost"?*

31. Richard II, 1.3.34, *What is thy name? and wherefore comest thou hither, before King Richard in his royal lists?*

32. The Comedy of Errors, 4.3.38, *Well met, well met, Master Antipholus.*

33. Taming of the Shrew, 4.5.72, *Who will of thy arrival be full joyous*

34. Twelfth Night, 1.3.48, *Good Mistress Accost, I desire better acquaintance.*

35. Measure for Measure, 2.1.160, *Varlet, thou liest, thou liest, wicked varlet!*

36. Othello, 3.3.416, *But yet I say, if imputation and strong circumstances, which lead directly to the door of truth, will give you satisfaction, you may have it.*

37. Twelfth Night, 1.1.14-15, *So full of shapes is fancy that it alone is high fantastical.*

38. Twelfth Night, 1.1.28-29, *the element itself, till seven years' heat, shall not behold her face in ample view*

39. King Lear 1.1.159-160, *Reserve thy state, and in thy best consideration check this hideous rashness.*

40. Hamlet, 1.1.33, *And let us hear Barnardo speak of this*

41. Twelfth Night, 2.4.70, *Give me now leave to leave thee.*

42. The Winter's Tale, 5.2.14-15, *a notable passion of wonder appeared in them;*

43. Henry IV, Part I, 1.3.1, *My blood hath been too cold and temperate,*

44. Richard II, 1.1.14, *Once did I lay an ambush for your life,*

45. Orthello, 3.3.340, *Not poppy, nor mandragora, nor all the drowsy syrups of the world, shall ever medicine thee to that sweet sleep which thou owedst yesterday.*

46. Henry IV, Part I, 1.2.35-36, *who would e'er suppose they had such courage and audacity?*

47. Macbeth, 1.4.56, *True, worthy Banquo. He is full so valiant,*

48. Hamlet, 1.3.72, *For the apparel oft proclaims the man*

49. Twelfth Night, 1.1.34, *in her sad remembrance.*

50. King John, 4.2.135, *Thou hast made me giddy with these ill tidings.*

51. Henry IV, Part 1, 5.2.15, *The better cherished still the nearer death.*

52. Lord Byron, Childe Harold's Pilgrimage, *let joy be unconfin'd;*

53. Henry VI, Part III, 3.2.58, *By many hands your father was subdued;*

54. Measure for Measure, 4.2.41, *Sir, it is a mystery.*

55. The Tempest, 2.1,187, *Well, I am standing water*

56. Twelfth Night, 1.4.14, *Therefore, good youth, address thy gait unto her;*

57. Macbeth, 1.1.6,12, *Upon the heath. Hover through the fog and filthy air.*

58. Macbeth, 3.1.55, *He hath a wisdom that doth guide his valor, to act in safety.*

59. Sonnet 73, 6-7, *As after sunset fadeth in the west, which by and by black night doth take away*

60. Henry VI, Part II, 1.1.10, *and humbly now upon my bended knee,*

61. Twelfth Night, 1.2.40, *till I had made mine own occasion mellow, what my estate is*

62. The Two Noble Kinsmen, 1.5.15-16, *This world's a city full of straying streets, and death's the market-place where each one meets.*

63. Julius Caesar, 1.1.4-5, *Upon a labouring day without the sign of your profession?*

64. Henry V, 3.3.1, *Once more unto the breach, dear friends, once more;*

65. Twelfth Night, 1.2.61, *I thank thee. Lead me on.*

66. Love's Labor's Lost, 4.3.28, *Nor shines the silver moon one half so bright*

67. The Tempest, 5.1.254, *This is as strange a maze as e'er men trod,*

68. Twelfth Night, 2.5.1, *Come thy ways,*

69. Aubrey-Maturin Novels, by Patrick O'Brian, *170 instances therein of, "There is not a moment to lose!"*

70. As You Like It, 5.1.10, *It is meat and drink to me to see a clown.*

71. Twelfth Night, 1,2.29, *And then 'twas fresh in murmur-*

72. All's Well That Ends Well, 4.3.69. *The web of our life is of a mingled yarn, good and ill together.*

73. The Winter's Tale, 3.3.16, *I am glad at heart to be so rid o' the business.*

74. A Midsummer Night's Dream, 3.1.24, *For Pyramus and Thisbe, says the story, did talk through the chink of a wall.*

75. 3 King Henry VI, 5.6.80, *which plainly signified that I should snarl and bite and play the dog*

76. Hamlet, 3.2., *See, what a grace was seated on this brow;*

77. Macbeth, 1.3.126, *The instruments of darkness tell us truths.*

78. The Wonderful Wizard of Oz, XI, Pg 89, *...through seven passages and up three flights of stairs*

79. Julius Caesar, 4.3.288, *Thy evil spirit, Brutus.*

80. The Taming of the Shrew, 1.1.118, *is it possible that love should of a sudden take such hold?*

81. Merchant of Venice, 4.1.47, *Some men there are love not a gaping pig*

82. Romeo and Juliet, 2.2.33-34, *Wherefore art thou Romeo?*

83. Twelfth Night, 2.4.50, *Come away, come away, death,*

84. Henry IV, Part II, 1.3.110, *We are time's subjects, and time bids begone.*

85. Sonnet 3, 9, *Thou art thy mother's glass, and she in thee*

86. Twelfth Night, 2.1.12, *My stars shine darkly over me:*

87. Macbeth, 1.2.36, *If I say sooth, I must report they were*

88. Romeo and Juliet, 1.5.43, *Oh, she doth teach the torches to burn bright!*

89. Romeo and Juliet, 5.3.181, *Poison, I see, hath been his timeless end.*

90. Macbeth, 2.3.30, *Lamentings heard i' th' air, strange screams of death,*

91. Sonnet 17, 7, *The age to come would say, "This poet lies,"*

92. The Tempest, 1.2.25, *More to know did never meddle with my thoughts.*

93. The Wonderful Wizard of Oz, Ch 12, Pg 113, The Search for the Wicked Witch, *I have been wicked in my day, but I never thought a little girl like you would ever be able to melt me and end my wicked deeds.*

94. Twelfth Night, 2.4.53, *I am slain by a fair cruel maid.*

95. Twelfth Night, 3.4.47, *Go to, thou art made, if thou desirest to be so--*

96. Romeo and Juliet, 3.5.104, *But now I'll tell thee joyful tidings, girl.*

97. Romeo and Juliet, 2.2.2, *But soft! What light through yonder window breaks?*

98. The Winter's Tale, 5.2.21, *Nothing but bonfires; the oracle is fulfilled;*

99. The Winter's Tale, 5.2.16, *The wisest beholder amongst them, that knew no more but seeing, could not say if the importance were joy or sorrow.*

100. Twelfth Night 2.5.114, *What should that alphabetical position portend?*

101. Hamlet, 3.2.66, *In my heart's core, ay, in my heart of heart,*

Chapter XV. The Discovery of Oz the Terrible

1. Julius Caesar, 1.1.30, *But indeed, sir, we make holiday to see Caesar and to rejoice in his triumph.*

2. Antony and Cleopatra, 5.1.15-16, *The round world should have shook lions into civil streets and citizens to their dens.*

3. The Winter's Tale, 4.4.372-373, *Your heart is full of something that does take your mind from feasting.*

4. As You Like It, 4.1.105, *Why then, can one desire too much of a good thing?*

5. Sonnet 116, 7, *It is the star to every wand'ring bark,*

6. As You Like It, 4.1.124, *Forever and a day.*

7. Twelfth Night, 1.5.45, *If it will not, what remedy?*

8. The Winter's Tale, 4.4.743-745, *I see the play so lies that I must bear a part. No remedy.*

9. The Merchant of Venice, 4.1.169, *You stand within his danger, do you not?*

10. Henry VIII, 3.1.32, *May it please you noble madam, to withdraw into your private chamber,*

11. Macbeth, 4.1.46, *Open, locks, whoever knocks!*

12. Romeo and Juliet, 3.3.114, *Thou hast amazed me.*

13. Othello, 1.3.135, *Then, in th' very moment*

14. Love's Labor's Lost, 5.2.118, *The third he caper'd, and cried, 'All goes well;'*

15. The Wonderful Wizard of Oz, Chapter XIV, Pg 123:
    Standing on your left foot speak, *"Ep-pe Pep-pe Kak-ke!"*
    Then standing on your right foot speak, *"Hil-lo, hol-lo, hel-lo!"*
    Then standing on both legs say, *"Ziz-zy, Zuz-zy, Zik!"*

16. Twelfth Night, 1.5.106, *By mine honor, half-drunk.*

17. As You Like It, 2.2.7, *They found the bed untreasured of their mistress.*

18. The Two Gentlemen of Verona, 5.4.125, *Forbear, forbear, I say!*

19. Twelfth Night, 2.5.47, *O, peace, peace!*

20. Measure for Measure, 3.1.200, *The hand that hath made you fair hath made you good:*

21. Twelfth Night, 2.3.108, *Thou'rt i' the right*

22. Othello, 2.3.11, *The purchase made, the fruits are to ensue:*

23. The Winter's Tale, 5.1.73, *She had just cause*

24. Julius Ceasar, 1.2.139, *Men at some time are masters of their fates;*

25. The Tempest, 5.1.104, *But yet thou shalt have freedom*

26. The Merchant of Venice, 4.1.185, *And earthly power doth then show likest God's when mercy seasons justice.*

27. Much Ado About Nothing, 3.4.48, *but God send everyone their heart's desire.*

28. Romeo and Juliet, 2.3.92, *Oh, let us hence. I stand on sudden haste.*

29. Measure for Measure, 2.2.33, *'Tis meet so,*

30. Cymbeline, 4.2.384, *Good faith, I tremble stiff with fear;*

31. Twelfth Night, 1.2.61, *I thank thee. Lead me on.*

32. Macbeth, 3.3.5, *The west yet glimmers with some streaks of day.*

33. The Wonderful Wizard of Oz, Ch XV, Pg 130, *"Who melted her?" asked the Guardian of the Gates. "It was Dorothy," replied the Lion gravely.*

34. Twelfth Night, 1,2.29, *And then 'twas fresh in murmur-*

35. Sonnet 58, 5, *O let me suffer, being at your beck,*

36. Coriolanus, 2.1.184-185 *A hundred thousand welcomes. I could weep and I could laugh, I am light and heavy. I could weep. Welcome.*

37. The Taming of the Shrew, Induction, 1.50, *Let one attend him with a silver basin full of rose-water and bestrewed with flowers.*

38. Twelfth Night, 2.5.35, *The Lady of the Strachy did marry the yeoman of the wardrobe.*

39. Hamlet, 1.3.101, *Pooh, you speak like a green girl,*

40. Hamlet, 2.2.125, *Doubt thou the stars are fire,*

> *Doubt that the sun doth move,*
> *Doubt truth to be a liar,*
> *But never doubt I love.*

41. A Midsummer Night's Dream, 4.1.185, *And by the way let us recount our dreams.*

42. The Merchant of Venice, 5.1.52, *How sweet the moonlight sleeps upon this bank!*

43. Twelfth Night, 2.3.49, *In delay there lies no plenty.*

44. Taming of the Shrew, 4.5.72, *Who will of thy arrival be full joyous.*

45. Twelfth Night, 1.5.240-241, *In your denial I would find no sense; I would not understand it.*

46. Richard III, 3.7.80, *Marry, God defend his Grace should say us nay!*

47. Twelfth Night, 2.4.86, *I cannot be so answer'd!*

48. Sonnet 144, 3, *The better angel is a man right fair,*

49. Twelfth Night, 2.2.35, *My state is desperate for my master's love.*

50. The Wonderful Wizard of Oz, Ch 11, Pg 96-97, The Wonderful Emerald City of Oz, *And if he is the great head, he will be at my mercy; for I will roll this head all about the room until he promises to give us what we desire.*

51. Twelfth Night, 2.3.129-131, *Sweet Sir Toby, be patient for tonight. For Monsieur Malvolio, let me alone with him. If I do not gull him into a nayword and make him a common recreation, do not think I have wit enough to lie straight in my bed. I know I can do it.*

52. Twelfth Night, 2.3.155, *For this night, to bed, and dream on the event. Farewell.*

53. Richard III, 3.7.59, *He doth entreat your Grace, my noble lord, to visit him tomorrow or next day.*

54. Twelfth Night, 2.1.8, *My determinate voyage is mere extravagancy.*

55. Othello, 1.1.123, *Transported with no worse nor better guard but with a knave of common hire,*

56. Romeo and Juliet, 2.3.92, *Oh, let us hence. I stand on sudden haste.*

57. Macbeth, 4.1.142, *Saw you the weird sisters?*

58. The Tempest, 1.2.138, *Wherefore did they not that hour destroy us?*

59. The Tempest, 1.2.25, *More to know did never meddle with my thoughts.*

60. The Merchant of Venice, 1.3.130, *Shall I bend low and in a bondman's key, with bated breath and whispering humbleness.*

61. Richard III, 3.7.68, *In deep designs, and matters of great moment, are come to have some conference with his grace.*

62. Twelfth Night, 1.5.73, *but he will not pass his word for two pence that you are no fool.*

63. Romeo and Juliet, 5.3.1, *Give me thy torch, boy.*

64. Romeo and Juliet, 5.3.73, *Open the tomb, lay me with Juliet.*

65. Twelfth Night, 2.5.181, *mark his first approach before my lady;*

66. Twelfth Night, 2.3.23-24, *of the Vapians passing the equinoctial of Queubus.*

67. A Midsummer Night's Dream, 3.2.116, *Lord what fools these mortals be!*

68. The Winter's Tale, 4.4.334, *Then whither goest? Say, wither?*

69. Twelfth Night, 1.5.270, *With an invisible and subtle stealth to creep in at mine eyes.*

70. Henry IV, Part 1, 1.3.4, *You tread upon my patience.*

71. The Winter's Tale, 4.4.808, *An it like your worship.*

72. Hamlet, 4.5.29, *He is dead and gone, lady, he is dead and gone.*

73. The Taming of the Shrew, 1.1.117-118, *I pray, sir, tell me is it possible that love should of a sudden take such hold?*

74. The Winter's Tale, 4.4.471-472, *And thou, fresh piece of excellent witchcraft.*

75. Twelfth Night, 2.4.70, *Give me now leave to leave thee.*

76. Henry IV, Part I, 1.2. 187, *And pay the debt I never promised.*

77. Romeo and Juliet, 3.3.13-14, *For exile hath more terror in his look, much more than death.*

78. Henry IV, Part II,1.3.77, *And come against us in full puissance*

79. Henry IV, Part II, 3.2.238, *O, give me always a little, lean, old, chopped, bald shot.*

80. Twelfth Night, 1.3.106-107, *Wherefore are these things hid? Wherefore have these gifts a curtain before 'em?*

81. The Two Gentlemen of Verona, 4.2.98, *Thou subtle, perjur'd, false, disloyal man!*

82. Macbeth, 1.2.36, *If I say sooth, I must report they were*

83. Twelfth Night, 2.5.47, *O, peace, peace!*

84. King Lear, 2.2.23, *Why, what a monstrous fellow art thou,*

85. Henry IV Part 2, 4.3.84-86, *left the liver white and pale, which is the badge of pusillanimity and cowardice;*

86. Henry IV, Part I, 1.2.111, *He will give the devil his due.*

87. Hamlet, 3.1.130, *I was the more deceived.*

88. The Winter's Tale, 4.4.517, *I am but sorry, not afeared;*

89. Henry IV, Part I,3.1, *And such a deal of skimble-skamble stuff*

90. Hamlet, 2.2.100-101, *That he is mad, 'tis true, 'tis pity, and pity 'tis 'tis true – a foolish figure*

91. Hamlet, 3.1.154, *God has given you one face, and you make yourself another.*

92. Troilus and Cressida, 3.3.243-244, *I see my reputation is at stake: my fame is shrewdly gor'd.*

93. Troilus and Cressida, 3.3.204, *I have strong reasons.*

94. Much Ado About Nothing, 3.5.25, *I would fain know what you have to say.*

95. Hamlet, 1.3.44, *Best safety lies in fear.*

96. Henry IV, Part 1, 5.4.34, *I fear thou art another counterfeit.*

97. Macbeth, 2.1.61, *I go, and it is done. The bell invites me.*

98. The Winter's Tale, 4.4.818, *therefore they do not give us the lie.*

99. The Winter's Tale, 4.4.819-820, *Your worship had like to have given us one, if you had not taken yourself with the manner.*

100. The Winter's Tale, 4.4.805, *Though I am not naturally honest, I am so sometimes by chance:*

101. Pericles, 5.2.6-9, *What pageantry, what feats, what shows, what minstrelsy and pretty din the regent made in Mytilene to greet the King.*

102. Othello, 5.2.149, *Thou art rash as fire,*

103. Twelfth Night, 2.3.11, *Thou'rt a scholar.*

104. Much Ado About Nothing, 2.3.69, *One foot in sea and one on shore, to one thing constant never.*

105. The Winter's Tale, 4.4.339, *Pedlar, let's have the first choice.*

106. The Winter's Tale, 4.4.598, *They throng who should buy first, as if my trinkets had been hallowed, and brought a benediction to the buyer.*

107. Troilus and Cressida, 3.3.96, *Here is Ulysses; I'll interrupt his reading.*

108. Twelfth Night 2.1.29, *Pardon me, sir, your bad entertainment*

109. Cymbeline, 1.6.21, *Boldness be my friend.*

110. The Merchant of Venice, 4.1.174-175, *The quality of mercy is not strain'd. It droppeth as the gentle rain from heaven upon the place beneath*

111. King Lear, 4.1.32-33, *And the worse I may be yet. The worst is not so long as we can say, "This is the worst."*

112. Hamlet, 1.4.68, *I do not set my life in a pin's fee,*

113. Hamlet, 1.4.1, *The air bites shrewdly; it is very cold.*

114. Twelfth Night, 1.2.44-45, *Till I had made mine own occasion mellow, what my estate is!*

115. Twelfth Night, 2.1.12, *therefore it charges me in manners the rather to express myself.*

116. King Lear, 2.4.149, *that you'll vouchsafe me raiment, bed, and food.*

117. Macbeth, 5.1.1, *I have two nights watched with you but can perceive no truth in your report.*

118. King John, 4.2.13-14, *To smooth the ice, or add another hue unto the rainbow,*

119. Sonnet 29, *Like to the lark at break of day arising from sullen earth, sings hymns at heaven's gate;*

120. Hamlet, 1.2.184, *In my mind's eye, Horatio.*

121. Hamlet, 5.2.10-11, *There's a divinity that shapes our ends, rough-hew them how we will.*

122. Hamlet, 5.2.12, *That is most certain.*

123. Much Ado About Nothing, 1.1.132, *No, I pray thee speak in sober judgement.*

124. As You Like It, 5.4.21, *I have promised to make all this matter even.*

Chapter XVI. The Magic Art of the Great Humbug

1. The Wonderful Wizard of Oz, Ch 16, *"Congratulate me," the Scarecrow said to his friends, "I am going to Oz to get my brains at last. When I return I shall be as other men are."*

2. The Wonderful Wizard of Oz, Ch 16, *"I have always liked you as you were," said Dorothy simply.*

3. As You Like It, 4.1.105, *Why then, can one desire too much of a good thing?*

4. Twelfth Night, 2.4.112, *She sat like patience on a monument,*

5. Hamlet, 3.1.57, *To be, or not to be? That is the question –*

6. The Wonderful Wizard of Oz, *How can I help being a humbug when all these people make me do things that everybody knows can't be done?*

7. Hamlet, 1.3.78, *This above all: to thine own self be true, for thou canst not then be false to any man*

8. The Comedy of Errors, 2.1.22, *Thou art indu'd with intellectual sense and soul*

9. Twelfth Night, 1.1.40, *Love thoughts lie rich when canopied with bowers.*

10. Henry IV, Part 1, 3.1.171, *valiant as a lion,*

11. The Merchant of Venice, 1.1.1, *In sooth, I know not why I am so sad: it wearies me;*

12. The Merchant of Venice, 1.1.80-81, *A stage where every man must play a part, and mine a sad one.*

13. The Tempest, 1.1.11, *You do assist the storm.*

14. The Merchant of Venice, 5.1.89, *So shines a good deed in a naughty world.*

15. Twelfth Night, 5.1.57, *Give me now leave to leave thee.*

16. Twelfth Night, 2.4.70, *I must catechize you for it, madonna.*

17. Twelfth Night Or: What You Will

18. As You Like It, 2.4.57, *Thou speakest wiser than thou art ware of*

19. Twelfth Night, 1.5.268, *How now?*

20. Twelfth Night, 1.3.19, *What's that to th' purpose?*

21. Twelfth Night, 2.3.158, *What o' that?*

22. Twelfth Night, 1.5.28, *How easy is it for the proper false in women's waxen hearts to set their forms.*

23. Twelfth Night, 2.1.25-26, *she bore a mind that envy could not but call fair.*

24. Macbeth, 3.4.70, *When all's done,*

25. Twelfth Night, 4.2.38, *I say, there is no darkness but ignorance,*

26. King Richard III, 1.4.101, *'Tis a point of wisdom.*

27. Much Ado About Nothing, 1.1.46-47, *He is no less than a stuffed man. But for the stuffing – well, we are all mortal.*

28. Twelfth Night, 1.5.140, *he's fortified against any denial.*

29. Much Ado About Nothing, 1.1.132, *No, I pray thee speak in sober judgement.*

30. The Winter's Tale, 4.4.116, *Then make your garden rich in gillyvors,*

31. The Winter's Tale, 4.4.85, *For you there's rosemary and rue.*

32. Romeo and Juliet, 2.3.15, *Oh, mickle is the powerful grace that lies in herbs, plants, stones, and their true qualities.*

33. Hamlet, 4.5.195, *There's rosemary, that's for remembrance.*

34. Hamlet, 4.5.200, *there's rue for you, and here's some for me; we may call it "herb of grace" o' Sundays.*

35. Twelfth Night, 3.3.14-15, *I can no other answer make but thanks, and thanks, and ever thanks.*

36. Twelfth Night, 2.5.83, *By your leave, wax.*

37. Henry VI, Part III, 1.4.185, *Off with his head, and set it on York gates;*

38. Twelfth Night, 2.2.165, *I thank my stars I am happy.*

39. As You Like It, 5.1.29, *The fool doth think he is wise, but the wise man knows himself to be a fool.*

40. The Taming of the Shrew, 1.1.117-118, *I pray, sir, tell me is it possible that love should of a sudden take such hold?*

41. Romeo and Juliet, 2.3.92, *Oh, let us hence. I stand on sudden haste.*

42. The Tempest, 1.2.279, *Knowing I loved my books, he furnish'd me from mine own library with volumes I prize above my dukedom.*

43. Twelfth Night, 1.2.61, *I thank thee. Lead me on.*

44. The Merchant of Venice, 3.2.64-65, *Tell me where is fancy bred, or in the heart, or in the head?*

45. Henry IV, Part I, 1.2.87, *if a man should speak truly*

46. Julius Caesar, 2.2.43, *Caesar should be a beast without a heart.*

47. Coriolanus, 2.1.119, *So do I too,*

48. A Midsummer Night's Dream, 1.1.237, *Love looks not with the eyes but with the mind.*

49. Blaise Pascal, The Mind on Fire, *The heart hath reasons that reason cannot know.*

50. Henry V, 4.1.45, *The king's a bawcock, and a heart of gold.*

51. Twelfth Night, 2.2.20, *For she did speak in starts distractly.*

52. Othello, 1.3.66, *But I will wear my heart upon my sleeve for daws to peck at.*

53. Twelfth Night, 2.1.12, *therefore it charges me in manners the rather to express myself.*

54. Measure for Measure, 2.2.164-165, *Go to your bosom, knock there, and ask your heart what it doth know.*

55. Henry IV, Part II, 1.1.19-20, *O Lord, who lends me life, lend me a heart replete with thankfulness.*

56. Twelfth Night, 2.4.114-115, *What dost thou know? Too well what love women to men may owe:*

57. The Wonderful Wizard of Oz, Ch XV, *I shall really be very unhappy unless you give me the sort of courage that makes one forget he is afraid.*

58. Hamlet, 1.3.43, *Be wary, then. Best safety lies in fear.*

59. Proverbs 9:10, *The fear of the Lord is the beginning of wisdom.*

60. King Lear 1.1.153-154, *Reserve thy state, and in thy best consideration check this hideous rashness*

61. Twelfth Night, 1.3.48, *I desire better acquaintance*

62. The Merry Wives of Windsor, 2.182-83, *unless he knows some strain in me, that I know not myself,*

63. Twelfth Night, 3.2, *For courage mounteth with occasion:*

64. Twelfth Night, 1.1.1, *If music be the food of love, play on;*

65. The Wonderful Wizard of Oz, Ch XV, *"You have plenty of courage, I am sure," answered Oz. "All you need is confidence in yourself. The True courage is facing danger when you are afraid, and that kind of courage you have in plenty."*

66. As You Like It, 2.2.7, *They found the bed untreasured of their mistress*

67. All's Well That Ends Well, 1.1.65-66, *Keep thy friend under thy own life's key.*

68. Macbeth, 1.2.36, *If I say sooth, I must report they were*

69. The Wonderful Wizard of Oz, Ch X, *"Oz keeps a great pot of courage in his Throne Room," said the man, "which he keeps covered with a golden plate to keep it from running over."*

70. The Wonderful Wizard of Oz, XVI, *which he poured into a green-gold dish, beautifully carved.*

71. The Wonderful Wizard of Oz, XVI, *What is it?*

72. Twelfth Night, 2.1.23-24, *But, come what may,*

73. Henry V, Part II, 5.5.52, *Presume not that I am the thing I was.*

74. The Tempest, 1.2.182, *Thou didst smile, infused with a fortitude from heaven.*

75. Romeo and Juliet, 2.2.28, *As is a wingèd messenger of heaven*

76. The Tempest, 1.2.225, *to ride on the curled clouds.*

77. The Merchant of Venice, 1.2.15-16, *I can easier teach twenty what were good to be done than be one of the twenty to follow mine own teaching.*

78. Measure for Measure, 1.1.17-21, *we have with special soul elected him our absence to supply, lent him our terror, drest him with our love, and given his deputation all the organs of our own power: what think you of it?*

79. Measure for Measure, 1.1.22-24, *If any in Vienna be of worth to undergo such ample grace and honor,*

80. Measure for Measure, 1.1.69-71, *your scope is as mine own, so to enforce or qualify the laws as to your soul seems good.*

81. Henry IV, Part II, 2.3.31, *Uneasy lies the head that wears a crown.*

82. Macbeth, 1.7.4-5, *but that this blow might be the be-all and the end-all here,*

83. Twelfth Night, 2.5.150-151, *for every reason excites to this, that my lady loves me.*

Chapter XVII. How The Balloon Was Launched

1. Romeo and Juliet, 3.5.21, *The vaulty heaven so high above our heads.*

2. The Tempest

3. As You Like It, 2.7.137, *I thank you; and be blessed for your good comfort.*

4. The Tempest, 5.1.110-111, *I drink the air before me, and return or ere your pulse twice beat.*

5. Sonnet 29, *Like to the lark at break of day arising from sullen earth, sings hymns at heaven's gate;*

6. The Tempest, 4.1.168-169, *We are such stuff as dreams are made on,*

7. Henry V, 3.1.32, *The game's afoot: follow your spirit, and upon this charge cry 'God for Harry, England, and Saint George!'*

8. Othello, 1.3.135, *Then, in th' very moment,*

9. Twelfth Night, 2.5.35, *The Lady of the Strachy did marry the yeoman of the wardrobe.*

10. Julius Caesar, 3.2., *Friends, Romans, countrymen, lend me your ears.*

11. The Wonderful Wizard of Oz, XVII, *now he is gone, and he has left the Wise Scarecrow to rule over us.*

12. Twelfth Night, 2.4.70, *Give me now leave to leave thee.*

13. Richard III, 3.7.68, *In deep designs, and matters of great moment, are come to have some conference with his grace*

14. The Wonderful Wizard of Oz, Ch XVII, *he was going to make a visit with a great brother Wizard who lives in the clouds.*

15. Romeo and Juliet, 2.2.30-32, *Of mortals that fall back to gaze on him when he bestrides the lazy-puffing clouds and sails upon the bosom of the air.*

16. Sonnet 28, 10, *when clouds do blot the heaven:*

17. Romeo and Juliet, 2.2.188-193, *'Tis almost morning. I would have thee gone. And yet no further than a wanton's bird, that lets it hop a little from his hand, like a poor prisoner in his twisted gyves, and with a silken thread plucks it back again, so loving-jealous of his liberty.*

18. The Wonderful Wizard of Oz, Ch XVII, *"Come back," she screamed, "I want to go, too!"*

19. Romeo and Juliet, 2.2.118, *Parting is such sweet sorrow.*

20. The Merchant of Venice, 1.1.61, *We leave you now with better company.*

21. The Wonderful Wizard of Oz, Ch XVII, *Still, for many days they grieved over the loss of the Wonderful Wizard, and would not be comforted.*

Chapter XVIII. Away to the South

1. The Merchant of Venice, 3.2.180, *Madam, you have bereft me of all words.*

2. The Taming of the Shrew, 1.1.117-118, *I pray, sir, tell me is it possible that love should of a sudden take such hold?*

3. Titus Andronicus, 3.1.6, *And for these bitter tears, which now you see,*

4. As You Like It, 2.7.137, *I thank you; and be blessed for your good comfort.*

5. Measure for Measure, 3.1.2-3, *The miserable have no other medicine, but only hope.*

6. Romeo and Juliet, 1.1.179-180, *This love that thou hast shown doth add more grief to too much of mine own.*

7. Macbeth, 3.4.70, *When all's done,*

8. Macbeth, 3.2.14, *what's done is done.*

9. Romeo and Juliet, 3.5.1, *Wilt thou be gone?*

10. Twelfth Night, 2.2.1, *Will you stay no longer, nor will you not that I go with you?*

11. Romeo and Juliet, 3.5.22, *I have more care to stay than will to go.*

12. Hamlet, 1.3.78, *This above all: to thine own self be true,*

13. Much Ado About Nothing, 3.4.48, *but God send everyone their heart's desire.*

14. The Winter's Tale, 4.4.182-185, *This is the prettiest low-born lass that ever ran on the green-sward: nothing she does or seems but smacks of something greater than herself, too noble for this place.*

15. Much Ado About Nothing, 1.1.132, *No, I pray thee speak in sober judgement.*

16. Sonnet 18, *But thy eternal summer shall not fade,*

17. Twelfth Night, 3.1.6, *my house doth stand by the church.*

18. Hamlet, 5.1.14, *Give me leave.*

19. Hamlet, 5.1.36, *I'll put another question to thee.*

20. Twelfth Night, 1,2.29, *And then 'twas fresh in murmur-*

21. Henry V, 4.1.45, *The king's a bawcock, and a heart of gold.*

22. Cymberline, 5.5.132, *Is he thy kin?*

23. A Midsummer Night's Dream, 3.2.198, *Most ungrateful maid!*

24. Twelfth Night, 1.3.51, *Is that the meaning of "accost"?*

25. Romeo and Juliet, 5.3.184, *There rust and let me die.*

26. Hamlet, 2.2.122, *I would fain prove so.*

27. Hamlet, 3.4.56, *See, what a grace was seated on this brow;*

28. As You Like It, 2.3.67, *But come thy ways, we'll go along together.*

29. Twelfth Night, 1.3.48, *Good Mistress Accost, I desire better acquaintance.*

30. Twelfth Night, 1.5.161, *We'll once more hear Orsino's embassy.*

31. Romeo and Juliet, 3.5.235, *Marry, I will, and this is wisely done.*

32. The Winter's Tale, 2.2.78-79, *upon mine honor,*

33. Macbeth, 1.4.56, *True, worthy Banquo. He is full so valiant,*

34. The Wonderful Wizard of Oz, Ch, XIX, *The next morning Dorothy kissed the pretty green girl goodbye, and they all shook hands with the soldier with the green whiskers, who had walked with them as far as the gate.*

35. A Midsummer Night's Dream, 1.1.180, *Godspeed, fair Helena!*

36. Measure for Measure, 1.1.79, *The heavens give safety to your purposes.*

37. Twelfth Night, 1.4.21-22, *Be clamorous and leap all civil bounds rather than make unprofited return.*

38. Twelfth Night, 2.4.114-115, *What dost thou know? Too well what love women to men may owe:*

39. Othello, 4.3.44, *'Tis neither here nor there.*

40. Sonnet 17, 7, *The age to come would say, "This poet lies,"*

41. Twelfth Night, 3.1.11, *To see this age!*

42. Julius Caesar, 3.2.89, *Did this in Caesar seem ambitious?*

43. The Winter's Tale, 4.4.372-373, *Your heart is full of something that does take your mind from feasting.*

44. The Taming of the Shrew, 1.1.117, *I pray, sir, tell me*

45. Henry VI Part 2, 3.1.50-51, *forgive my rudeness,*

46. Much Ado About Nothing, 2.1.326, *Go in with me, and I will tell you my drift.*

47. Othello, 3.3.136, *I prithee speak to me as to thy thinkings.*

48. Twelfth Night, 1.3.124, *Confine! I'll confine myself no finer than I am:*

49. Julius Caesar, 3.1.100, *is the only question we concern ourselves about.*

50. Twelfth Night, 1.1.16, *Will you go hunt, my lord?*

51. Measure for Measure, 2.2.115, *Ay well said.*

52. King Richard III, 1.4.101, *'Tis a point of wisdom.*

53. Macbeth, 3.4.25, *But now I am cabined, cribbed, confined, bound in to saucy doubt and fears.*

54. Twelfth Night, 1.1.20, *like fell and cruel hounds ere since pursue me.*

55. Twelfth Night 2.1.29, *Pardon me, sir, your bad entertainment.*

56. Hamlet, 3.1.34, *Her father and myself (lawful espials) will bestow ourselves that, seeing unseen,*

57. Macbeth, 2.1.54, *Alarumed by his sentinel, the wolf, whose howl's his watch, thus with his stealthy pace,*

58. Richard II, 2.1.7, *Where words are scarce, they are seldom spent in vain,*

59. Macbeth, 1.2.33, *began a fresh assault.*

60. As You Like It, 2.4.39-40, *Alas, poor shepherd, searching of thy wound, I have by hard adventure found mine own.*

61. Henry IV, Part I, 3.1.100-101, *In a new channel, fair and evenly. It shall not wind with such a deep indent,*

62. As You Like It, 3.5.74, *Where, in the purlieus of this forest stands a sheepcote fenced about with Olive trees?*

63. Henry IV, Part I, 3.1.96, *And cuts me from the best of all my land*

64. Hamlet, 5.2.279, *I do confess 't.*

65. The Merchant of Venice, 2.2.122, *I'll take my leave of the Jew in the twinkling.*

66. Hamlet, 3.2.350-352, *'Tis now the very witching time of night, when churchyards yawn and hell itself breathes out contagion to this world:*

67. Twelfth Night, 1.5.287, *Even so quickly may one catch the plague?"*

68. Measure for Measure, 3.2.236, *He professes to have received no sinister measure*

69. Henry IV, Part I, 4.2.56, *I am as vigilant as a cat to steal cream.*

Chapter XIX. Attacked by the Fighting Trees

1. Twelfth Night, 3.2.13-14, *since before Noah was a sailor.*

2. Julius Caesar, 5.1.124-127, *Why then, lead on. Oh, that a man might know the end of this day's business ere it come! But it sufficeth that the day will end, and then the end is known. – Come, ho! Away!*

3. Twelfth Night, 3.1.114, *After the last enchantment you did here,*

4. Macbeth, 4.1.142, *Saw you the weird sisters?*

5. The Tempest, 1.2.308-309, *The foul witch Sycorax, who with age and envy, was grown into a hoop.*

6. King Lear, 1.1.221, *I know no answer.*

7. Romeo and Juliet, 2.3.15, *Oh, mickle is the powerful grace that lies in herbs, plants, stones, and their true qualities.*

8. Macbeth, 3.4.129, *Stones have been known to move, and trees to speak.*

9. Twelfth Night, 2.1.12, *therefore it charges me in manners the rather to express myself.*

10. Romeo and Juliet, 5.3, *A churchyard; before a tomb belonging to the Capulets.*

11. Twelfth Night, 2.5.121-122, *The cur is excellent at faults.*

12. Henry V, 4.1.1-2, *'Tis true that we are in great danger; the greater therefore should our courage be.*

13. Twelfth Night, 1.4.14, *Therefore, good youth, address thy gait unto her;*

14. Two Gentlemen of Verona, 4.2.41, *Is she kind as she is fair?*

15. Henry IV, Part I, 3.1.197, *One that no persuasion can do good upon her?"*

16. Measure for Measure, 2.1.114, *All this is true.*

17. Othello, 1.3.135, *Then, in th' very moment,*

18. The Taming of the Shrew, 1.1.117-118, *I pray, sir, tell me is it possible that love should of a sudden take such hold?*

19. King Lear, 4.6.24, *Topple down headlong*

20. The Tempest, 5.1.51, *But this rough magic I here abjure*

21. Romeo and Juliet, 5.1.39, *I do remember an apothecary – and hereabouts he dwells*

22. The Comedy of Errors, 2.2.185, *They'll suck our breath, or pinch us black and blue.*

23. The Wonderful Wizard of Oz, Ch XIX, *"The trees seem to have made up their minds to fight us, and stop our journey," remarked the Lion.*

24. Henry IV, Part I, 2.3.9-10, *out of this nettle, danger, we pluck this flower, safety.*

25. The Wonderful Wizard of Oz, Ch XIX, *except Toto who was caught by a small branch and shaken until he howled.*

26. Romeo and Juliet, 1.1.22, *But thou are not quickly moved to strike.*

27. Hamlet, 4.5.179, *let the great ax fall*

28. A Midsummer Night's Dream, 3.2.413, *Follow me then to plainer ground.*

29. Romeo and Juliet, 3.1.3, *And if we meet we shall not 'scape a brawl,*

30. Twelfth Night, 1.5.72, *Sir Toby will be sworn I am no fox,*

31. Julius Caesar, 5.5.28-29, *It is more worthy to leap in ourselves than tarry till they push us.*

32. Henry V, 3.6.25, *That stands upon the rolling restless stone -*

33. Romeo and Juliet, 2.3.92, *Oh, let us hence. I stand on sudden haste.*

Chapter XX. The Country of the Quadlings

1. Henry V, 1.1.67, *grew like the summer grass,*

2. As You Like It, 5.3.17, *That o'er the green cornfield did pass,*

3. As You Like It, 5.3.21, *Between the acres of the rye,*

4. Henry V, 1.1.62-64, *The strawberry grows underneath the nettle, and wholesome berries thrive and ripen best neighbored by fruit of baser quality;*

5. As You Like It, 4.1.1, *I prithee, pretty youth, let me be better acquainted with thee.*

6. Henry IV, Part II, 5.3.1-3, *Nay, you shall see my orchard, where, in an arbour, we will eat a last year's pippin of my own graffing,*

7. As You Like It, 5.1.10, *It is meat and drink to me to see a clown.*

8. The Taming of the Shrew, 1.1.117-118, *I pray, sir, tell me is it possible that love should of a sudden take such hold?*

9. Measure for Measure, 3.1.200, *The hand that hath made you fair hath made you good:*

10. The Comedy of Errors, 2.1.50, *Spake he so doubtfully, thou couldst not feel his meaning?*

11. King John, 5.1.46, *But wherefore do you droop? Why look you sad?*

12. As You Like It, 4.1.15-19, *it is a melancholy of mine own, compounded of many simples, extracted from many objects, and indeed the sundry contemplation of my travels, in which my often rumination wraps me in a most humorous sadness.*

13. As You Like It, 4.1.20-21, *A traveler! By my faith, you have great reason to be sad. Then to have seen much and to have nothing is to have rich eyes and poor hands.*

14. As You Like It, 2.4.39-40, *Alas, poor shepherd, searching of thy wound, I have by hard adventure found mine own.*

15. As You Like It, 4.1.24, *I have gained my experience.*

16. As You Like It, 4.1.25, *And your experience makes you sad.*

17. Richard II, 2.3.46-47, *I count myself in nothing else so happy as in a soul remembering my good friends.*

18. As You Like It, 1.1.4, *and there begins my sadness*

19. As You Like It, 2.4.75-77, *My master is of churlish disposition, and little recks to find the way to heaven by doing deeds of hospitality.*

20. The Wonderful Wizard of Oz, Ch XXII, *Before the gates were three young girls, dressed in handsome red uniforms trimmed with gold braid;*

21. Henry IV, Part II, 1.1.1, *Who keeps the gate here, ho?*

22. The Wonderful Wizard of Oz, Ch XXII, *Why have you come to the South Country?*

23. Twelfth Night, 3.1.43, *I mean she is the list of my voyage.*

24. The Wonderful Wizard of Oz, Ch XXII, *To see the Good Witch who rules here. Will you take me to see her?*

25. Henry IV, Part II, 1.1.3, *What shall I say you are?*

26. Henry IV, Part II, 1.1.4-5, *Tell thou the earl that the Lord Bardolph doth attend him here.*

27. Love's Labor's Lost, 5.2.119, *The fourth turn'd on the toe, and down he fell.*

28. Twelfth Night, 1.1.26, *So please my lord, I might not be admitted,*

Chapter XXI. Glinda, The Good Witch of the South

1. The Merry Wives of Windsor, 3.5.64-65, *I was at her house the hour she appointed me.*

2. Twelfth Night, 1.5.94, *'Tis a fair young man, and well attended.*

3. Twelfth Night, 2.3.152-153, *the expressure of his eye, forehead, and complexion,*

4. Twelfth Night, 1.2.56, *I prithee – and I'll pay thee bounteously –*

5. Macbeth, 4.1.142, *Saw you the weird sisters?*

6. Sonnet 110, 1, *Alas 'tis true, I have gone here and there -*

7. Romeo and Juliet, 2.2.66, *How camest thou hither, tell me, and wherefore?*

8. Twelfth Night, 1.3.48, *Good Mistress Accost, I desire better acquaintance.*

9. Much Ado About Nothing, 3.5.25, *I would fain know what you have to say.*

10. The Taming of the Shrew, 1.1.117-118, *I pray, sir, tell me is it possible that love should of a sudden take such hold?*

11. Henry VI, Part II, 1.1.19-20, *O Lord, that lends me life, lend me a heart replete with thankfulness!*

12. Hamlet, 1.3.78, *This above all: to thine own self be true,*

13. Henry VI, Part I, 5.3.29, *My ancient incantations are too weak*

14. Hamlet, 1.5.22, *To ears of flesh and blood.*

15. Henry V, 4.1.45, *The king's a bawcock, and a heart of gold.*

16. Twelfth Night, 2.4.101-103, *There is no woman's sides can bide the beating of so strong a passion as love doth give my heart.*

17. Much Ado About Nothing, 3.1.113, *What fire is in mine ears? Can this be true?*

18. The Tempest, 5.1.70, *The charm dissolves apace,*

19. Twelfth Night, 2.3.99, *Is it even so?*

20. Twelfth Night, 1.5.24, *Apt, in good faith, very apt.*

21. Othello, 3.4.60, *'Tis true. There's magic in the web of it.*

22. Othello, 1.3.135, *Then, in th' very moment,*

23. Twelfth Night, 3.1.11, *To see this age!*

24. Two Gentlemen of Verona, 2.1.131, *How now, sir? Are you reasoning with yourself?*

25. Twelfth Night, 1.1.34, *in her sad remembrance.*

26. Henry IV, Part I, 1.2.73-74, *Dauphin, I am by birth a shepherd's daughter, my wit untrain'd in any kind of art.*

27. Romeo and Juliet, 2.2.184, *So loving-jealous of his liberty.*

28. Much Ado About Nothing, 1.1.132, *No, I pray thee speak in sober judgement.*

29. Henry IV, Part I, 3.1.197, *One that no persuasion can do good upon her?*

30. The Two Gentlemen of Verona, 5.4.131, *Come not within the measure of my wrath.*

31. Othello, 3.3.170, *Oh, beware my lord, of jealousy! It is the green-eyed monster which doth mock the meat it feeds on.*

32. Romeo and Juliet, 5.3.181, *Poison, I see, hath been his timeless end.*

33. Measure for Measure, 2.1.41, *Some rise by sin and some by virtue fall:*

34. Romeo and Juliet, 3.3.13, *For exile hath more terror in his look, much more than death.*

35. Twelfth Night, 1.1.18, *Oh when mine eyes did see Olivia first,*

36. Macbeth, 1.5.1, *Enter Lady Macbeth, alone, with a letter*

37. Macbeth, 3.4.129, *Stones have been known to move, and trees to speak.*

38. Romeo and Juliet, 3.5.105, *And joy comes well in such a needy time.*

39. The Merchant of Venice, 5.1.89, *So shines a good deed in a naughty world.*

40. Henry V, 1.2.147, *As did the former lions of your blood.*

41. As You Like It, 2.7.1, *I think he be transformed into a beast,*

42. Othello, 5.2.360, *Then must you speak of one that loved not wisely, but too well.*

43. Romeo and Juliet, 5.3.308, *See what a scourge is laid upon your hate,*

44. Henry IV, Part 1, 5.4.34, *I fear thou art another counterfeit.*

45. Romeo and Juliet, 5.3.181, *Poison, I see, hath been his timeless end.*

46. Hamlet, 4.7.100, *Did Hamlet so envenom with his envy*

47. Twelfth Night, 1.5.18, *You are resolute, then?*

48. Macbeth, 1.2.36, *If I say sooth, I must report they were*

49. The Merchant of Venice, 4.1.169, *You stand within his danger, do you not?*

50. Hamlet, 1.1.132, *If thou art privy to thy country's fate,*

51. The Merry Wives of Windsor, 3.5.80, *As good luck would have it,*

52. Sonnet 17, 7, *The age to come would say, "This poet lies,"*

53. Twelfth Night, 1.3.32, *By this hand,*

54. As You Like It, 5.4.105, *Then is there mirth in heaven when earthly things, made even, atone together.*

55. Measure for Measure, 2.1.114, *All this is true.*

56. Twelfth Night 2.1.29, *Pardon me, sir, your bad entertainment.*

57. Twelfth Night, 2.1.35, *Fare thee well at once.*

58. King Lear, 2.4.149, *that you'll vouchsafe me raiment, bed, and food.*

59. Sonnet 18, 9, *But thy eternal summer shall not fade,*

60. As You Like It, 1.2.79-80, *The more pity that fools may not speak wisely what wise men do foolishly.*

61. Much Ado About Nothing, 1.1.86-87, *when you depart from me, sorrow abides and happiness takes his leave.*

62. King Lear, 2.4.280-283, *No, I'll not weep. I have full cause of weeping, but this heart shall break into a hundred thousand flaws or ere I'll weep.*

63. Sonnet 104, *To me, fair friend, you never can be old, for as you were when first your eye I eyed, such seems your beauty still.*

64. Twelfth Night, 2.4.118, *I am all the daughters of my father's house, and all the brothers too.*

65. Julius Caesar, 5.1.116-120, *And whether we shall meet again I know not. Therefore our everlasting farewell take. Forever and forever farewell, Cassius. If we do meet again, why, we shall smile. If not, why then this parting was well made.*

Chapter XXII. Home Again

1. The Wonderful Wizard of Oz, Ch XXIII, *Take me home to Aunt Em!*

2. The Tempest, 5.1.110-111, *I drink the air before me, and return or ere your pulse twice beat.*

3. King Lear, 4.6.24, *Topple down headlong*

4. Romeo and Juliet, 1.4.14-15, *You have dancing shoes with nimble soles.*

5. The Wonderful Wizard of Oz, Ch XXIII, *The Good Witch Grants Dorothy's Wish, just before her was the new farmhouse Uncle Henry built after the cyclone had carried away the old one.*

6. The Wonderful Wizard of Oz, Ch XXIII, *The Good Witch Grants Dorothy's Wish, Uncle Henry was milking the cows in the barnyard,*

7. The Wonderful Wizard of Oz, Ch XXIV, *Home Again, Aunt Em had just come out of the house to water the cabbages*

8. Twelfth Night, 2.4.12, *and play the tune the while.*

9. The Wonderful Wizard of Oz, Ch XXIV, *folding the little girl in her arms and covering her face with kisses.*

10. Henry VI, Part I, 1.4.102, *Whence cometh this alarum and the noise?*

11. The Wonderful Wizard of Oz, Ch XXIV, *Home Again, "From the Land of Oz," said Dorothy gravely. "And here is Toto, too. And, oh, Aunt Em! I'm so glad to be at home again!"*

Epilogue

1. As You Like It, 5.4.211-213, *Good plays prove the better by the help of good epilogues.*

2. As You Like It, 3.2.173, *O wonderful, wonderful, and most wonderful, wonderful!*

3. The Wonderful Wizard of Oz, Introduction, L. Frank Baum, Chicago, April, 1900

4. Hamlet, 3.1.80, *The undiscover'd country*

5. Hamlet, 1.3.78, *This above all: to thine own self be true,*

6. As You Like It, 2.4.39-40, *Alas, poor shepherd, searching of thy wound, I have by hard adventure found mine own.*

7. The Wonderful, Wonderful Wizard of Oz, Ch XX, The Country of the Quadlings

8. The Wonderful Wizard of Oz, Ch XXIV, Home Again, *"From the Land of Oz," said Dorothy gravely. "And here is Toto, too. And, oh, Aunt Em! I'm so glad to be at home again!"*

The Cast

In Order of Appearance